Death Reckoning

WYATT PARKS

This is a work of fiction. Unless otherwise indicated, all the names, characters, businesses, places, events and incidents in this book are either the product of the author's imagination or used in a fictitious manner. Any resemblance to actual persons, living or dead, or actual events is purely coincidental.

Published by Wyatt James Parks

Cover Artwork by David Haynes

ISBN: 978-0-578-72672-4

DEDICATION

To my parents, for giving me a childhood boring enough to write about.

CONTENTS

ACKNOWLEDGMENTS

I feel like young writers, myself included, have an inclination towards trying to re-invent the wheel. Luckily, I had my editor and mentor, Kay Hill, to always remind me that the wheel of the novel has been spinning a lot longer than me. Without her endless patience and belief in both myself and this story, it would never have made its way into your hands.

One short sleep past, we wake eternally

And death shall be no more; Death, thou shalt die.

-John Donne, "Sonnet X"

CHAPTER ONE

He rolls down the driver's side window sticking his head out as far as his body will allow without having to remove the seatbelt. "Safety first" as his mother would say. His efforts are rewarded with a line of traffic as far as the eye can see. He slumps back into his seat and beats his head against the steering wheel. Once. Twice. Three times. On the third time his head accidentally connects with the horn, letting off a loud "hoooooooonnkkkk".

He sighs.

Death hates commuting.

Glancing up at the rearview mirror, Death catches a look at his reflection. Long black hair that can only be described as a complete mess, not enough to warrant the effort involved in actually cutting it, but enough for it to be something he would complain about if prompted. As he blows the loose strands out of his face, it reveals his eyes to the mirror. Death stares into them and they stare back at him. The gray irises constantly shift and change like the first drops of food coloring in a clear glass of water. Gray ocean waves crashing over one another, sometimes a pale, smoky color, other times a dark, stainless steel. Growing up, Death's mother had tried to get him corrective lenses for it.

"You'll never amount to anything with eyes like that. What kind of girl wants to marry someone with a light show for eyes? And what if you date someone prone to epilepsy? You could kill a girl. Do you really want that on your conscience?"

Eight-year-old Death was not entirely confident in regards to his mother's understanding of epilepsy, an opinion seconded by the optometrist.

"You must be kidding me," Death's mother had said in a huff, "Look at those eyes. They need to be taken care of. He could kill a girl!"

The poor angel optometrist was naturally confused and after a good deal more arguing and bluster from Death's mother, they were back home with no corrective lenses and a bad mood.

"I tell you, I hate those stupid angel doctors. They hate us. If only I was one of those stay at home moms and we were both angels he wouldn't have even thought twice about giving us those corrective lenses whether you needed them or not."

Death's mother straightened out, puffed up her chest, tucked in her chin and narrowed her eyes, then began to speak in an overly deep and official sounding voice.

"Why yes madame of course I can help you with that. Corrective lenses, why yes we do have those, and just in the boy's size, what a wonderful coincidence. Well, here you are. My assistant can take your card up front. Hey sport, you want a sucker? Here you go. Cute kid, looks just like his mom. Haha, of course, not a problem at all. Have a blessed day."

Death's mother reverted from her frightening impression of the average angelic professional and back to her standard look. Slightly above average height for a woman, serious expression and hard features, black hair with a streak of grey. Eyes the same as Death's sans the dreaded color shifting.

This is why people don't like me.

Those eyes have witnessed the fall of young and old, rich and poor, saint and charlatan, yet they are devoid of any affection. People often complain that it feels like he is staring right through them.

Death's prominent cheek bones, long nose, thin features and naturally sunken look has been mythologized for eternity as a skeleton wrapped in a dark cloak and wielding a fearsome scythe, which is kind of embarrassing for Death because he's a little insecure about the way he looks. Granted, he is quite thin and if you pair that with the panic of a near Death experience, things can get misconstrued and rumors can spread. It's understandable, but that doesn't make it any less hurtful.

Death does wear the cloak for work sometimes, but the scythe is more of a prop than anything else. It was originally meant as something to keep Death from biting his nails. It was kind of fun to carry it around in years past, but it takes more than a sharp stick to scare people nowadays.

Death switches his view to the upper corner of the mirror, trying to get a better view of the line of cars behind him. The highway stretches towards an endless horizon paved with cars of various makes and models. The surrounding area is just as endless in a sense because everywhere he looks there is nothing but steel, rubber and cement. An underpass is the best place to be stuck in a traffic jam so, naturally, Death is about ten feet away from it. Glancing around, the urban infrastructure bears down on him like an angry God. Monolithic buildings and endless shops and cars and honking and shouting and *people.* Not that these people can see him, but Death can certainly see them. There are a lot of differences between angels and demons, gods and men, but one of the things that bind them all together is rush hour. Everyone needs to be somewhere and it just so happens, in a rather irritating fashion, that they all need to be at this "somewhere" at the same exact time. If he were a different kind of person, Death would probably try and write a poem or something about the sanctity of rush hour. About how it represents something greater about the connectedness of the mortal and the sacred realms, but right now all he can think about is how close he is to the underpass and the sweet reprieve it'll provide from the beating sun.

Death notices an irritated shifting of wings in the car behind him and turns to see an angel scrolling through his phone, occasionally looking up, taking a big huff of a sigh, and then going back down to the phone. He looks kind of familiar, although to be fair they all kind of look the same. Death hates people who check their phones in the middle of traffic. Especially people who check their phones the wrong way. The proper way to check your phone at a traffic stand-still is to bring it up to your eyeline so you can keep an eye on traffic with your peripheral vision. If you check your phone in traffic by resting it on your thigh and look down, Death feels perfectly justified in believing you should be chemically castrated and removed from the gene pool alongside airplane clappers. Not only is it dangerous and irresponsible to check your phone like that, it's also disrespectful to the other people on the road.

Stupid punk.

As Death shifts in his seat, something draws his gaze off to the side.

A flower.

More of a sprout than a flower really. A little ways off the road, it rests in the shade of the underpass. If its delicate petals were not protected from the wind, the feeble plant would almost certainly have been carried off by the slightest breeze. It's not especially large, but it's certainly like none he has seen here in a long time. Death can't remember the last time he saw a flower, or anything resembling one, on this road. The people of Heaven prefer artificial flora so the place is covered in AstroTurf and nothing grows in that. Hell is similar except Satan uses artificial plants because nothing can grow there in the first place besides bitterness, daddy issues, and the occasional gnarled shrub. Also, onions.

This is different though. This is neither tree nor grass, moss nor weed. This is a flower and a pretty one at that. It resembles a daisy with delicate, white petals and a warm yellow center on a thin, green stalk. Death feels an odd sense of familiarity with the flower as if he has seen it before.

And just like that, Death is no longer in a car stuck in traffic.

A small balcony, its translucent curtains fluttering in the breeze. Gazing out past the balcony and the curtains, he can see an endless orange horizon. Citrus.

The last one is not an image, it's a smell, but whenever those images come to Death's mind, he can't help but smell it. It's difficult to place as it doesn't smell like any citrus fruit he's ever eaten. It's strong and it causes a fuzzy, cold feeling to creep through his nose, but Death has never been able to call it anything but citrus. Almost like some kind of mental set.

Death grew up around flowers, his mother being a rabid gardener, and he remembers looking out his window as a child to see his mother toiling away day after day. She would be out there when he woke up in the morning and she would be out there when he returned from school in the afternoon. Watering the petunias, trimming the tomatoes, picking the mint, and overall putting in much more diligence than what is required of an amateur gardener such as herself. Death wouldn't have minded all the gardening had it not been for the constant salads and vegetable-based dishes she made. A vegetable dish every now and then is one thing but a young boy, no matter how well behaved, can only take so much zucchini pasta, oven-roasted asparagus, and kale chips before something bad happens deep inside.

Death watches the daisy until his eyes start to hurt and glaze over. With a sigh, Death turns back to the line of traffic which of course has not changed in the slightest.

At least I'm not at the very end of the line.

A rare bit of optimism from the Grim Reaper.

The car in front of him is a large black SUV. Back when he was picking out a car, Death had considered getting one just like it. The extra back seat would have made transporting souls a lot easier. However, they're too tacky and cumbersome and he didn't do any transporting anymore. This left a pick-up truck, a sedan, or a smart car as his only real choices. The truck would have been nice, but he knew if he came home with a truck, people would always be asking him for help moving and he could think of no worse fate. A sedan is good on gas mileage, but they are rather boring. The smart car was the obvious choice but Death knew that his life was forfeit if he got into even the slightest fender bender and decided against it. During the third round of pros and cons lists, this one centering around potential resale value, Satan stepped in and gave Death a car of his own choosing, stating that "cars would no longer exist" by the time he came to a decision.

And so, Death came to drive a bright red sports car with black leather interior and a suspiciously absent muffler. It's a two-seater, although there is technically a "backseat" he would not wish that fate on even his worst enemy. Death would rather drive just about anything else, except perhaps a Jeep, but when he begins to think about what he would get instead, he hits the same roadblocks as before so the gaudy sports car remains.

Closing his eyes, Death thinks of home. His bed, his kitchen, his paints. He has never wanted to be there more than he does now. Except for maybe the last time he was stuck in traffic. Just as he begins to settle deeper into these happy thoughts Death hears a loud "hoooooooonnkkkk" from behind.

The cars have begun to move.

CHAPTER TWO

Death is the only one to turn off at the exit. The sports car with its aerodynamic design bounces around as soon as the road becomes anything other than perfectly crafted asphalt. The sounds of irate angels and demons nursing their car horns slowly fades away into a distant background chorus. These sounds have not always been present in this little corner of the universe.

Once upon a time, the afterlife was a place of timeless beauty uninhibited by the soul crushing march of technological progress. Some people complain about the shift, but those dissenters should try and manage the lives and fates of seven billion *living* people, let alone the roughly ninety-eight billion *dead* people without the aid of modern digital convenience. God may be an omnipotent, omniscient, omnipresent Being of indescribable knowledge, goodness, and beauty but He's not some kind of wizard.

When things started getting tough to handle, God looked into the future to see what those tricky humans would come up with. They were already doing a good job with stuff like crossbows and the Pear of Anguish, but God needed something a little more than that. And "more" is what he found. Filing cabinets, computers, and God's favorite invention of all, bureaucracy.

God had tried His hand at creating original tech several times in the past, all of them resulting in horrifying monstrosities such as a television that displays your deepest darkest desire causing more than a few permanent psych ward stays, an AI assistant that tried to take over the universe and ascend to godhood, and a portable toaster that caught fire when exposed to fabric.

After the toaster, God gave up on trying to perfect His own technology and just left innovation to the humans. He had always been better with living things and there was just something about circuits and wires that never really clicked. The designs were left with the angels for them to figure out. It took a while because angels are not astoundingly intelligent but they eventually figured out how to assemble their first computer, and so it was that cars, televisions, obesity and other wonders of the modern world were introduced to the denizens of Heaven and Hell quite some time before a human ever thought to themselves, "Wow, I really wish there was a magic slab I could look at to tell me the morning news".

Death pulls onto the dirt path and into the miniature parking lot. He calls it a "miniature parking lot" because there are three spaces and one of them has a handicap sign in front of it so there are really only two spaces. The handicap space is the closest to the entrance so Death parks in the furthest spot. After all, handicapped vehicles often have ramps and other things like that and you never know how much space they may need. One of Death's greatest fears is using a handicapped parking space or bathroom and then an actual handicapped person needing it. As a child, he had once accidentally used the women's restroom at a Costco and the embarrassment nearly killed him. The shame, and sheer unbridled awkwardness of being caught using a handicapped anything would surely devour his will to exist.

Granted, he had never seen a handicap vehicle in this parking lot before, but you never know what could happen. Death parks and sits for a moment, running through the script in his head and muttering along, lowering the sunshade and using the mirror to give himself the once-over. He has shed his usual attire of a stained hoodie, t-shirt and jeans, instead donning the closest thing to a suit he could find in his closet. This amounted to black slacks and a gray plaid button-down shirt.

Why do they make gray plaid?

The shirt was a birthday gift from his mother several years earlier paired with a declaration that it would match his complexion "quite well", which he was skeptical about, but there was nothing better to wear in his closet.

Death shuts his eyes and takes a deep breath before stepping out of the car and begins to walk towards the end of the lot where two smaller paths split off from the main dirt road. The crossroads give him the chills. A thin layer of mist hangs in the air even on the best of days, giving it a foreboding aesthetic.

I hate that word: aesthetic.

He had once been a regular here but nowadays his presence is a rare occurrence at best. Death doesn't mind. Even after millennia of going up and down these paths the feelings never change. Trying to pinpoint his distaste for this journey has proven unsuccessful each time.

His eyes flit over the weathered wooden signpost with its two arrows pointing in opposite directions.

It's the color of the wood.

Each part of the signpost is made of the same uncured cedar that has fallen into such a desperate state of disrepair like those old run-down cabins you sometimes find in the woods that are guaranteed to be either a drug den or a serial killer's murder house. There's just something about that dark, cracked wood with moldy spots all over it. Almost like leprosy for timber.

The top arrow points to the left, the bottom arrow to the right. On each arrow is a little carving. The top one pointing to the left is a circle and the on the bottom one pointing to the right is something resembling a triangle.

The road to the left is lined with trees whose branches arch inward to make a natural tunnel of sorts. Light floods through the leaves specking the narrow dirt road little sunspots that shift and dance in time with the sun and the clouds, cavorting about like organisms under a microscope.

The path is always silent except for the sound of the wind in the leaves. It has a calming effect on human souls. Many are distressed to learn they have died when the day finally comes around, and they often shower him with questions about what's happening to them and where they're going which gets annoying. This anxious line of questioning tends to continue until they reach this path where it melts away and they instead walk in silence. Death is happy to bid the chatter goodbye but leaves and other little tree bits often fall on his head and the sound of windblown branches puts him on edge.

Nowadays there is no need for him to transport any souls. That part of his job has been taken over by the busing system that God and Satan put together as a way of "maximizing efficiency". While some people would likely get offended by corporate suddenly outsourcing important aspects of a job with no warning, Death doesn't mind so much. He's never been in love with his work so he doesn't particularly care how he gets it done. A job is a job no matter what way you do it. There is no real upside to his role being outsourced either because it just gives God an excuse to pile more work onto his plate under the reasoning that he has "plenty of extra time", though it often feels like the entire universe is against him having spare time.

No excuses. It has to be today.

Death has been planning this for months. His original idea was to schedule an appointment, but he had a feeling that wouldn't help matters. It might irritate Him to show up unannounced, but it might increase his chances of getting the answer he wants.

Hopefully God is in a good mood today.

CHAPTER THREE

"It doesn't have to be expensive! I'll pay for it, Eric, wait!"

The door slams shut with a resounding crash.

Emily's heart sinks into her stomach.

Oh my god the neighbors probably heard that.

She can still hear him shouting and cursing to himself as he walks down the hallway.

If I'm able to hear him all the way down the hall now, then everyone on our floor must have heard us before.

Emily stands frozen in the entryway and lets the waves of nausea crash into her and fill her throat and lungs and stomach until, finally, she begins to feel like she can move again.

They're probably talking about it right now.

If Emily had paused and thought clearly for a few moments she would have realized that at this time of day most people were either already at work, rushing around because they were late for work, or they were high off their kite and had no idea what the noise was but found it almost as intriguing as the talking bird on the windowsill. Either way, too busy to care about the screaming couple down the hall.

At the moment, Mr. Mustard is perched atop the couch watching over what has just transpired. There are always two things that people first notice about Mr. Mustard. First, the orange tabby cat is extremely overweight. So much so that there is a permanent dent in the couch where he likes to spend most of his time. The second thing is the perpetual mean look on his face that denotes his namesake. Mr. Mustard has never liked Eric so he hopes this is a sign of things coming to an end.

Regaining her composure, Emily takes a few breaths and does the only thing she can: get ready for work. She wants to cry. She wants to cry really badly. But today is not the day for that.

I have leftover dumplings in the fridge. I guess I'll have that instead of going to El Caballo's tonight…I don't know. I really wanted Mexican today.

Emily begins to sigh but catches herself.

No. None of that.

As she walks out the door Emily glances at small collection of cards propped up on the kitchen counter and smiles. The biggest and most gaudy of them all reads "HAPPY BIRTHDAY" on the outside, and on the inside, "Hoping your 26th is as one of a kind as you -Love, Nana".

CHAPTER FOUR

It's a brisk five-minute walk from the crossroads to the Heavenly checkpoint where the path opens up into a well-manicured clearing from which the gates are visible. It's hard to miss them, really what with their gaudy exterior. The Pearly Gates are constructed entirely of gold and encrusted with pearls and gems which adds to the façade of decadence. A façade because Death knows for a fact that the main gate is the only part that contains any pearls, gems, or gold. The rest of the gate spanning the perimeter of Heaven is just cheap wood with a gold varnish and those plastic jewels you find at the dollar store thrown on. Precious metals don't grow on trees after all, and God has bills to pay.

One-hundred and fifty feet or so in front of the gate is a guardhouse with an adjacent boom barrier. The barrier, even when lowered, does not cover the entire pathway so if one wanted to bypass it, all they'd have to do is take a couple steps to the right and keep walking. The clearing is rather peaceful, but that will end in a couple of hours when the buses arrive and the chatter of new arrivals begins, plunging the clearing into the chaos of impatient souls. Death shudders at the thought, but right now the only noise is the oddly aggressive pre-recorded harp music playing from a set of speakers disguised as rocks. The guardhouse is solitary and a complete and utter waste of space. Nonetheless, it remains.

Michael the Archangel is sitting in the little guardhouse on his hard, wooden stool reading a magazine (from where Death is standing it looks like it was something about the "Habits of Highly Effective Angels"), all while maintaining impeccable posture. Michael glances up at the approaching figure and a look of panic flashes across his face as he folds up the magazine and tosses it under the counter. Death acts as if he didn't see anything.

Michael is still sporting his trademark close cut blonde hair. The two have known each other since kindergarten and Death cannot recall ever seeing him with a different haircut. Even though it compliments his tight lipped, sour expression perfectly, you'd think he would try something at least little different at some point. Laugh lines are very common on angels and the other denizens of Heaven, but Michael has none. Instead he has an exhausted and empty stare. Some things never change.

Michael is very rule-following even as angels go and he was always getting in good with teachers during his school years. Death assumed Michael was always trying to garner the approval of his authority figures because he felt no love from his parents growing up. By following the rules, getting good grades, dressing right, and overall being an insufferable little shit he felt he could somehow fill the hole he felt deep down that screamed and shouted that he was completely unlovable. Death had considered presenting his theory to Michael in the past, but the opportunity has yet to arise.

Michael is wearing his gray guard's uniform sans the ball cap. Michael is a stickler for rules and dress codes, but his hatred for hats exceeds all else.

Wings hang from the back of the uniform. When fully extended they reach about a hand's-length further than the tips of Michael's middle fingers. The dull gray of the uniform causes the white of the wings to stand out even more.

They are a sight to behold when in flight and Michael's wings in particular are known to have struck fear and wonder into the hearts of those that faced him in battle. It's been some time since his last battle, and though still beautiful, Michael's wings look weaker and smaller since Death last saw them. The faintest hint of bald spots forming on some choice edges. Angels form bald spots on their wings from age but the main culprit is usually disuse.

"What are you doing here? I thought your day off was tomorrow?" Michael says as he crosses his arms.

"I thought I'd stop by, you know, say hello to everybody. I don't get to come by much these days, but more importantly how are you today, Michael? How's the book coming?"

Death throws a toothy smile and chipper inflection there at the end. At the mention of his book, Michael's expression softens.

"It's going quite well, as a matter of fact. I wrote a couple of pages this past week and it's really starting to take shape...you know, I think I might have a couple here...let me have a look."

Michael begins rummaging around under the counter.

Oh no why did I ask about the book, why did I have to do that? I don't have ten years to work through your fucking complex.

"Oh no, it's uh, it's just, I'd really like to but I'm kind of...um, I mean I'd rather just read the finished project. You'll probably make changes before the end so...you know."

That was weak, even by Death's standards, but it seems to work because Michael stops rummaging under the counter and sits back up in his stool before releasing a massive sigh.

"Yeah, you're right. I just want someone else to read it because I'm just really worried that no one will like it, you know?"

"Oh, uh, I'm sure that won't happen."

"I sent my rough manuscript to Him and I received a copy and pasted message from his secretary."

Michael looks past Death, lost in thought.

Come on, don't lose me. Not today.

A shout sounds from a ways off towards the gates.

"What are you doing over there, Michael? Get back to work."

Death turns to the right and catches sight of him.

The holy father of uselessness himself: Saint Peter.

The little loser is standing in front of the pearly gates in an ill-fitting business suit which does a subpar job of disguising his hideous form, with clipboard and attached pen in hand, tapping his foot in impatience like a supremely pissed upper middle class white woman awaiting the arrival of the manager she demanded to see. Death has to wonder how anyone could find him appealing in any capacity. Even from this distance he can feel himself becoming more irritable simply from the presence of the short, pudgy first pope.

Michael turns toward Death and looks at him with that exhausted, empty stare.

"My apologies. That was very unprofessional. I'll send you on through."

Michael presses the button and the boom barrier begins to rise and Death waits for the barrier to go all the way up before stepping forward. Turning his head to glance back at Michael, he watches the barrier lowering at a snail's pace and Michael's downtrodden expression as he once more withdraws his magazine. Michael is annoying, but he means well.

Death's unhappiness increases the less distance there is between him and Peter. The former Apostle has a large square head with small features which just makes him look even more pouty and cartoonish than he already does. All of this is accentuated by his balding head which has gotten worse over the years. It's a divine mystery how he keeps losing hair even though he resides in the realm of eternal youth and happiness. Peter's massive head rests on the shoulders of a short, stocky, overweight body. Somehow, he remains overweight after not having a solid meal in thousands of years and the bags under his eyes look as if he's never heard of skincare. The guy just looks plain unhealthy.

"Why are you here? Your day off is tomorrow. You should be working."

Why does everyone need to know why I'm here? It's not like they ever care whether I'm doing my work or not anyway.

Death puts on a big grin.

"Oh, yes. I just decided I would come up and visit because I never get to see any of you. It's always in and out without a chance to talk."

Peter does not look convinced as he scratches the knuckles on his right hand.

"Well if you're not on the job that means there are souls that still need to be dealt with. And if that's true then why are you dilly dallying around?"

I should've left this asshole upside down on that cross where he belongs.

"My shift doesn't start for another hour and a half."

As much as he would have preferred to just punch Peter in the jaw and move on, they are in Heaven and whether anyone likes it or not he oversees the pearly gates and that's not changing any time soon.

"Yes, of course. Have a nice time socializing. I am assuming you will be speaking to Him this morning?"

Death forces a smile and brushes past.

Stupid piece of useless garbage.

Death hears Peter pick up the walkie-talkie attached to his muffin-top waist, say something vapid and stupid into it, and the gates begin to open.

CHAPTER FIVE

Death can hear the singing before he is even inside the gates. Heaven is a gated community for a reason. Most assume this is because they are snobby and pretentious, but in truth, God's chosen are simply too rowdy to be allowed to mill around without boundaries. If they aren't singing, they're dancing and if they aren't dancing, they're singing. It's an absolute nightmare.

Most of them are fat because they tend to have puritan consumption habits in their earthly lives so as soon as they make it inside the gates, they beeline for the first all-you-can-eat buffet in sight. Something about that restraint in life results in complete and utter lack of decorum in eternity. Drinking, partying, and lewd behavior pretty much summarizes the lot of the saints. Last time Death was here he was accosted by a rather inebriated pair of elderly nuns who wanted to "show him a good time".

What really kills Death about the whole city is just how downhill it's gone. Heaven was once a shining bastion of culture and hope. Death is fully aware that he does not always have the "most positive attitude", which tends to make him biased towards things in a negative way, but even he was impressed with Heaven in the early days. Now the place is coming apart at the seams with rowdy humans who put a whole new meaning to the words "urban decay" and God is doing nothing about it.

That's what He always does. Or doesn't do.

Death is unsure whether God or the angels actually do anything anymore. Back in the day they were always doing something. What they were doing wasn't always great, and God really dropped the ball right off the bat by just smoking the entire planet. But those were the bad days. The good days involved battling demons, appearing before mortals in visions, and even taking a couple days off now and then to file paperwork. Whether they were making mistakes or doing real work, at least something was happening. Not anymore.

They've all become so clouded by their own holiness and sanctity. When you're constantly surrounded by the pure and holy you become sick of it and nothing feels sacred anymore. When nothing is sacred...well, there you go. It all comes out in the behavior of the saints.

They traipse about in overly revealing robes that might as well be considered straight-up lingerie. Death finds all of this disgusting because he was always taught that people are obligated to dress with at least an iota of dignity, or at least the common decency required to wear a robe properly.

While the humans dress like prize sows on a beach day, the angels are always immaculate. Suits, ties, cufflinks, and egos as large as an eighteen-year old white guy referencing Nietzsche out of context.

As Death enters the main office building he is greeted by the smell of old coffee and aftershave. Death remembers when they first got a coffee machine up here and none of the angels had no idea how to engage with caffeine. The first one to try the drink hawked it out like it was Satan's very own piss. That is, until he threw some milk and sugar in.

Now every angel takes their coffee the same way, three creams three sugars so you have to specify if you want something different. The angels love the idea of coffee because they think they keep working hard throughout the whole day without ever getting tired. This would only be helpful if they actually accomplished anything throughout the day. They're under the impression that they're doing something though, and boy do they take it seriously. The angels were always kind of self-important assholes back in their heyday, but at least they had some room to talk. They were out killing demons and shit which, even though it accomplished nothing in the long run, was at least kind of impressive. Nowadays they just do meaningless office work that none of them understand the purpose of but are too scared to ask about for fear of looking stupid.

The angels are bustling around, yelling at each other and throwing back cup after cup of terrible tan coffee. Even the receptionist, an attractive young angel with high cheek bones and thin lips, is barking into a receiver. Something to do with lost inventory or incorrect data input.

Death loiters around the reception desk for a bit, waiting for the receptionist to ask his name or reason for visit. After a few minutes of no such luck he just walks past the desk and towards the large office door at the end of bullpen. The angel isn't going to hang up anytime soon and Death knows his way around. The office is designed like a grid with narrow pathways of that so-thin-it's-almost-hard-wood carpet separating the desks from one another. Several angels push past Death without a word and continue along with their work as if nothing is amiss.

I've worked for Him for as long if not longer than most of them have existed and I still can't get so much as a damn "hello"?

Death shakes his head as he arrives at the large office door. It's made with real wood of a rich red coloration. God is not a fan of what He deems to be too ornate, so the door reeks of wasted potential even if it's well made and high class.

Death knocks, gently but with purpose.

A gruff voice shouts from within.

"Come in."

Death takes a deep breath, grabs hold of the handle and pushes; smiling with all his might.

"Hello, sir! How are you doing today?"

Death figures this is a good way to start things off.

"What are you doing here?" the deity growls.

If you are impressed by the door to God's office, you're bound to be even more impressed by the office itself. It's not what you would expect from the one true God, a bit on the smaller side, but it is certainly something. No windows and not a speck of wall space uncovered by books and bookshelves. The shelves line the walls, filled with a wide variety of volumes, all of them hardcover and fiction. The fiction part seems odd until you realize God knows everything else off the top of His head. The office is not large, but the shelves reach the ceiling. This specific feature has always given Death a claustrophobic feeling, making his rare visits somehow less enjoyable than they already are.

God's desk is just as orderly as the shelves.

"What are you doing here?" God growls once again.

"I just wanted to stop by and say hello. I can't remember the last time I made my way up here."

"I can."

"Ha-uh, um, so how have things been?"

"Busy."

"Busy with what?"

"You know what."

God plucks a fountain pen from the pen holder on his desk and scribbles his signature on a handful of documents, then hands them off to the smaller desk on his right.

"Look these over and give them to the first numbskull with wings you can find."

Seated at the smaller desk is that damned kid. Death hates him. Death hates him as much as he knows how. It's not because he's a bad person, which wouldn't really a problem for Death. After all, Satan is the most egotistical, self-obsessed person he knows, yet Death still talks to him just fine.

This is different. The kid is just insufferable. An idiot savant who gets by on nothing other than who his dad is. Always on his phone typing away at God only knows what. And even He probably doesn't know. It's irrelevant, however, because at the end of the day he's just a useless, insufferable punk and Death still needs to talk to God.

The kid looks away from his phone to glance at the papers before returning to the soft glow of the backlit screen.

The room is dim, with most of the light coming from the lamp on God's desk. It's an older lamp with that sickly, green translucent glass/porcelain *thing* covering the bulb that, as much as Death may want to deny it, compliments the mahogany wood desk quite nicely. The light from the phone illuminates the soft face gazing into it, bouncing off its owner's eyes and giving them the slightest sparkle.

Eyes that shift from color to color, the retinas often containing more than one at a time. Irises in a perpetual gradient state. The exact same eyes as his Father. Not a single difference. Death knows a lot of people who are just like their parents in some way, whether it be ears, nose, eyes, or terrible personality, but there's always something about them that's different. If you take the time to give them a good hard look you'll usually find a freckle, a millimeter's worth of cartilage, or maybe even a speck of brown in a blue eye. Not God and His son. Not a speck of difference.

In their eyes at least.

Other than that, Jesus looks nothing like his Father. The former wears a white button down with a loose blue tie and he always manages to wear things that actually fit him. The latter does not understand that being able to get something on your body does not equate to it fitting you. So even though God is rather well dressed, it's all much too big for him. This wayward professor look is not helped by his bald godhead and a nearly perfect shave. Death can just barely make out a patch of stubble near the upper end of God's right jaw, the place where He always scratches when He's stressed or worked up. Jesus lacks the blonde hair, blue eyes and beard that everyone loves so dearly, instead having short, curly brown hair, a dark complexion, a clean-shaven face now that he's no longer a poor carpenter, and those technicolor eyes. Father and Son.

Death speaks up.

"Do you have a minute? I actually needed to speak with you about something important."

God looks up from the papers and removes his thin wire glasses, staring straight into Death's eyes. He looks impatient.

"If it is so important then why are you not already speaking?"

Death opens his mouth to speak, closes it, and glances at the kid and back at God.

He's not supposed to be here. That damned kid and his blank stare.

"Well, if I could speak to you alone…"

"Anything you are going to say to me you can say in front of him. If he's going to take on the job after me, he needs to learn."

"Again, sir, I would really prefer—"

"Speak."

There is no way out of this. Death takes a deep breath.

"Well, if you insist…"

"I do."

Death licks his lips involuntarily.

"How long have I worked for you sir?"

God turns to his Son.

"What do we say to that?"

Without looking up from his phone the kid replies in a simple, matter of fact, almost bored tone.

"Get to the point."

"Atta boy," God turns back to Death, "So. What's the point?"

All of his planning hinged upon the build-up. Death would ask a question, God would answer, he would ask another question, God would give another answer, so on and so forth. This would put God in the right state of mind to grant his request. His plan was akin to the Titanic: unbeatable, unsinkable, perfect in every way. Safety measures taken, back-up plans made. Every possible event was planned for, except for a giant fucking iceberg by the name of Jesus H. Christ.

You have to go for it. There's no point waiting around now, you just have to do it.

"I would like to formally request that you, God of the universe, grant me an assistant. I have taken on a much larger workload this past century due to the..."

Mismanagement.

"...unforeseen and unfortunate circumstances that have occurred. I have done so with no complaint and an abundant level of joy, but it is tiresome. For me to continue with this quality of work, I am requesting you enlist an assistant for me from the ranks of the humans. I have no preference as to whom so long as they are literate. I will provide all accommodations and any other necessities they may require. I firmly believe that if you grant me this, then my productivity and therefore my usefulness to you will increase. Making it a beneficial decision for both of us."

It sounds a bit rigid when he actually says it out loud. Like a proposal straight from an international political document or something written by a Brönte sister, but it gets Death's point across in a manner he feels is concise, reasonable and easy to understand.

"No," God answers.

"I have the details ironed out, and if I missed anything, I apologize. I can answer any of your questions, it won't cost you anything, all I really need is a signature. I have the paperwork all prepared and I can print it off if you'll give me the permission. I just thought it might be presumptuous to bring it along with me, but I can send you the full proposal if you would prefer to sleep on it but—"

God raises his hand in demand of silence.

"That won't be necessary. The answer will remain the same."

"I'm sorry but, um, I fail to understand why. Everything is in order."

"That's where you're wrong. Everything is not in order. You do not have my approval, and I have never given any indication that you would ever receive my approval. It is simply not feasible."

Death tries to speak, but the words catch in his throat.

"But..."

"No buts. It's not going to happen. Do you think I just have souls laying around, waiting for me to give out like party favors? This isn't some kind of charity. This is a business. A business I intend to keep in perfectly good working order so I can pass it on to my Son. Now what kind of example would I be setting if I just started compromising the rules for one selfish employee? Is that any way to run a business? No. The answer is no.

And if my memory serves, aren't you getting a day off tomorrow? Do you believe that is easy to manage?"

He wasn't supposed to answer like that.

"And I am appalled that you would think me gullible enough to just give you something you know you can't have by dressing it up like a humble request."

He was supposed to listen.

"Moreover, I have been noticing more and more of this behavior from you. You are blessed immeasurable and yet you still have the gall to come and ask me if you can have an *assistant*? Where in your job description is there any sort of prescription for an assistant? To save you the time, the answer is: nowhere. The reason being the fact that it is unnecessary. You do not need it. You have been doing your job just fine for quite some time now, and if you think you need someone to help you do it, then you are sorely mistaken."

There's a nicer way to say it.

"And don't think I don't know what this is all about, because I am completely aware. You and Satan both have been opposed to this from the start. But whether you two like it or not, my Son is taking over."

Why does everything always come back to that? Enough with your vain self-importance.

God takes a deep breath and massages his temples.

"Get out."

Death takes the invitation gladly and wheels around and as he does so, notices *him* again.

It looks like the kid has finally decided to look up from his phone. He was watching the whole time with those arrogant, knowing eyes of his.

He probably enjoyed it.

"This isn't over," God calls out in an icy tone.

Death shuts the door behind him. Leaving God and his Son to do what they do best: administer.

CHAPTER SIX

"Emily?"

"Hm?"

Emily snaps out of her distracted state.

"What?"

Anita sighs and begins refilling her cup with the watery teachers' lounge coffee. Emily blinks, letting the dull, cold pressure of her headache push against the dip where her forehead ends and her nose begins. It feels like her head could split apart at any second. It's becoming a bit much to handle so Emily switches her focus over to Anita. She's tall with black hair that goes down to just above her shoulders, resting in stark contrast to her white blouse.

"Is something wrong? You seem out of it today," Anita asks, tightening the plastic lid on her cup and taking a sip.

Emily presses the bridge of her nose between her thumb and forefinger, staunching the flow and pushing back the pressure.

"Me? Oh, yeah, no, I'm fine. I'm just really tired and I feel kind of nauseous honestly. One of the kids must have given me something."

Anita twists her lips into that thin smile of hers. Aloof and always judging. For as long as Emily can remember, she and Anita have been best friends. Always together, they remained that way until Emily moved out west for college, but the two agreed to go to the same school and be roommates. It didn't work out at first, but fate would have it differently. Emily's original assigned roommate dropped out mid-semester because she tried to kill herself. It was so sudden and frightening that Emily almost didn't know how deal with it.

Emily remembers being excited to live with Anita but she felt sorry for the girl. Emily wanted to be a teacher whereas Anita originally wanted to be photographer before she changed her major to education. They took all the same classes, graduated side by side, and by some miracle got a job at the same elementary school teaching just down the hall from one another.

Anita takes a sip and places her finger atop the papers Emily is in the process of grading and slides them away, forcing Emily to look up at her face rather than averting her eyes back towards the desk.

"What's wrong?"

Emily forces a smile.

"N-Nothing it's uh, I just didn't sleep much last night. Mr. Mustard wasn't feeling well so I stayed up with him."

"On your *birthday*? Come on, Emily, you should've had Eric do it."

"Haha, yeah I guess. It's fine though. He had a long day of work and it's not like twenty-six is anything special."

Anita continues to stare through Emily with that blank, chill look of hers. Emily never knows how to feel about Anita. Part of her fears the woman, while the other part doesn't know what she would do without her.

"Are you sure, Emily?"

The coldness shifts to warmth. Anita has always had a way of seeing through Emily, and she usually appreciates it. But not today, Emily doesn't have the energy.

"Yep. Just fine."

The pressure in her forehead returns once more.

CHAPTER SEVEN

It must seem a little strange for an eternal demi-god-like being to ask his boss for somebody to pass the time with. And it does seem strange to just about everyone except Death. For him this is the most un-strange thing that he could think of. Being Death is not an easy job and when you do it for several millennia it takes a toll. You see, he's always been a lonely kid, an only child raised by a single parent. Plenty of people come from this environment perfectly well adjusted, however, he had always been different from the other kids. Death may well have been perfectly normal, but he had certainly *felt* different, and sometimes that's more important than whether you actually are or not.

There is something that happens to a child when they grow up lonely. A wound forms over countless hours of playing in a room by yourself. The wound deepens each time the watercolor paints touch the nice printer paper spirited away while mom is on the phone. A wound that grows at the muffled sound of children laughing and feet hitting the pavement.

The wound is painless but deep, cutting from the tip of your right-hand middle finger straight to your heart. The wound heals but most of the time it doesn't heal properly. Sort of like a deep cut that never gets stitches. It gets cleaned and taken care of, no infections or threat of death here, but it never gets stitches. It never gets what it really needs so it heals wide open and becomes hard and strange looking. It's painless, but something about it is just not right. Most children go on without noticing something is wrong. After all, nothing really is wrong. That is, until you get older.

That's when you start to notice it. No longer a child, you begin to realize that there is something hard inside where your vital organs are supposed to be. Its edges perfectly smooth from years of weathering. Its polished surface deflects everyone and everything all the while keeping the thing inside of it safe: the bloodied, long dead corpse of a fetus with the umbilical cord still intact. It does not remember how it found itself in such a place, but it seems to faintly recall the something hard beginning to form around it at a slow and methodical pace. It was warm and quiet inside so it didn't fight back. Then one morning it opened its eyes and there was nothing but darkness. The something hard had completely encased it.

Silence.

Suffocation.

Death.

Death's wound has not healed properly. He noticed it one day while eating a ham sandwich over the sink and, though unsure how he got it or what it was, he figured it would probably be best to take care of that dark, cavernous, empty feeling. Death did what any sane person would do and typed out a quick internet search. A few things came up: get busy, spend quality time with loved ones, and dedicate time to hobbies.

Throwing himself into his work lasted for all of about a week. People who find meaning in their lives from work must have far more interesting and meaningful jobs than Death because he found himself wanting to die more by the end of it than he did at the start.

Bonding with family and friends is great until you realize your mother's only joy is gardening and your only "friend" is literally Satan.

Hobbies lasted surprisingly long. Not that Death really has many hobbies. Reading is alright once in a while but he refrains from doing it too often because he dislikes most characters. Death likes music but he can't perform anything beyond the simple scales that his mother forced him to learn in elementary school. Death has always enjoyed painting but he would never consider doing it as more than a casual hobby.

One time in high school he began having some wild dreams of selling his paintings and living a bohemian lifestyle somewhere exciting like Maine. Death had shown his mother one of his works and she very lovingly told him that it was, "the kind of thing that hangs in motels and exists only to make a stained beige wall look less offensive."

Art is out of the question.

Death is still searching for the answer to his problems, but the trouble is that he never has the time to dedicate towards a solution. This is where the need for an assistant comes in. Death's workload is massive. If Death has an assistant then he can finish his daily quota faster, which leaves him with the extra time needed in order to figure out why he feels empty.

He wants a human assistant because angels are useless and pretentious, and demons are more trouble than they're worth. Humans can be the same way, but they are generally obedient to people like Death so it would make their initial learning curve easier to overcome. He also just has this feeling that it needs to be a human. Every time he considers the possibility, he can't imagine it any other way.

It takes some time for Death to process what God said. Everything is a blur as he walks out of Heaven, the voices like distant, muffled shouts. He put so much work into his speech and his arguments that he had convinced himself that God would have to comply. How could He not? Death does not ask for anything, not even that day off. Death had simply received an email one day informing him that he was being given the day off and he was not to refuse, and why would he? Death had never had a day off before and it was nice to have something to look forward to, but it was not his idea.

Everything he said is true. Death is financially capable of taking on an assistant and it would certainly increase his productivity. Death is a good worker, but he could be much better if he had the time to figure out what is wrong with him.

Death looks up to see the end of the road in sight.

Death once again experiences an immense disquiet as he approaches the crossroads sign.

Back again.

Death still lacks any real words to describe the feeling the signpost and the crossroads give him. Maybe…soft despair. Asserting Death as completely in the *Pit of Despair* would be completely absurd and over the top. All things considered, he was not in the most pleasant situation. So soft despair it was.

Well with that disaster behind him, he only has one option...

God is not the only who can grant wishes.

CHAPTER EIGHT

Kids these days.

The boy will one day inherit the Heavens and the Earth and here he is, fiddling around on his phone, not paying any mind to the work they need to get done. Not that any of it really matters, nothing anyone does in this office matters. If God wants something to happen, He makes it happen, if He wants something not to happen, he makes it not happen. That's the perk when you're the one making the rules. The job does have its downsides.

"Son."

Jesus looks up from his phone.

"Hm?"

"You can head out early today. Tell them to leave once they've done enough for the day and not to bother me."

Jesus looks at his father with one of his trademark stares. Those two eyes of ever shifting techni-color hue that urge you to continue talking, to share more, to open up, to divulge your deepest, darkest secrets and regrets. If he had a third eye then his irises would create an organic ellipsis. Three circles that refuse to let you leave without saying what you really want to say.

I hate it when he does this. It's creepy. I don't know who taught him how to do it.

Apparently satisfied for now, Jesus rises from his desk, finishes typing something on his phone and stows it in his pocket as he saunters over to the door. As he's exiting, Jesus turns on his heels to face his father and stares him dead in the eyes. No emotion, rapt attention, those rainbow eyes.

"Don't work too hard."

The closing of the door the punctuation mark ending the sentence. What exactly he meant is a mystery to God, but there were several words spoken which never left the boy's mouth.

I suppose he's not really a boy anymore.

God shakes his head and stands up from His desk, trying to ignore the pain resonating from His lower back and locks the office door before sitting back down slowly and with great care only letting out a breath once He's comfortable and the pain has subsided a bit.

I'm getting old.

He can hear the sounds of the angels jostling around and laughing as they all pack up and begin leaving the office.

Lazy bastards.

God stares at the office phone on His desk until the sound of angels fade out and eases the building into complete silence.

He takes a deep breath and picks up the receiver. He hates making these calls. Today He will stand his ground and get what He needs. He is God after all. He will not give an inch. God dials, bringing the receiver to his ear and listening as it rings. The call connects and a polite elderly voice speaks.

"Hello?"

"Hello, Agnes, it's me."

There is a long period of silence.

"Agnes?"

"Yes?"

"Are you there?"

"Oh, yes I just wanted you to have to speak first. What do you want? I'm very busy you know. I'm working on a new blanket for Thomas even though he never likes the colors I pick. This time I'm going for a nice peach colored yarn which is going to look just stellar with the mint green one. I've also been catching up on the more recent soap operas on television. And before you say anything I know, they're *so* banal, *but* that's what I like about them. Everything is so much simpler, unlike real life. People are so funny...oh I'm sorry I just went off again. I've been doing that so much lately I really must stop before it becomes a habit. What was it you needed again?"

The polite tone is completely gone, replaced with a voice so sardonic and condescending that God can literally see a smirk in his mind's eye. Somewhere deep within God, a pot begins to boil.

"It's about your brat. He came in today to ask me if he could have a *companion*. Now what do you think about that?"

"What did you tell him?"

"No of course."

"Then it's over. Why are you calling me?"

The boiling intensifies, bubbles popping as they rise to the surface in greater numbers.

"I'm calling you because he's *your* son and you said this would be dealt with."

"It *is* dealt with."

"Are you certain? Because from where I'm standing, it looks like nothing has changed."

The line remains silent. The bubbling begins to quiet.

"I'm not sure I like your tone."

"You don't have to like my tone. You just have to take care of your end of things."

"Maybe if you were more careful then I wouldn't be forced to clean up your messes."

The rumbling of the pot as bubbles begin rushing to the surface.

"Just keep an eye on him. I don't want to have to do anything about him."

"That seems to be the case with most things you pretend to love."

The water in the pot is still and mirrorlike, revealing the reflection of an aging and decrepit mannequin figure falling apart at the seams like peeling ash.

"Just make sure it's dealt with."

Silence.

"That means we're done, Agnes."

"Oh, I know we are."

Before He can say anything Agnes hangs up.

God puts the receiver back in its place and remains devoid of thought for a time. The silence is deafening to the point where He cannot think or feel even if He wants to.

Once He's had his fill of silence, God organizes the documents on His desk into a neat pile and, withdrawing his pen, gets back to work signing papers and reviewing reports. It's a lot of work being God and it comes with a great deal of responsibility. The job has its perks.

CHAPTER NINE

The bus smells of urine and weed.

Public transportation. That's one thing about moving to the city that Emily has never been able to get used to. Not that she dislikes it or anything, it's just so different. Everyone owns a car where she grew up because public transportation is relatively non-existent. This results in no one using what little public transportation there is because it's bad due to lack of funding. It lacks funding because local government puts all the funding into road maintenance and police enforcement of traffic laws because everyone drives a car. It's something of a cycle. A lot of people when they move to the city from a small town miss ease of driving alongside the general feeling of safety, or more accurately, the assumption of safety.

Emily's next-door neighbor was murdered by a serial killer when she was eleven. Not a lot of people can say that. Not that it's a good thing, it was a horrible thing really but Emily's parents told her about a year after the fact. They were vague with the details and she never really found out, but she was able to infer that the murder had happened at night, while she was in bed asleep. If she was asleep then that means she was thirty feet away from the murder when it happened. You could look into that poor little boy's room from her window.

Sometimes if she was sitting at her desk doodling with her window open she would look up and see him at his little desk playing with action figures and their eyes would meet and he would grin real big and wave and

Emily would wave back. She was supposed to babysit him the following year when she turned twelve. He was so little. He *is* so little. He never got bigger. Emily refuses to remember his name right now. She can't do it. Remembering the name makes it a bit too real. Emily's parents never made her remember and that's alright.

Emily's grandmother was worried when she first moved to an apartment in the city after college because she thought it was unsafe to live alone there. She has never once felt unsafe in the city surrounded by people. Emily only ever feels unsafe when she's alone, when it's quiet and the only sound she can hear is her own breathing. Emily went home to her grandmother one Christmas soon after she had started living on her own and the first night almost killed her.

The silence of the suburban evening filled her lungs, dripping down her esophagus like Drano, eating away at the muscle and stealing Emily's ability to breathe. Inky black tendrils coursing through her blood from a small spot just behind the base of her lungs. She didn't sleep until she got back to the city. The sound of the cars, the shouts, the footsteps of upstairs neighbors, the moaning of the stoner couple next door, someone dropping something on the stairs and the clanging that grows faint as curses ring through the stairwell and into the ears of Emily on the precipice between being asleep and being awake, between dreams and nightmares, between numbness and having to feel anything at all.

The college aged boy to Emily's left with the wisp of hair on his upper lip and headphones in his ears shifts in his sleep and rests his head on Emily's shoulder. He looks to be about nineteen. Dark blonde hair, naturally tan but looks like he hasn't really done anything outside in a while. His mouth is open a bit and after a minute or two Emily notices a faint spot of drool forming on her blouse.

Emily turns her head towards the window. People are milling about beneath the setting sun. Men in suits, women in baggy jeans and beanies, happy looking dogs with their unhappy owners, angry dogs and their friendly looking owners, a homeless man singing opera at the top of his lungs in front of a laundromat as an elderly Korean woman half his size approaches with a nasty looking broom and fire in her eyes.

The bus smells of urine, weed, and body odor.

Emily smiles.

CHAPTER TEN

Hell is rather drab for Death's taste. The city limits are too hustle and bustle and the people are obnoxious. Demons are a whole problem in and of themselves without even taking into account the human souls housed there. Contrary to more orthodox religious belief, Satan has a considerable amount of freedom when it comes to how things run day to day in Hell. The only thing he must do is ensure that souls be punished for their sins against God. This allows for a great deal of creative freedom on Satan's part and there is nothing he loves more than creativity.

Many great artists of human history have at least once dabbled into something concerning Hell. Painters, musicians, writers, no art form is exempt. They love to imagine things about Hell because whether they believe in it or not, deep down humans want to know what it's like there. They are all wrong.

These explorations of Hell are usually quite vain on the part of the artist. It feels good to present yourself as if you're the bearer of some insightful knowledge or understanding about something no one has ever seen before. Also, there's a degree of safety which comes part and parcel with artistically exploring somewhere you're not even entirely sure exists.

The Divine Comedy is one of the biggest smear jobs in all of human history. No hard feelings towards Dante or anything, but his book is complete and utter fabrication. It's not all his fault though, God is pretty good at manipulation, and it makes Him look better if Hell appears to be, well, a Hell-hole. The only thing Dante really got right about Hell is structure. Satan likes things to be organized and logical, and this was one of the main philosophies he kept in mind when restructuring to meet the demands of the information era.

Dante's journey through Hell is best compared to an American journalist's guided journey through North Korea. The unwitting poet was only shown what God wanted him to see. For instance, if Dante and his buddy Virgil had passed through at later times in the day, he would've seen demons and humans alike drinking together after a day of hard work, enjoying each other's company as if atrocious acts of torture had simply not happened. Instead, God made sure that Dante always missed the fun and only saw the especially grisly, stringing-people-up-on-meat-hooks kind of business. Nobody denies that stuff happens, but a good work of journalism should show every aspect of the story and get the full picture. Wide shot, you know? Professional integrity and truth and stuff. But hey, if God wants someone to think something, what can you do?

Satan wants things to run smoothly in his little corner of the universe and he is willing to employ any means possible to make that happen. Satan sent out some of his most trusted lieutenants to gather information on the greatest cities. Hell has only ever had one city, but it might as well have been twenty. For a time, Hell resembled Babylon, then Athens, then Rome, and he stuck with Constantinople for a while before trying out Paris. Then Satan took a brief vacation to Las Vegas. The sights, the sounds, the smells. Satan fell in love and decided it was time for a change.

New things started popping up mere days after his return. Neon lights, casinos, and rather tame suburbs. The demons and fallen angels changed out their tunics for suits and streetwear ushering in a new era in Hellish living. Satan loves fashion so the Champs-Élysées is another great inspiration for Hell and it creates an oftentimes unsettling contrast between the chintzy farce of Vegas and, well, Paris. It confuses and bothers Death to no end.

The damnation happens in the Tower of Hell at the far end of the strip where everything important exists. It rises taller than any other building and the obsidian exterior reflects any and all light, giving off a sinister glare. The various sins are punished on a different level depending on their severity. Damnation goes nine to five and runs like absolute clockwork.

Included is a sample schedule.

8:30 AM: Satan arrives on site, waves hello to the main receptionist, takes the elevator up to his office.
8:46 AM: Demons show up, clock in, set up at their assigned stations.
8:58 AM: Sinners, officially referred to in Hell as Valuable Company Assets (VCAs), arrive, sign in, report to their assigned stations.
9:00 AM: Damnation, officially referred to in Hell as Asset Behavior Correction (ABC), commences.
12:28 PM: ABCs halt and VCAs are allowed lunch from 12:30 AM to 1:15 PM.
12:30 PM: Tormenters, officially referred to in Hell as Behavioral Correction Associates (BCAs) clean supplies.
12:45 PM: BCAs take lunch.
1:15 PM: VCAs and BCAs return to facilities and continue with ABCs.
4:45 PM: VCAs clock out and depart, BCAs clean supplies and facilities used to complete ABCs.
5:00 PM: BCAs clock out and depart.
5:15 PM: Receptionist departs.
9:00 PM: Satan departs.

It's planned and organized to be as humane and functional as possible. No one damned for the wrong crime, nothing lost in the shuffle and, Satan's slogan: no mistakes. It's more for him than anyone else, but the words still ring true. It's beaten into the thick skulls of demons during training along with the endless list of regulations concerning how they interact with VCAs. Coincidentally, the treatment of VCAs is perhaps biggest inaccuracy in the entire *Divine Comedy*.

Even if Satan wanted to torture souls 24/7, it would be a Herculean feat of management and charisma. Even demons need a break every now and then, and the denizens of Hell have the median attention span of a butterfly. With this standardized work schedule, Satan is able to manage the type of people he employs while still maintaining good conditions for the human souls. Whether he admits it or not, Satan feels a level of responsibility towards those God-forsaken sinners.

Death has never understood why people assume everyone is just jumbled together in some melting pot of fire. Their Bible tells them they are cast into a lake of fire but how anti-climactic would that be if you were stuck to burning every second of every day for eternity?

It would be terrible and pointless from a punitive viewpoint because people can get used to anything. No matter the living conditions, people can find a way to enjoy it. Sure, a lake of fire is a little different than an apartment downgrade, but you give people enough time and there will be block parties, beach days, rec leagues, potlucks, you name it. Death wouldn't put it past people to start building cities and having wars because if you leave people in a room for long enough with nothing to do, for better or for worse, they'll find a way to send that shit to the moon.

As Death finishes walking through the main strip and nearing his destination, the sights and smells remind him of how much he dislikes the city.

A demon, short and squat with a pointed tail and spindly goat horns waves to Death with a smile of rotting teeth as he opens up shop for the day and a pungent odor wafts outward. Though Death is unsure as to what's being sold, he is certain it would break health code violations. The trouble with Hell is more the fact that no one takes care of it. The place could be good, but whenever Death goes down it feels like he's visiting an elderly uncle who hasn't taken out the trash in two months. Nothing in its right place, trash everywhere, shops and stores in no discernible order. It's chaos and no amount of flashy architecture can help it. Although Heaven is ornate, tacky and chaotic, at least they keep it clean.

It's before work hours so Death knows where Satan is. Death can hear the shouts and laughter coming from the bar as he approaches. Above the door in big, jagged letters, "Holy Church of the Damned". In Hell if you ever hear a demon tell you they're "going to church" and would you like to tag along, always ask which one because you may arrive in your Sunday best and find yourself sorely disappointed.

The bar is constructed like none other. A cathedral in the structural sense, yet it's more intricate and, technically speaking, beautiful than any cathedral on Earth. All the windows are stained glass of the utmost quality, depicting scenes of great triumph for the Devil with the occasional historical or technical detail omitted for the fun of it. Looking straight up from his position at the front door, Death can see the gargantuan rose window. Pink, purple, pale blue, cherry red, unlike anything Death has yet to see elsewhere. Chartres and Notre Dame pale in comparison.

Yet it lacks something they possess, something of that transcendental quality. That is, sincerity. At first glance you're just like "wow, this is one of the most amazing structural masterpieces I've ever seen. Wow, just, wow" but upon further inspection, the whole thing feels like a Vegas knockoff. You look closer and notice in the bottom left corner of one of the windows Satan is engaged in lewd and lascivious acts with the Virgin Mary and the whole thing loses a bit of its initial resonance.

He's so theatrical it's sickening

Death sighs to himself as he pushes open the gigantic wooden doors.

The interior of the "Church" is spacious and decorated with custom renditions of famous paintings and sculptures. Calling them self-insert parodies might be offensive to the Devil, but it's not far off the mark. There is a *David*, a *Lady Liberty Leading the People*, a *Venus*, and if you look hard enough there's a *Mona Lisa* hidden somewhere near the bathrooms.

There is also one especially vulgar painting of Satan crashing DaVinci's *The Last Supper* in a not so savory way. Besides the portraits and various nude sculptures, Satan has an awful eye for interior design. It all clashes far too much for Death's tastes. Satan is the type of person who thinks that if a bunch of artists he likes make a song together, it will inherently be good.

Satan's design philosophy reflects this character flaw.

The furniture resembles something out of a Victorian men's club. Garish couches that don't exactly appear comfortable which clashes with the concrete floors and wallpaper.

Yes, wallpaper, actual fucking wallpaper. No, it's not the 80s, it's Hell. It's a faded maroon with a design of Queen Victoria within a chipped and faded gold frame decked out like a nineties hip-hop star and throwing signs. Sometimes it feels like her eyes follow you.

Pool tables are scattered around the spacious interior, and a large number of demons are milling about between the pool tables, couches, and bar. Seeing as work starts soon, the demons are all dressed in business casual attire which matches their horns, tails, and cloven hooves about as well as slacks and button downs match the wings of their angelic counterparts. If Death were to come back that evening they would all be dressed like hypebeasts and there would be about twice as many because free time, especially after work hours, is usually spent at the bar. And they all smoke so the air has a certain *texture* to it.

It wasn't always like this, but an anonymous demon accidentally walked in on Satan stress smoking one time during the 40's and overnight every demon across Hell was smoking two packs a day. This means the air inside any building has a permanent Los Angeles smog. The demons also never learned the concept of "inside voices", so the laughing and chatting of the crowd compounds into a perpetual deafening roar. In a cruel example of linear thought, they all seem to think if they speak louder they'll certainly be heard.

Most bosses wouldn't want their employees drinking and partying right before work, but Satan is not most bosses. So long as they do their job Satan doesn't really care what they do, and Death can't help but agree with this frame of mind. Plastered or not, their quality of work cannot get any worse.

Demons believe they're far above the angels because they consider them pompous jerks with no clue about anything. Themselves? Smart as Hell. They know what's up. They follow Satan and he is much cleverer than God ever was or could be, and he isn't totalitarian. Stick it to the man, right? The demons don't view Satan as their ruler, even though he quite literally is. Through a good degree of effort on his part, they are all under the impression that they have some kind of deep personal relationship with him. If you pulled any demon aside and asked them, "hey, are you and Satan close?" they'd all reply in an instant with an emphatic "of course". It's shocking at times considering many have probably never had so much as a word with him. The angels have the exact same complex with God which results in internet comment section arguments that make Death want to hurl himself off a bridge.

The demons are laughing and enjoying one another's company, except for the Devil. Satan is known for his flamboyant personality. He's a truly likable guy if people are being honest with themselves, yet he has some reserved tendencies. One minute, Satan will be playing pool with the demons, chuckling and having a good time, and the next minute he'll be off by himself in the corner sipping a drink and staring off at something. When he is off by himself, it is an unspoken rule among the demons that no one is to bother him. It's the least they can do.

As Death scans the interior, he spies Satan lounging in the farthest corner of the cathedral sipping a drink and checking his suit for lint. There are rumors in Heaven that Satan brews his own beer using supposed "dark energy" from the souls in the Hell. Satan is the king of evil, not some heathen beast who ingests human souls for fun, and anyone who knows him particularly well knows that he much prefers fine red wine, although no-one would ever catch him admitting to it.

Death moves towards the back as fast as possible, keeping his head low and avoiding eye contact. The last thing he wants right now is to attract attention. Demons are friendly, but they're that aggressive kind of friendly like the old women that greet people at the front door of those especially quaint Evangelical churches. Friendliest people alive, truly wonderful and beautiful people, but there is such a thing as being *too* friendly. Death and Satan have known each other for some time and are fairly close friends so Death has unwittingly achieved some form of unspoken legend status among them. Death is always treated with an unsettling degree of courtesy when he's in Hell and everyone is always trying to get him to join in on their drinking. He always refuses. Death knows they're just trying to get close to Satan. Death hates a lot of things but one of the things he hates the most is dishonesty.

Demons really are idiotic.

As Death nears where Satan is seated, he takes notice of the pensive expression on the Devil's face. That expression which says he's looking for something that isn't there. Satan happens to glance in the direction of Death's awkward advance and immediately puts his drink on the wood table, rising with a wicked grin on his face.

"Long-time no-see, buddy, how's it going?" Satan asks, gesturing for Death to have a seat at his table. Death accepts and responds to his question with an incoherent stream of mumbles. Satan chuckles and waves at the bartender, raising his index finger.

"Somebody needs a drink."

"I really do not need a drink."

"If you came all the way down here just to look all mopey at me, at least do it with a drink in your hand."

A stout demon with an especially serious face appears at the table, beer in hand. Although his mouth is hidden behind a thick beard, Death knows he is frowning. He is very tall for a demon, and the ram horns that sprout from the top of his forehead and wrap around near his temples make him an even more imposing figure.

"Haven't you had enough to drink?" the demon growls, more as a statement than a question. Satan glares at the demon and then breaks out into a long and hardy laugh before responding.

"It's for Death, don't worry." Satan says and continues to chuckle a bit as the demon glances at Death and then back at the Devil. The stout demon does not budge. Satan turns back around in his chair.

"You can give him the beer, Jeff."

"Who's paying?"

Satan waves him off.

"Just put it on my tab."

"That tab hasn't been paid in twelve-hundred years, you bastard."

"Then one more drink won't make much of a difference, will it?"

Jeff grumbles and slams down the beer bottle with his massive red hand and trudges back to the bar, muttering to himself. Satan shakes his head, smiling, and turns back to Death once more.

"Jeff's a bit rough around the edges but he's fantastic if you take the time to get to know him. You know what I mean. It's a shame you two never got to know each other better, I think you'd get along great."

Satan looks over at Jeff and waves, the surly creature scowls and writes something down on a piece of paper which Death can only assume is Satan's twelve-hundred year old bar tab. Satan and Jeff have the same altercation just about every day and most employers would not take that kind of disrespect, but once again, Satan is not most employers. Also, there's a history.

When Satan was cast out of Heaven, an event which he refers to as being "fired", no one liked him much down here. You can't really blame them. A strange ex-angel shows up one day with a bunch of suitcases, high hopes, and a paper saying he's in charge. Not that there was much to really take over, more just a bunch of demons milling about doing weird shit and messing with the humans. But it's the principle of the thing and demons don't do well with being told what to do.

It gets lonely being the person in charge, especially if the people below want nothing to do with your leadership. Not only that, but no one believed in him. Not God, not his "friends" back home in Heaven, and certainly not the demons in Hell. All except Jeff. Jeff was Satan's across-the-hall neighbor in his first apartment in Hell and, he was the only one who treated him at all well. Satan doesn't admit to this part, but Jeff took care of him. Satan was just a scared kid and Jeff saw his potential, and rightly so. Satan built an empire from nothing, created a legacy from a punishment meant simply to get him out of the picture, and no one can take that away from him.

Satan finally takes his eyes away from the glass and back up at Death, leaning in close with a wicked grin on his face,

"You wouldn't know it just by looking at him, but Jeff absolutely adores opera."

Satan leans back in his chair and laughs. Death remains expressionless, staring at the beer in front of him now wet with condensation.

"Come on, buddy lighten up a bit. What's gotcha so down?"

Still no response from Death.

"Why did you come here if you don't want to talk? Is it the roads? I know we need to take better care of them and the trip is awful both ways. I promise we'll get to work on them as soon as we can, and I'm even trying to bully those angels into having them put in some work on their end of things, it's just been a real busy season with all the plagues and wars and-"

Death looks up from the wet beer bottle and right into the eyes of

Satan.

"One soul. That's all I want."

Satan's cheerful demeanor fades.

Oh no. I should not have said that. What am I thinking? You can't just blurt things like that out.

Death looks at Satan and his eyes have clearly changed. They've shifted from the usual, cheerful look into something more serious. These are now the eyes of someone that has something to lose. Satan is the first to break the silence by speaking in an artificial version of his previous tone as he fiddles with his drink, except now it's out of nervousness rather than boredom.

"What makes you say that?"

"I've just been thinking about it lately, and I think that might fix the problem."

Just at this moment Death's phone buzzes. He reaches into his pocket and pulls it out, only to see a text from Peter that reads, "Where are you?"

Death sighs.

"Sorry, I have to go. I'm late for work."

Satan looks relieved.

"Yeah you should get going, he hates it when people are late. Here, let me walk you out."

The two rise, with Death turning and trudging towards the door. As they pass the bar, Satan stops and gestures toward the taps.

"Want one for the road?"

Jeff is behind the counter cleaning a glass and he looks Death square in the eyes. That cold, disdainful stare he always gets from Jeff.

"No thank you. I'm already late as it is."

Satan shrugs and walks with Death towards the entrance, chattering all the while about something pointless. Death glances over his shoulder while he's being ushered out the door and notices the scowling figure of Jeff still staring at him. Satan is still jabbering and he hears something that sounds like "-welcome anytime", and then the door is shut and he is once more alone on the dusty streets of Hell.

Death lets out a sigh.

CHAPTER ELEVEN

Satan rests his hands against the door to the bar, closing his eyes and taking a deep breath. In through the nose, hold a moment, let it out slow. Once, twice, three times.

Alright, this is manageable.

Satan opens his eyes and makes his way towards the bar with a newfound determination. Satan pulls up the wooden slab blocking off the entrance, gives Jeff a look that says he needs to remain undisturbed, and enters the door behind the bar, shutting it behind him. Satan takes those deep breaths again.

This is still manageable. Just need to remove the responsibility. If I do nothing then it's all on me, and if it's all on me that's just one more excuse for Him.

The room is small and it functions as a sort of secondary office for Satan. The Devil's main office in the Tower of Hell is of course massive and a sight to behold, but this one is more comfortable. Different work requires a different space. The room is centered around a mahogany desk of reasonable size with two leather armchairs against the wall opposite it and a small table between them with a glass set and bottle of liquor atop it. Bookshelves line the walls to the left and right of the desk. Satan doesn't like to read, but there's something about the books being there that calms him. There's a warmth and coziness here that his main office fails to provide.

On the desk is a wireless handset which stands out against the almost nostalgic design of the room. God always uses this terrible old phone in his office which Satan will never understand because the thing itself is dreadful. You're the God of the Universe and you choose to use a crappy phone? It's too quiet and if the person on the other end speaks too fast the audio comes out sounding kind of distorted. Aesthetic or not, it just feels pointless to Satan. It's like those people that prefer vinyl to digital. Satan knows that digital sounds objectively better, so why would anyone make such an effort to listen to a worse version of music?

Satan takes a seat at the desk, picks up the handset and begins to dial. The beeps come to a sudden halt as Satan's thumb hovers over the dial button. The Devil grits his teeth, jams the button and raises the handset to his ear.

The dial tone sounds and the ringing begins. It rings and rings and rings.

You're kidding me. I know you're available.

On the final ring, the call connects and a gruff voice answers.

"What?"

"It's nice to hear from you as well."

"Cut it out. You called me."

"Yeah, I was calling to try and be of some help, contrary to my better judgement."

"If you're going to be a child, I'm going to hang up. I have a lot to do."

"Sure, sure."

"Did you call for a reason or am I just going to hang up?"

Satan takes a deep breath, trying his best to bottle up his next array of abuses into an airtight mason jar and hide it somewhere he won't try and grab it.

"Yes...so Death came by today right before his shift to ask me if he could have one of the souls. I told him no, obviously, but he doesn't look so good. I feel like we should talk about some way to deal with this because I have a feeling this isn't going to-"

"Death will be just fine."

"Yes, but-"

"No buts. Death will be fine. You followed orders like you're supposed to, souls are not bargaining chips. You're calling to inform me that you did your job?"

"No. I'm to calling to inform you of something that pertains to you-"

"I'm fully aware. He came to see me about it this morning. I've taken care of it. I have no patience for ungrateful employees who cannot find it in themselves to be happy with what they have been given. We're done."

The line goes dead.

Satan holds the handset away from his head before putting it back in its place and rises. Jeff enters as Satan is finishing pouring himself a drink from the glass bottle of liquor.

Jeff says nothing as he often does in situations like these. Just standing there, his mere presence acting as all the words he could possibly need to say. Satan rounds the desk, drink in one hand and resting his other on the back of the fine leather chair. He speaks to Jeff without looking at him.

"I was just trying to help. Not even help. I was just trying to push any implication of guilt off of me and onto Him. And I know how selfish and immature that sounds, but you know why I do it, right? You of all people do. If I give Him even an inch, so much as a speck of earth in my direction, He'll take all of it. Everything. Every single day since I've been here he's been looking for an excuse to get me into that pit. To toss me into that pitch-black eternity like some kind of used condom. Well I'm not going anywhere. He's such a prick."

Satan downs the drink in one gulp and roars as he hurls the glass against the wall. It breaks into countless pieces, bits of glass landing on Jeff's shoulder as the rest scatter about the floor. Satan takes up the lamp on his desk and begins pounding it against the corner, the lightbulb shattering and the lampshade completely unrecognizable. Satan takes up the handset and bashes it into its port again and again and again until the dialing becomes akin to the labored breaths of a dying cyborg.

"Are you done?"

Satan, breathing heavily, nods and adjusts his tie.

"Good. You had best head in, if you're late they'll panic."

Satan continues to nod as he finishes adjusting his tie, checking every piece of his costume and exiting at a fast, but decided pace, closing the door behind him.

Jeff glances at the pieces of glass on his shoulder and brushes them off as he takes in the destruction. Jeff sighs and exits the room, returning with a broom and dustpan.

"I should've never gotten him a new phone after the last time."

CHAPTER TWELVE

Death's first destination is a filthy apartment in a filthy part of a filthy city. He's not very fond of cities as a rule because they're too crowded, too noisy, and they smell terrible. And just to add to Death's bad mood, it is an unholy hour. Like, it's technically morning but it's black as night out. All the annoying jobs take place in the dead of morning. Death struggles for a few minutes to parallel park between a sedan that looks like it might have been washed with water and hand soap once about a decade ago and a blue and white sports car that can only have been parked by a blind man with the fine motor skills of an obese toddler. Death gets out and begins making his way up the steps and towards the apartment complex, huffing and puffing as he goes along.

Death sees a very angry looking man in his late twenties, the worst kind, exiting the complex on a collision course with Death so he moves to the side.

Asshole.

It's not really this person's fault that they didn't move to the side first, and it's not as if they should because Death isn't some big authority figure or anything and it's kind of arrogant to think that someone should do something like that for you when at the end of the day, you're just as obligated to move for them as they are for you. Well, either way, the living can't see Death so it's kind of a null point. It's a trick that everyone who works in the afterlife picks up after a while, but one that Death uses the most. Angels and demons rarely need it because when they show up it's always to make a point, but Death needs to be able to move around without the living knowing he's there, not that if they saw him it would make much of a difference. People tend to forget him unless he has a big cloak and a scythe.

While able to make himself less visible, Death can also make himself presentable to people. Usually it's for if Death wants a coffee or something. Most of the demons, and even some of the angels, would just take what they want. It's just one coffee after all, what's the harm? And it's not like anything these humans do actually matters. But Death finds that excuse so stupid it makes his head hurt. Really? You're a demon or an angel and you can honestly say that it doesn't matter what humans do? It's almost comedic in scale.

Death has always been of the mind that even though he doesn't particularly like humans, he at least has to treat them like they're worth something. He is Death after all. His entire life's work has, and continues to, rest upon the actions of humans. They're kind of pointless on a day to day personal level but they obviously matter to God, and He makes the rules.

"Hey! Is this your car?"

Death feels his stomach drop out.

He shouldn't be able to see me. No one's supposed to be able to see me, unless...

Sometimes living people can see Death even when he doesn't want them to. The downsides of living in the world of a triune God is that He loves a good paradox. Some people can see Death, but they're usually unsavory. No matter how much people see the effects of Death, it's not until they begin to love Death himself that they can see past his disguises. This doesn't apply to those who want Death for themselves, because usually they just want to escape the burning building so to speak. Lesser of two evils type stuff. Not these crazies. Death would usually give it a couple minutes before he collected the souls of the girls that got killed by the Ted Bundy types. They tend to treat Death like a celebrity but they're creepy as hell and make him really uncomfortable. This is not the kind of person that he wants to talk to today.

Death turns around. It appears the blind man with the fine motor skills of an obese toddler was not in fact a blind man with the fine motor skills of an obese toddler, but rather the very angry looking man in his late twenties who is now yelling at a pedestrian across the street. Due to how the angry looking man had initially parked his car, Death was forced to park his in such a way that makes it nearly impossible for the angry looking man to get out. Death takes a deep breath to calm himself.

That's his problem.

Death turns back around towards the apartment complex.

"I'm talking to you, fucker. Is this your car?"

Death turns back around.

The pedestrian glances up from his phone at the man and keeps walking.

Death looks at his car and then back at the man. His hair is too long and tied back in a loose ponytail that hangs just below his shoulders. This does nothing but show off his unflattering face. It's not that the man is ugly. In the right lighting, with better clothing and a proper hair cut he would be moderately attractive. There is just something mean about him that seems to go deep down to the core. Like, if you were to cut him open and peer inside, there would be something gnarled up and hard in there. A wrought iron heart, barbed wire veins, and petrol blood. It's sad, really. Death is pretty good at reading people, but he knows there is no skill involved in this observation. This man is as transparent as you can be. All you have to do is look in his eyes and you can feel the unhappiness and inadequacy.

"Not gonna answer me, huh? I'll take that as a yes. Piece 'o shit..."

Death turns once more towards the apartment building and

continues walking, tuning out the obscene remarks coming from behind him.

The apartment complex is about as nice as one would expect with denizens like the angry man. The main entrance door has bars and one of those loud buzzer systems which Death bypasses with ease.

He isn't exactly someone you can keep out.

It's not like Death can phase through walls or anything weird like that, he's not some sci-fi villain after all. Death just finds that doors open for him. If something is locked, Death opens it. Nothing too complicated or special. People have been trying to stop Death from doing his job for a long time and next to none have ever succeeded, and those who did never used a padlock.

The elevator smells of piss.

Death knocks on the door of apartment 233 out of politeness. People are generally more amicable if they feel in control of the situation, but it also helps with creating a first impression. Simply walking into someone's locked home is rarely a good place to start.

Silence.

Death knocks again.

Silence.

If there's anyone there, they either don't want to talk to him or don't know he's at the door. Even though he doesn't particularly want to talk to them either, the former possibility really bums Death out.

This is what I get for trying to be polite.

Death turns the knob slowly and opens the door, wincing as the door lets out a horrific squeak like a mouse subjected to Medieval torture. A rank smell emanates from the apartment, hitting Death like a city bus. It's the smell of letting oneself go. Death peeks into the living room and kitchen, finding nothing but old wrappers and dirty clothes. Dust is present in varying degrees on just about every surface in the place. Down the hallway, Death spies a single door cracked open. Treading with care, Death creeps forward and pushes open the door. The wall is splattered with a distinct red substance that has pooled on the desk and drips onto the now stained carpet. Slumped at the desk is a man's body.

Death rolls his eyes and glances away, he hates the sight of blood. After regaining his composure, Death pokes his head back into the room and sees the man's spirit sitting on the bed, staring at his body and crying in that silent kind of way. Tears flowing from his red eyes like a faucet that was not turned off quite right, running down his haggard face until they finally drip off onto the carpet below.

Death approaches.

No signs of recognition.

Death takes his hand and puts it in front of the man's eyes, waving it back and forth.

The man's gaze remains locked onto the corpse, the silent weeping uninterrupted. Death scans the room with a hand over his mouth and his eyes ready to look away at any second. As expected, there's a gun. It doesn't look like an especially legal purchase, and Death has a feeling he'll be meeting with whoever sold it to the kid sooner rather than later.

The guy is still crying, but Death is able to get a good long look at his face. The man is young. Death can barely call him a man. A boy, he's a boy. The boy has a mop of light red hair and freckles sprinkled across his face. Although red and puffy from all the crying, Death can see that his eyes were brown. A dull, dark kind of brown. Although Death hates dull people, he is far less concerned with the color of his eyes than he is with the crying.

I hate it when they do this...it makes everything so damn difficult...

Souls that don't want to go make Death's job more unbearable than it already is. Dead people are just like regular people, and this means it is nearly impossible to make them do something they do not want to do. It is difficult enough with regular people but at least there's always a bargaining angle. "We'll kill you", "We'll steal all your money", "We'll kill your kids". There's always something to use, no matter how small. Can you kill a dead person? The answer's no. You can't, people have tried and it doesn't work. Money is irrelevant when you die and, contrary to popular belief, Death has never encountered someone who thought for an instant that their money would help them. It's kind of funny when you think about it. Not that Death knows what being funny is, but he's seen enough TV to get the general idea.

Threatening to kill their kids doesn't work much either. People like to imagine that when they die their final thoughts will be of family and friends. Those people and moments most formative and dear. School, learning to drive, first kiss, getting into trouble, starting college. Maybe you'll remember your first love, maybe your second, definitely not your third, before finally the one you were meant to be with, and then the one you ended up actually being with. Maybe you'll remember your parents. Maybe you'll remember the birth of your children. How could you not think of stuff like that?

The hard truth is that people do not think of any of it when they meet Death. The first thing on their minds is, without fail, "holy fuck". No Friends. No family. No gods. In that moment of realization it is all about them and nothing else. It's selfish, but can you really blame them? They just died, it's a lot to take in. Part of Death's job is cutting through that and get them back on track.

Let's get to work.

Death takes a seat next to the boy on the bed. Not too close, and right on the edge of the bed so he can get up and leave that much faster should things get awkward. The boy has yet to take notice of Death, still staring with a vacant intensity at his own corpse.

Ok, this is just getting rude.

If someone walks into your room, you're generally supposed to give some kind of response. Whether you tell them to get out, glance at them and go back to whatever you're doing, or smile and greet them like a well-adjusted member of society, there's some degree of acknowledgement involved. This guy is literally too out of it to notice the person sitting right next to him.

Death reaches into his cloak and retrieves a small, thick, leather bound superhero notebook as well as a pocket magnifying glass. There is a lot you can say about Death, but you can never call him disorganized. When Death was growing up, his mother referred to his stellar organizational skills as "weaponized anxiety". Death flips to today's date and goes down the list.

"When I was a young man starting out on my life as God, someone very important to me gave me a notebook as well. It helps to keep your thoughts organized, and for what you'll be doing organization is of the utmost importance."

God had opened his desk drawer and pulled out the pocket encyclopedia sized leather notebook. It was completely normal except for the various "BAM!", "POW!" and miscellaneous off-brand superheroes scattered across the cover. Death vividly remembers being surprised and kind of taken aback, looking up at God with a puzzled look. God went right on the defensive.

"I don't really know what kids your age like so I just went with what my Son likes. You two are around the same age. He's eight and you're..."

"Twelve."

"Yeah. Twelve. Close enough. You like superheroes too, right?"

Death did not.

"Yeah, it's fine."

It was not fine.

Death has yet to get around to asking about a replacement more befitting his age, but if the past is any indicator, God is not one to go back on His decisions. Death was given a bright blue superhero themed notebook, and a bright blue superhero themed notebook he would continue to use. Death hates superheroes, but he also hates ungrateful people.

Death finds the handwritten entry.

Tuesday, October 15th:

~~21:58-Carlos Santana, 31, likes board games.~~

~~Stabbing. Heaven.~~

~~22:46-Josephine Miller, 45, jogging.~~

~~Breast cancer. Hell.~~

23:20-William (Willie) Bartek, 20, likes Thai cuisine.

Suicide. Hell.

23:57-Andrew Brock, 23, likes reading.

Car accident. Heaven

Death glances up at the sobbing ginger slumped on the bed and then back down at his book.

Willie Bartek. Almost done, but now for the hard part.

Death clears his throat, loosens the tension in his shoulders, turns to Willie and frowns.

"Hey, Willie."

Death's strategic somber syllables seem to pass right through Willie like water through a strainer. Yet, as they are leaving his other ear, it's like an invisible hand reaches out and pulls them back into his mind. Willie's tears falter and his eyelids flutter as if waking up and he slowly turns to face the figure to his right. Death is not a familiar face to Willie. There is not an ounce of recognition in those swollen, red eyes and that's just how it is for some people. Not everyone has a tragic childhood.

Death smiles at him.

I hate doing this, it just feels so disingenuous. It's not as if I actually know him or care very much about his feelings, but here I am pretending we're best buds.

Death manages to power through the smile. There was a movie Death watched once and hated, something cliché about father and son, but the father character had smiled in a very particular way when he was telling the son that everything was going to be alright. Death has no idea if he's hitting the mark, but humans put a lot of stock in facial expressions. It has something to do with some psychology bullshit that Death could not care less about. If people's feelings are paint, a smiling face is a blank canvas.

On second thought, it may have been a dog movie.

The crying stops and Death speaks.

"So, uh, how are you doing?"

"Not too great," Willie looks away from Death and back at the body slumped at the desk covered with pooled blood, holding his gaze for several seconds before looking back at Death.

Silence fills the room. Death can hear footsteps shuffling around upstairs and a muffled, but very panicked, voice speaking on the phone.

This is going to get busy fast. Why couldn't this asshole just hang himself like everyone else?

"You know, I think we should get outta here. There isn't much to come from staying."

Willie keeps staring at his old body.

"Why did I have to do this..."

"What? I can't hear you, speak up."

"I hate this...why am I so stupid..."

Death's smile vanishes like a candle being blown out.

"Willie, I have half a mind to leave you here if I'm being completely honest right now. I've been all over the world today, jumping from time zone to time zone, oftentimes in more than one place at once because you people are apparently incapable of calming yourselves down and not killing one another for a few fractions of a second. Someone earlier today got stabbed by someone I have an appointment with next week over a pack of gummy bears at a convenience store. A couple days back, this guy broke his neck trying to jump a riding lawn mower over a ramp. Why did I need to force myself to get out of bed, drive all the way over there only to have to listen to an inbred homunculus explain to me why I should give him a new lease on life because, and I quote, 'I know what I did wrong and I can totally make it this time.' This is what I deal with every single day and right now I am not in the mood. So, can you please just do me a favor and cut it out with all the whiny crap so I can be done for today?"

It is at this point that Death realizes Willie's not listening and has instead returned to staring at his own corpse. Death frowns and watches Willie stare and cry for a considerable amount of time, allowing himself to mentally check out a bit as well.

Honestly, it's like dealing with a fish. Why am I even here? I could be home right now. But no. Every single day filled with enough of these pointless bullshit people.

Death takes a deep breath and lets out a long, heavy sigh.

"It's not your fault, Willie. Everyone let you down, especially her.

She would have been much happier with you than him. She was blind. You're going to a better place, and I know it hurts and you don't believe it, but the people you're leaving behind will miss you dearly and she'll think about you every day."

Willie turns away from the body almost immediately and listens to Death with rapt attention.

"Is that all really true?"

"Yes."

No, you boring sack of shit.

"I just need you to sign here, here, and here."

Willie looks down as Death reaches into his bag and retrieves a clipboard with several documents attached. Willie glances back and forth between him and the clipboard until he finally takes it and pretends to read it. Death holds out a pen which Willie takes and uses to give his messy, almost childish signature. Whereas most adult signatures have a level of refinement to the squiggles from constantly having to sign for things, Willie's is like that of a middle schooler who just learned cursive. Rigid and inexperienced but trying its damnedest to appear otherwise.

Death gently takes the clipboard and tucks it back into his bag, retrieving a small slip of paper and an ink stamp, fills out the required fields, slaps on the stamp of approval, pulls out a brochure, folds the slip inside and puts the brochure in Willie's hand. All of it happens as one smooth movement, a singular action, a routine that Death can do with his eyes closed but loathes with such an overpowering hatred that he doesn't even have the slightest desire to try, because if he were to try then there's the slimmest possibility that he could mess it up and then he would have to do it all over again and having to do it even a single time more than he already has to is the worst possible thing he can imagine.

You really shouldn't sign things without reading them. You never know what could be on there.

Willie is back to staring at his corpse.

"This is your pass to the afterlife. One way. The brochure lists various bus stops. Find your nearest one and get on it within seventy-two hours of now or else they'll send an exorcist after you. If they catch you then you'll be sent to purgatory to serve some time before beginning your eternity. If you have any questions or concerns make sure to call the number on the back of your bus pass, also if you fill out the customer satisfaction survey on the inside flap of your brochure and hand it to the driver before getting off you will get 10% off your next order at any participating Yam of God location. Enjoy your stay in the afterlife."

Death double checks to make sure he has everything and leaves. Nothing much else for him to do here. But something stops Death as he passes through the doorway.

"Do you know who I am, Willie?"

No response.

"Willie, do you know who I am?"

Willie turns his eyes from the corpse and meets Death's gray lava lamp irises with a look of confusion.

"You're the Reaper."

Death nods his head as if reassuring himself.

That I am.

CHAPTER THIRTEEN

Emily sits on the first set of stairs leading to her apartment complex watching the people as they go by. After aimlessly riding the bus for a while, Emily decided she had gone over her transportation budget just enough to justify it as a birthday present to herself, but not enough to be dangerously irresponsible so she got off at a stop about two miles from her apartment and walked the remaining distance. She sits and watches the people, Emily considers what her grandmother would say about this. The poor woman would definitely be worried about Emily's safety and most certainly would have scolded her. It's not as if it were a massive risk, it was two miles, but at the thought of her grandmother's worrying she gets a little feeling of warmth in the center spot below and behind her lungs.

For as long as Emily can remember, something has been draining out of her. Slowly, like a pinprick that doesn't heal. Every couple minutes, the smallest drop of blood falls to the ground and so on and so forth for twenty-six years. Emily has tried everything she can think of to staunch the flow and nothing works for long.

Emily checks the time on her phone.

1:34 AM

The numbers blur as Emily looks instead at the background photo. Her cat, Mr. Mustard, grouchy as ever, in her lap with Eric behind her eating cold pizza out of a box. Both of them laughing. It was their first night in the apartment and there had been a mess-up with the movers so none of their things were going to be there for another week and a half. With the last of Emily's graduation money they had ordered a large no topping pizza. Even though Emily is fairly certain the pizza was ketchup and shredded cheese melted on a circular sheet of corrugated cardboard, it was the best meal she has ever had.

Emily clicks the phone off. No need to dwell on things too much.

The phone vibrates, startling Emily.

Incoming Call: *Anita*

Emily smiles when she sees the contact photo for Anita: her sitting in the next seat over at some seedy bar, looking into the camera with that faint, wry smile of hers as she nurses a glass of water.

"Well, a great big evening hello to you," Emily bellows in a deep voice.

"You're always so awkward answering the phone."

"I do my very best."

Anita laughs on the other end before shifting tone like a flash of lightning on a rainy night.

"So, Emily, what's wrong?"

"What do you mean? There's nothing wrong."

"Seriously?"

"I didn't get very much sleep last night."

"That's obviously not true. I mean, talk about a cry for help. 'Oh, uh, no I just didn't get much sleep last night haha'. Come on, Emily. I've known you too long for this, what's wrong?"

"I, uh...phhh. Why are you so good at this?"

"Because you're not that hard to read."

"I'll have to work on that. I just, I don't actually know. He's been so distant lately, and honestly kind of cruel. He's never been one to open up much, but he was always at least putting forth an attempt, you know? Like, I don't know, just *trying* to be good, you know? I mean, I know he's never been good, but he was *good* you know? Like, he was good and nice and he had a heart. He may have been bad but he was never *bad* but now he doesn't feel like anything. He's always gone, and when he's here he's not even really here he's just grouchy and mean and I feel like it's my fault."

"How would any of that be your fault?"

"Well, I just, I mean I talk about myself so much like right now. It's always about me and no one else. I know I'm a selfish bitch but I try really hard not to be. I try so hard because I don't want to be like I was, you know? I've been feeling it get bad again but I'm not too worried. It feels better than in the past but like, it's just shitty but I also know it'll work itself out. Does that make sense?"

There is a momentary pause and for an instant, Emily can hear Anita's faint breathing.

"You're exhausted. It's currently…1:47 AM. I'm assuming you haven't had a good night's sleep in a while, and you've never done well without sleep. I'm also assuming from the background noise that you're not at your apartment. Go home, get some sleep."

"I'll do that. Thank you for talking."

"Honestly, Emily, it doesn't seem like you needed to talk. I think you've finally outgrown me."

Emily smiles.

"I could never outgrow you. I'll call you tomorrow, buh-bye."

"Goodbye."

Anita hangs up first and Emily stares at the call log before getting up from the steps and making her way towards the apartment building. As Emily walks, the smile fades and she retreats at a creeping pace back to the gray matter cubbyhole inside her skull so that by the time she arrives at her door she is right back where she started. The same woman with that same feeling behind her lungs. Anita's words help, but she would have to be with her all the time for it to make any difference. When it gets bad, it continues to get worse until something drastic happens. That's how it's always been.

I can't be drastic now. I'm not a teenager, I'm not a child. If I crack, then my entire life cracks with it. You've got to be strong, Emily. You've got to deal with it like a grown ass woman instead of running away like you always do. Stupid stupid stupid.

Emily opens the door and makes her way through, quiet and slow like a kid who snuck out. Emily closes and locks the door behind her, depositing her keys and wallet in the little basket in the entryway and scans the dark apartment.

No Eric.

Emily creeps over to her bedroom and peeks her head in.

No Eric.

Emily lets out a sigh of relief even though she knows she should wish he's here. But now she'll be able to get to sleep before him and she can worry about everything tomorrow and that makes her feel a lot better.

Tomorrow.

Emily tosses her phone onto her bedside table and throws herself onto the bed, closing her eyes as she fidgets around and gets herself under the covers. She must be more tired than she initially thought because the usually thirty to forty minute task of falling asleep is happening almost instantaneously. Emily waltzes on the precipice of sleep as she enters her own little world of dreams and she teeters on the edge preparing to fall. As she tips over and gravity takes her into the dreamy black pit of sleep, a thought passes through her mind. She notices the thought as she's falling and glances up to see it soaring above like a bird.

The door was unlocked.

CHAPTER FOURTEEN

Death gazes into the eternal spiral of his squeaky ceiling fan. The Reaper can't sleep and it had been a longer day than usual. After leaving Willie's apartment, Death found his driver's side rear tire slashed. He assumes it was the angry pony-tailed man, but it could have been a monstrous racoon for all it matters because in the end, Death had to change a spare and it took him longer than it should have because he was tired and then by the time he got in the car he still had a few more stops to make which just made the final hours of work more miserable on a rather profound level. When he was driving around, all he could think of was sleep and his bed but now he's here and the respite isn't.

Death used to love the peace and quiet of these moments before sleep. The serenity and fulfillment of being able to sit in silence and have a good long think was never lost on Death. Those moments as you drift off to sleep were always his favorite. There's something transcendent about it, taking the plunge into the world of the subconscious. Now Death fears those moments, those not-even-seconds, with the whole of his being. When he was younger, they were like dunking your head under the water and opening your eyes up to take everything in before returning to the surface. The peace, the stillness, the silence.

Now when Death takes the plunge, he closes his eyes, pinches his nose, and throws himself into the ready embrace of a sinking sense of danger. An implacable anxiety that roots itself somewhere just behind his lungs and stretches its cold, inky tendrils up into the grooves of his brain and starts to burn and burn and burn and burn and burn. And yes, before you ask, you can freeze and burn at the same time.

He still feels like a child, but more in the sense that once he's jumped into the pool he feels the impending fear of being attacked by a shark. Death knows that he is in a swimming pool hundreds of miles inland from anything even resembling a shark, but that changes absolutely nothing. The tendrils still take hold and he has to fight back or else he will be dragged underneath without time to even think.

Why do kids always think there are sharks in swimming pools?

It doesn't make any sense. Why would there ever be a shark in a swimming pool? And if someone did manage to sneak a shark into your pool while you were gone, chances are it's not even the dangerous kind. It would likely be one of those little ones that have more in common with puppies or kittens than any sort of man-eating sea monster.

It's not any sort of logic that makes a child believe there is a shark in the water, but rather when they jump in the water and realizes they are alone. Their mom went inside to finish up a load of laundry, their brother is taking a nap, their dad is at work, and there is no-one but them and the shark. It's that implacable feeling that if you were to get bitten by a man-eating sea monster right this instant then no one would be there to help. The deck chairs are empty. No sight of anyone through the window. Just the child alone, face to face with their own personal shark and no one around to help. The child feels a pure aloneness they do not understand, that they cannot explain, but they know it makes a five-foot pool a horrifying trench of sinister depth and darkness from whence sharks emerge in order to gobble little children up skin, bones, heart, soul and all.

There's nothing like those final moments of lucidity to make you feel like a bigger piece of shit.

Death rolls over in his slightly-too-small bed. Why a grown man still has a twin bed is beyond even him. It was there when he moved in and he's never had the energy to fight anyone on it.

The hushed jazz piano track isn't helping.

When Death stopped being able to sleep, he tried listening to music. Death knew that you're supposed to just still your body and not look at screens so on and so forth, but none of it really worked. Death would just lay in bed, staring at his ceiling fan on the lowest setting going round and round and round, hypnotizing him into an almost trance-like, yet very awake, state. When Death is in that trance-like, yet still very, very awake state he can't help but consider just about everything.

Oftentimes, he will get trapped on a specific subject and then go in circles with it until he gets so sick of the loop that he just has to get up and do something. Death will imagine a conversation or a course of events, and then play it out to its logical conclusion based on his knowledge of people and things. It's a game that he's been playing since he was young, and although the basic rules of the game have stayed the same, the end result has changed a good deal. It used to be a good way for him to pass the time while waiting for his mother somewhere, long car rides, and most of all as he was going to sleep. Death's mother had actually been the one to suggest he try it when she noticed he was finishing her sentences. She had of course yelled at eight year old Death for being rude and told him he would never get a girlfriend if he interrupted people like that, but after the obligatory scolding, told him he should use rather rude talent to practice talking to people so that he wouldn't, "sound like such an autistic freak".

She was right.

It started out as something to help Death learn how to ask for his meal at a restaurant without scaring the waitress and slowly turned into a way to keep himself from curling up into a ball, covering his ears, closing his eyes, sucking in all the air he could, and holding his breath so the only sound he could hear was the dull beating of his heart.

Elementary school was hard.

Even though he employed such methods of distraction as a child, Death had since then done his best to avoid them. Self-inflicted distraction is one of the things that Death hates, but as the music plays and the fan whirs and squeaks he sighs.

Since when did I become the kind of person that can't sit in silence?

CHAPTER FIFTEEN

Bureaucracy has an interesting capacity to fuck up in the simplest ways possible. A well-designed system can run almost completely independent of any leadership or thought for years. Everyone just does their little mundane jobs each and every day and it runs like clockwork. A well-oiled machine, a factory of mass production, a towering monument to a collective shirking of responsibility. However, as with most finely tuned machines, a well-placed mote of dust is enough to send it spiraling to the ground in flames faster than the speed of light.

In this case the well-placed mote of dust goes by the name of Raphael. In preparation for Death's day off, Saint Peter planned for a massive joint operation between Heaven and Hell to pick up the work, because whether Peter likes to admit it or not, Death is quite good at his job. Raphael is one of many angels hand-picked by Peter to process a number of souls bound for Heaven. Peter has been spending his off hours fine tuning the plan so that everything will run without a hitch because if it goes well, maybe God will fire Death and give Peter's top-notch team the job instead. A saint can only dream. The issue with a top-notch team is that it relies on other people doing their job.

Raphael is not looking forward to filling in for Death. Raphael does not like Death. He loves his job at the office and doing all of his important work, Raphael is never able to explain what it is when people ask but he knows it's important, and to him this whole filling in for Death thing is a waste of his precious office time. Toiling over this dilemma, fill in for

Death (something he does not want to do) or not fill in for Death (something he wants to do), Raphael decides to call in sick.

As the angel opens his laptop he realizes that if he calls in sick right now, early evening the day before, Peter will likely ask him to find a replacement. Peter had made it clear to everyone on the team that all of his time today would be spent going over each and every detail, every single soul, and making sure all the details are right and nothing is missing. There would be no mistakes, not one. Raphael does not want to find a replacement because he's already done for the day and that would be extra work to do at home. No matter how important your work is, a good work/life balance is necessary. So, Raphael waits.

And waits.

And waits.

And waits until the clock is just about to strike midnight and sends an email to Peter.

"Sick. Can't come in tomorrow."

Raphael feels this is sufficient and he has done his part as a good employee. The angel goes to sleep without a care in the world as the message shoots through whatever it is emails shoot through and pops up on Peter's laptop causing him to halt his work like a deer in the headlights.

Peter feels as if he could throw up. Frantically typing, he replies demanding that he come in.

No response.

Another email.

No response.

A flurry of emails.

No response from the angel, who is sound asleep, dreaming of all the fun things he would do with his hard-earned day off.

Peter begins to sweat, dropping what he is doing and going through his countless contingency documents. The trouble is that almost all of his contingencies are for things like, forgotten clipboards, mixed up routes, and recording data incorrectly. Peter never expected anyone on his team would let him down. The other Apostles had always gotten on him for his trusting personality, for always assuming that if someone said they would do something they would in fact do it. This was supposed to show them, this would show everyone that not only are Peter's ideals are capable and valid, but so is Peter.

Finally, Peter arrives at the final contingency: Plan Z

Peter steels himself and sets about reworking his entire plan, changing schedules, sending new emails, combining groups and shifting numbers and doing a pretty fantastic job considering the circumstances.

Such a fantastic job in fact that he completely forgets about what he was doing previously. If Raphael had sent that email just a little bit earlier, maybe Peter would have had more time and remembered, and maybe if he had sent it a little bit later then Peter would have finished it. There's no way of knowing for sure but one thing is certain, Peter had completely missed a soul. One name with a suspicious lack of details. Who are they? What do they love? And most importantly, which eternity are they bound for?

CHAPTER SIXTEEN

*The eternal setting sun, the cloudless, orange juice sky. The sound of crashing waves. Death gazes down from the balcony as they curl into themselves, the resulting sea foam a deep, inky black. Death can feel a light sea breeze on his face. His breath is light and he feels rested and full. His eyelids aren't heavy. Death takes a deep, full breath of the salty air, allowing it to fill his lungs, free of the strange thing that once lived just behind it. There is a faint smell of citrus. Death turns around and catches a glimpse of the veil fluttering against the breeze and just beyond it-*RINNNNNGGGGGGG.

Death slams the alarm clock resting on his nightstand. He had forgotten to disable it for his day off, though it wouldn't have made that much of a difference. If you wake up at four in the morning for tens of thousands of years, then alarm or not, you will wake up at four in the morning. Death rests his head on his singular pillow and looks up at the textured ceiling finish. He often finds himself lost in the random patterns, each one as different as a snowflake. If he stares at them for long enough they'll begin to blend together and form shapes and constellations. A plaster Rorschach blot. Sometimes he finds a mask, other times a great beast glowering down at a young boy, and other times a funny little lizard. If he so desires, Death could gaze up at his ceiling all day. It would be a waste, but it would be his waste and that wouldn't be so bad. He stays longer than usual and gets out of bed when he feels ready. Strolling into his kitchen, starting the pot of coffee he had prepared the night before, and checking the refrigerator and pantry for something to eat.

Orange juice, yogurt, an old sub, a bag of pretzels, microwave popcorn and hot pockets. Should be fine for today.

Although not some of Death's favorite foods, his real goal for today is to not leave the house. Today is a day for watching television, reading, and painting. It's been so long since Death painted anything, and now he finally has something to add. Death takes a seat on his couch and turns on the TV as the faint hissing of brewing coffee is drowned out by the blathering of some polarized news channel. The attractive-if-you're-a-housewife news anchor is saying something about rigged polls and under the table deals, but that lasts all of two and a half minutes until he passes things over to coverage of a local dog show. Changing the channel a few times, Death finally settles on one of the several channels playing *Seinfeld* reruns. Back when they were in high school, Satan had discovered human sitcoms and it was love at first sight, with *Happy Days* being his personal favorite. Many lunch periods were spent comparing people they knew to characters from the shows. Although Death had begun watching them because Satan all but forced him, eventually it became a pastime. He likes the simplicity of the characters and although their actions border on irrational and/or psychotic at any given moment, it's an irrationality that makes sense in the given world. You can feel the emotional highs and lows without having to work too hard.

The hissing of the coffee maker stops so Death pours himself a cup and stands by the sink, gazing at the screen and sipping from his mug. Taking his time, not rushing, tasting the bitterness of the coffee until the cup is empty.

Alright. It's time.

Death sets down the mug, turns off the TV, and strides past the couch and up to the singular closed door down the hallway adjacent to the kitchen. It looks just like the other doors in his house but this one has something important inside. He turns the knob slowly and with intent as if to avoid waking something within. The studio. Paintings half-finished and complete alike strewn around the room. You would think upon entering that you had, in a rather silly fashion entered the home of someone else and were not in fact in the house of the Grim Reaper. Everything is so out of character with paints and palettes, canvas and cloth, and most of all, clutter.

No one is allowed inside besides himself, although Death has yet to enforce the rule because no one knows about his studio. In the far corner there is a single window that allows a beam of light into the room. Death's eyes follow the beam from its origin in a downward motion, focusing on the motes of dust swimming in the air made visible by the light until his eyes make their way to the final destination. The center of the room.

A solitary easel with a canvas board resting on it.

Death has been painting for a long time and it was one of the only things he enjoyed as a child. Not that his paintings were worth anything, but he liked doing it. The way he could stop thinking and let his hands do all the work. Generally speaking, he either finishes a painting in the first sitting or gives up and never comes back to it. However, the one resting on the easel has a thin layer of dust on the top of it.

The painting depicts a small room. To the right, there is a four-poster bed with a blue and white patterned quilt on it.

Death had started it several years ago when he began to have the dreams. His first image of the room was of the curtain tossing softly in the wind and he remembers it like it was yesterday. He was seated at the kitchen table in his mother's house listening to her drone on about something petty like daytime television or gardening. In a subconscious attempt at a daring escape, Death had turned his head to look out the window all the while nodding his head like some broken toy when all of a sudden he was somewhere else. This Somewhere Else had a curtain and he was looking at it from a seated position. Death could hear the faint but steady crash of waves, feel a light breeze, and see the thin veil fluttering playfully in the breeze, almost inviting him onto the balcony. He leaned towards it and found himself leaning towards his mother's sink instead. She had not skipped a beat and was still lecturing him on proper tomato care in her usual fashion. He was shaken at the time, but he attributed it to sheer boredom. A simple, one-time thing.

Death is prone to seeing it in his day to day life, but he always sees it when he dreams. The first time it happened, he didn't think much of it. Then he had the same dream the next night. And the next night. And the night after that. It's been five years and he still has the same dream every night. Sometimes bits and pieces change, but it is always in that room, the black waves are always crashing, and the smell of citrus is always in the air. Whenever something new happens in the dream he adds it to the painting.

As Death began to have these recurring dreams and daydreams, it went from something that piqued the interest of his creative fancy to an all-consuming obsession. Death is not one to have all consuming obsessions, but here he is, working on the same painting of the same image that continues to grow in his mind year after year. The Grim Reaper intends on finishing it some day but he has yet to explore the entire room and get all the angles and material he needs. Death is only ever there for what feels like a few seconds and sometimes he'll miss details and you can't very well have a good painting without details. This makes every single vision of great importance.

Death's studio, though an organizational atrocity, has an odd sense of order to it. Even though nothing is in a logical place, he knows where everything is. Digging underneath an array of used paint tubes he finds one with just enough black paint to add the waves. Death's palette and a fresh brush are resting on a precarious stack of books next to the easel. When he is done painting, he always makes sure to leave a fresh brush next to the palette. Something of a courtesy to his future self.

He takes the palette in hand, squeezes out a reasonable amount of paint, dips his brush, and brings his hand up to canvas...

Ringggggggggg.

Death's hand hovers inches away from the canvas. Waiting until the ringing stops.

Whoever it is can wait. Today is my day off.

He brings the brush in once more.

Ringgggggggg.

I can't focus like this.

He waits out the second call, letting it ring all the way through.

On the third call, Death slams down the palette and storms over to the wall-mounted phone in his kitchen entryway.

"What."

"Death, I need you to come in," Peter blurts out over the line.

"No."

Death makes to hang up.

"Wait, wait, wait! Death, seriously, I need you to come in. It's an emergency."

Death holds the phone in front of his face and closes his eyes, clenching the receiver in his hand.

"It's my day off. Why are you calling me about an emergency? Isn't it your job to take care of those?"

Silence.

"It doesn't matter what happened, what matters is there are a good number of souls with no one to process them. I'll send you the list, but you need to come in."

"Absolutely not. This is my one day off. I'm going to spend it the way I want to, and believe it or not, that does not involve swooping in to save your ass. Goodbye."

Death makes to hang up once more.

"W-wait, wait, wait! If you don't come in, Michael will take the fall for it."

"What?"

Peter is stuttering up a storm by this point.

"Y-you heard me. Michael was in charge of organizing who was assigned where. He made a mistake."

"That was your job, Peter."

Silence.

"...He'll believe me. He doesn't like Michael very much anymore."

"You're a piece of shit you know that, right? And aren't you supposed to be a little more subtle if you're trying to blackmail people?"

"It's not my fault Michael made a mistake."

Death takes an internal time out.

Let's think about this logically. In the end, it's not my problem. It's not my responsibility that Peter wants to be a piece of trash. It's not my responsibility to keep useless old Michael from taking the fall for a mistake he didn't make. Today is my day off. My first ever vacation, and even though I know they're using it to not-so-subtly mask a trial run without me, I'm happy to have whatever vacation I can get. What's the point in fighting something that only helps me? If this crashes and burns like it's bound to, then I come out with net positive results and if anything it just improves my case for actually getting what I want so really what I should tell Peter is to-

"Send me the list. I won't have time to copy it into to my notes."

"Thank y-"

Death hangs up and lets out a sigh.

And today was going so well.

CHAPTER SEVENTEEN

Emily wakes up later than usual. Mumbling something about her alarm, she rolls out of bed and makes her way into the kitchen. The best way to start a lazy Saturday is always with a cup of coffee and a toaster waffle. Emily is filled with a slothful anticipation for the day to come. Television, movies, maybe she would get take-out. She hasn't had Chinese in a while.

She notices a slip of paper on the counter as she plugs in the coffee maker.

In Eric's childish scrawl, "Be gone for a few days, have some work to take care of."

It's decided then. First up, coffee and see what's on TV, next get to reading that awful novel her book club chose this month, and then movies to close out the evening. Emily needs a break, this week had been difficult, and with Eric gone she can get the rest she needs with no interruptions.

Emily suddenly realizes she didn't water her plants yesterday. Emily has always been terrible with plants. If having a green thumb means that you're good with plants, then Emily has...

What's the opposite of green?

Emily ponders it as she walks out on to the balcony of her apartment, picking up the watering can resting on a table near the door.

A cluster of spider lilies are blooming in a small garden box attached to the handrail. These are the only plants that Emily has ever been able to take care of. Emily has tried her hand at gardening countless times in the past and even managed to kill a cactus, but she's had good luck with her spider lilies. After watering them, Emily turns around to find a man with a messenger bag standing in the entryway to her apartment. Tall and thin with deep circles under his eyes and a haggard expression, the man has dark hair that hangs just above his eyes. To compliment the brooding art major aesthetic, he's wearing a black t-shirt and ill-fitting jeans accented with the occasional paint splatter here and there.

Strange men wandering into her apartment is not a common occurrence for Emily, so she's not entirely sure how to handle the situation. Should she call the police? Should she scream? Should she say hello? He doesn't look all that threatening, but he's still a strange man who has entered Emily's apartment without permission. He's obviously here of his own free will but in kind of a funny way, the man looks as if he would rather be anywhere else.

Emily decides to break the silence herself.

"Hello?"

The man pulls a cell phone from his back pocket and scrolls through it, glancing up at Emily and back down with a puzzled expression.

"Excuse me, um, who are you? Why are you here? And, uh, how did you get in?"

The man looks up at Emily and leaves his gaze there, clicking the phone off and returning it to his back pocket. Then he speaks.

"Name?'"

"Um, Emily. Why do you need to know?"

"You don't know who I am?"

Emily thinks for a moment and comes up empty.

"I don't believe I do. Now are you going to tell me who you are or not?"

"You're sure you don't know who I am or why I'm here? No clue whatsoever? They usually know."

"*They usually know*? What does that even mean?"

The man sighs and mutters something about incompetence then begins looking around the apartment. Peeking behind couches, opening doors, he even looks inside the refrigerator. Emily feels the natural urge to tell him to stop, after all, going through a stranger's home is quite rude, however she has no desire to do so. The man notices Mr. Mustard on the couch in his usual spot deep in a morning nap and makes sure to avoid disturbing the oversized pancake of a cat while he searches under and around the cushions. The man goes about his search as if it were the most natural thing in the world, only stopping when examining the counter.

"What's this note?"

Emily glances at the note Eric left on the counter.

"My husband left it. He goes out of town a lot for business."

The man nods.

Finally, he comes to Emily's bedroom, takes one look inside and immediately shuts the door. He pulls out the cell phone and swipes through it, becoming visibly confused, then he clicks it off once more and strides closer to Emily. She is now able to get a good look at his eyes. A somber gray, at first glance they are an almost depressing color. However, the longer she looks, the more Emily notices something shining through from behind the gray. Almost like a little LED candle in a restaurant is just barely able to shine through an opaque candle holder. The gray moves and shifts about like the contents of a lava lamp, moving freely between different shades.

The man reaches into his bag and pulls out a pen and a slip of paper.

"Do you have any idea whether you were a good or bad person? I need to know what to write down here."

"Um. I mean, I'm not perfect but I try to do good things. I've never killed anyone, if that's what you're asking."

"Yeah that doesn't help me much."

The man begins scrolling through his phone and muttering again.

He lets out a deep sigh and shakes his head.

The man looks exhausted and Emily finds it almost distracting to watch. As he looks down at the phone, Emily watches his irises move about like lazy, iridescent jellyfish. Tired behind the eyes, a weariness centered in his chest, Emily sees it with infrared intuition. Emily has never been good at much, but she's always had a knack for finding those in pain, and this strange figure in her apartment is in pain. A not especially unique kind of pain, but pain nonetheless.

It probably feels unique to him.

"Can I get you something?" Emily asks.

The man is muttering something about how this is why he needs a day off and how incompetent someone by the name of Peter is. Then he stops and looks at Emily with a puzzled look.

"What?" He replies

"Can I get you something?"

"What do you mean?"

"Like, coffee or a cup of water or something. You look exhausted."

Then Emily remembers what's in her freezer and smiles.

"I also have toaster waffles in the freezer. It's early, have you eaten yet today? I know they're kind of kiddy, but they're really good especially if you put a little syrup on them because it gets in the grooves and stuff and it just adds so much and like, if I have any oranges they taste really good with-"

"Come with me."

He turns around and began walking towards the apartment door.

Emily is just getting more and more confused. The opening moments of her day were quite normal. She was going to spend a free Saturday doing whatever she wanted and now a strange man is telling her to come with him and the especially strange thing is that Emily wants to. She actually wants to go with this stranger who appeared, creeped around, and then told her to come with him.

Nana would be so angry with me.

What had he seen in her bedroom? Emily walks up and puts her hand on the door handle, beginning to turn it.

"I wouldn't do that if I were you."

Emily looks over at the man who is standing in the entryway. His expression is different than before. Before, there was a level of annoyance on his face and in his tone as if speaking to her was a chore. However, right now there is a touch of concern. In that moment his disdain for her does not matter. Emily can see it in his eyes and knows that whatever is on the other side of that door will do her no good.

"You were nice to my cat, so I have a good feeling about you."

The man gives her a puzzled look and shrugs as he walks out of the apartment.

Emily waits a few moments then follows.

It's a good thing that Emily heeded Death's advice. If not, she would have opened the bedroom door to find herself lying peacefully in a mess of sheets and pillows with dark bruises on her neck and bloodshot eyes gazing up into the eternal spiral of the ceiling fan looking for something, or someone, that isn't there.

CHAPTER EIGHTEEN

As they drive down the road, Emily is in a strange mood. Death would consider himself a relative expert on how people work but, he's a bit stumped with her. She's not hysterical, nor is she particularly somber. The woman is more along the lines of pensive than anything else. He is not used to dealing with composed people in times like this.

The list that Peter sent me just flat out missed her. Non-existent. I had her location and nothing else. That's bad. Really bad, and I need to get this figured out soon. Whether she consciously knows it yet or not, she's dead. Not only is she dead but she has not been assigned a destination yet and even if she doesn't realize her situation, it's abnormal for a person to be a wayward soul. She may be composed now, but when it hits her it'll hit hard and she's going to crash.

Death has no problems with people feeling bad and stuff, but he does have issues with people dragging him into those feelings.

People have changed. It was much better back in the day when if you were sad or had some other emotional issue you just pushed it deep down until it eventually manifested itself into some kind of complex. Don't drag other people into it. It's the principle of the thing.

Death has very strong principles.

That's when he realizes she's sitting in the front seat.

Wait why the hell is she in the front seat? Why did I let her sit in the front seat? Did I?

Death thinks back over the previous fifteen or so minutes. He had been too caught up in thought to notice that she hopped into the front seat without any sort of inquiry as to whether that was okay.

What a rude person.

This is especially irritating to him because it's too late to have her sit in the back now. If they get out of the car and go to get back in it'll be awkward if he tells her to sit in the back. She would certainly ask why, if she sat up front before, does she have to sit in the back now? Death's head begins to swim.

In the front she stays.

Until Death can figure out what to do with her, she is just going to have to stay with him. He still has a good few names left on his list and because he had a late start the Reaper cannot afford to waste time.

"There's some work I need to take care of. You're going to have to tag along for a bit."

The woman turns her head.

"Oh, ok. What do you do?"

Death blinks once, twice, three times.

"What do I do?"

Emily nods.

"I, um...I serve paperwork."

"Cool. You must get to meet a lot of interesting people that way.

Death sighs as he pulls up in front of a small suburban home. An idyllic place, all things considered. Though not far from the city, it somehow manages to retain an air of calm and quiet. The road in front is busy but the cars go at such a speed to where you'd feel safe letting your kid play outside. The home has a white picket fence and flowerbeds adjacent to the front porch. It reminds Death of his mother's house and he feels imminent sense of dread.

"You'll wait in the car."

The woman nods.

Death removes the keys from the ignition and makes sure the doors are locked before making his way up to the house. As Death puts his hand on the gate, he blinks and hears the faint sound of crashing waves, smells the distinct scent of citrus and feels the soft sea breeze. And in quite literally the blink of an eye it's all gone. Death sighs and turns on his heels back towards the car. Death unlocks the door, puts the keys in the ignition and turns the air conditioning on. Death hates it when people leave pets and children in cars without air conditioning.

"Once I shut the door, make sure you lock it. I don't need this thing getting stolen, okay?"

The woman smiles and nods.

Death shuts the door and watches through the window to make sure that she actually locks the car and then pushes through the gate, retrieving the cell phone from his back pocket as he goes.

08:40-Charles (Charlie) Wu, 9, likes basketball.

Fatal fall, Heaven.

Death groans.

I hate kids.

Death has never really understood why kids automatically get into Heaven. The only people who would ever assume that all kids deserve to go to Heaven are those who have never met a child before. God has a child, an especially bratty one at that, so he should understand more than most.

Besides, Heaven is not the most child friendly place out there. It's just a bunch of freaks who think they're really good because they simply avoided doing one thing or another. Death knows that "Jesus", although he prefers "bratty kid", is the only reason fellow brats get in. Nowadays, Jesus makes the call on who gets in or not. At least when God was doing all the work there was some kind of stable leadership. Do bad thing, go to Hell. Do good thing, go to Heaven. Simple, easy, clean-cut. Now everything is all about "loving others" and "faith" or other buzzwords like that. It's all so vague and inclusive that Heaven is full of a bunch of riff-raff. The whole point of Heaven was to sort the good people out from the bad ones. But now there are all these cheesy loopholes like mothers praying their kids in, people redeeming their spouse, deathbed conversion and other cheap shit like that. Why can some people work hard their entire lives to achieve something and then just anyone can show up dressed like a vagabond and nothing but a forgiveness prayer under his belt? It irks him to no end.

Death knocks on the door out of courtesy and the door flies open to reveal a small boy with messy black hair and a confused look on his face. Peering behind him, Death spies his little corpse with limbs at awkward angles, a big wound on his head, a grisly halo of dried blood, and a crimson streak starting from around the middle of the steps going down.

Parents are probably at work and the kid walks himself to the bus stop. How irresponsible can you be?

Death shakes his head.

Hearing the sound of a television in the background, Death peers over the other side of the child to find that he is watching cartoons, and the really loud and obnoxious ones at that.

"May I come in?"

"I'm not supposed to let strangers in."

"I'm not a stranger, I just need your help with something."

The kid does not break his emotionless gaze on Death's face.

"That's what the creepy man in the video at school said and we were supposed to tell him 'no, I can't help you' because he might be a kidnapper. Are you a kidnapper?"

"No."

The kid ponders for a time.

"A kidnapper would probably say that."

"I'm not a kidnapper, so just let me in."

"No."

"Listen, kid, I am starting to get really tired of this and I have had a long day. Please just be considerate, make my job easier, and let me in to your house. I don't need to ask for permission."

The kid starts to look scared.

Wait, shit, that's something a kidnapper would say.

Death is feeling irritated. Things are starting to get in the habit of upsetting his plans. He had been hoping to do absolutely nothing today, then he met an annoying woman and now he's speaking to an annoying child and after all of this is over he's going to have to speak to even more annoying people and then when the whole entire workday is over he's going to have to deal with this annoying woman and almost certainly have more annoying conversations with even more annoying people the next day and the day after that and the day after that forever until it's decided he's no longer useful and he's thrown into the Abyss.

Everything begins to weigh down on Death like a ten-gallon hat cast from iron. All he wants to do is go home and sit in the peace and quiet and figure out what's wrong with him. If he never figures it out then he'll never be able to fix it and if he's never able to fix it then he doesn't know how much longer he can last living like this day in and day out feeling like everything is just outside of his control like a home that gets messier and messier until finally it's so messy that it becomes too much to clean and you have to just live with it and move the mess around because you've gone too far and going back is not an option because there is nothing you can do to stop it and even if you were to stop it then would that ever really-

"What's your name?"

Death looks down to his left to find Emily crouched at the boy's eye level, a soft smile complimented by a warm look in her eyes. The child seems a bit put off by this genuinely friendly adult who Death can only assume does not give off kidnapper vibes.

"Charles...but that name is really lame, so you need to call me Charlie."

"Alright, Charlie, nice to meet you," the woman holds out her hand for a shake, "can my friend and I come in?"

Charlie looks between her and Death, continuing to hold a suspicious glare on the latter until he nods his head and shakes the Emily's hand. She smiles even brighter.

"Thanks, Charlie. What are you watching on TV?"

Charlie's face lights up and he grabs her hand, leading the woman over to the television set and blabbing all the while about whatever the mindless garbage playing on the television screen is. Death hovers in the doorway for a few moments before crossing the threshold and closing the door.

Is it my face? It would be understandable if I was wearing the cloak and carrying the scythe, but I'm not.

Death concludes that he will never understand children.

There are two couches in the living room. The woman and Charlie sit on one, Death on the other. Charlie's choice between the two of them is made quite clear. As the other two are chattering on about whatever it is children care about, Death undoes the clasps on his bag and begins pulling out and organizing the necessary paperwork to get Charlie and himself going their separate ways. As he begins to open his mouth, Emily looks at him and slightly raises her hand from her lap and shakes her head. There is a look in her eyes that Death has not yet seen today. Determination.

Death waits to see what happens.

After a few minutes the woman taps Charlie, who is engrossed in the television screen, on the shoulder.

"So, Charlie, my friend and I need your help with something. Do you think you can do that for me?"

Charlie turns from the screen and looks around at the two of them with an apprehensive and confused expression.

"What do you need my help with?"

Death sees his chance and slides the paperwork across the coffee table between the couches.

"I need you to sign here, here, and here."

Charlie looks at the woman.

"He means write your name, Charlie."

Charlie nods his head and gets up, walking into the kitchen. Death can here the sound of someone rummaging around in a drawer.

"I have a pen right he-"

The woman gestures at her neck for Death to stop speaking and, leaning forward, speaks to him in a loud whisper.

"Just let him get one himself."

"Why? I have one right here and it's certainly better than whatever he's going to find in a junk drawer."

"Sure, but kids like to do things themselves. It won't hurt to just let him get his own pen."

Death thinks it over for a second.

"Wait, why are you even here right now? I told you to wait in the car."

The woman hangs her head and looks away as she answers.

"I got lonely."

"You got...lonely?"

"Yeah is that such a problem?"

"I don't know, did you lock the doors?"

A look of surprise forms across her face and Death's heart sinks. He hurries to the window, pushing the blinds out of the way. The car is thankfully still there. Charlie makes his way back into the room as Death sits down on the couch and Emily avoids eye contact. The boy withdraws the pen he found, it appears to have robots on it, and looks at the papers.

"Here?" Charlie points to where Death had shown him before.

Death nods.

Charlie writes his name in a form of chicken scratch that might pass off as print if you took the time to decode it, however, ensuring the quality of signatures is not part of Death's job description. Death takes the papers, slips them into his bag and takes out a bus ticket, copies Charlie's information down and stamps it. This stamp contains the words "Unaccompanied Minor" enclosed in a red ink box. Death hands the slip to Charlie and begins going over it while he packs up his things.

"Go to any of the locations found on the back of that slip and get on the bus number listed on the front. Just do what everyone tells you and you'll get where you need to go. The next bus for you will arrive in about thirty minutes."

Death is already at the door as he finishes the last syllable. Death has given that same speech more times than he can count. It's the nature of the job. As Death is stepping outside, he notices that the woman has yet to get up from the couch and is instead staring at him with an incredulous look.

"What? Let's go."

"We can't just leave him here."

"He's fine. His parents must let him walk to the school bus alone all the time."

"And look how that turned out," the woman said as she gestures to the mangled little corpse at the foot of the stairs.

"Well, I can promise you that won't happen again."

The woman glares at Death.

Charlie speaks up.

"I can walk myself to the bus. I'm a big kid."

"See? He's a big kid. He'll be just fine. Let's go."

Death never hangs around longer than he can help it. There's a point at which it just gets awkward. After all, his job is done and it's not as if he's out here trying to make friends.

"I'm not leaving him," the woman says as she stands up, "We should at least bring him to the bus stop."

Death looks down at his watch.

The stop isn't far. We can walk him there and then I can get back to finishing this list so I can deal with this whole strange-woman-with-no-destination situation...More like, strange-and-extremely-annoying-woman-with-no-destination-situation.

"Fine. Let's go now then."

The woman smiles and Charlie rolls his eyes.

This is why I hate kids. They always cause me problems.

***

There were a handful of other souls at the bus stop, and it was weird for Death to not be the one who sent them there. Peter's taskforce has been going around processing souls today as well. Mostly elderly people, a few other kids, and one middle aged man. Charlie started chatting with the kids right away so it was easier to convince the woman to leave him. The other souls were all eyeing Emily so it was important to get her out as fast as possible. Most souls pick up pretty fast on who Death is and once they're in the afterlife, people become pretty loose lipped. After all, there's nothing in the world left to lose and Death cannot afford any big talkers in Heaven right now.

Once the two got back in the car Emily began to get mopey and now she's staring out the window, watching the trees pass by in a blur of green.

"That little boy was dead back there."

"Mhm."

"It was so sad."

"Mm."

"Why did he have to die like that. He was so young. He didn't even care."

"Mm."

"What was that?"

"What?"

"Whatever that was back there. Who are you?"

"Who do you think I am?"

The woman pauses. It's as if she does not want to say it.

"You're Death."

Death nods his head.

"So that means..."

Death does not respond.

Silence.

"For some reason I don't even feel sad. Do most people feel sad?

"Some."

"I feel more sad about that little boy. Is that normal?"

"I suppose."

Silence.

The woman turns back toward the window and Death can hear the faint sound of someone who desperately needs to cry but does not want to be heard. Death focuses on what's playing on the radio: Something loud, garish and poppy, of course. Death turns it up a bit and waits. After a few seconds he can hear it. Faint and muffled but very much there. Death stares straight ahead and focuses on the music. That's when Death feels his heart drop deep into his gut.

I forgot to tell her to sit in the backseat.

CHAPTER NINETEEN

The rest of the day is spent finishing Peter's list.

Death ends up making Emily go in with him on the jobs. As much as he hates it, he can't afford to have his car stolen and leaving her with that kind of responsibility is just asking for disaster. Plus, people take to her rather fast. Most of Death's time on the job is spent arguing with the souls and trying to get them to sign paperwork. There was once an old man who refused to sign anything until he was able to read the whole the entire document. The man spent about five minutes looking for his glasses and then another thirty or so reading the contract from front to back.

Death encountered no such issues today with Emily around. Simply by her presence, the souls were more relaxed and willing to sign whatever paperwork was given to them without having to read it over first and wasting everyone's time.

If she wanted, she could have had a very lucrative career in criminal interrogation.

After the uncomfortable episode with the crying, Death is even more unsure how to interact with her. Stiff upper lip is something highly valued in the afterlife. There are parts in the Bible where important people weep and do emotional stuff like that, but when it says they cried it doesn't mean that literally. It's like when someone posts an emotional scene from a movie or TV show on social media with the caption "I am CRYING". Nine times out of ten they are not crying. In fact, they usually look quite the opposite.

Death has never been comfortable with other people's tears, which poses an issue in his day to day work. However, it just shows how different he is from Emily. She might be nice enough but she doesn't pay attention and there is so little understanding of the crucial fact that she shares space with others. Death finds it difficult to say that she's mean-hearted. It feels more like ignorance than disregard.

Death hates inconsiderate and imposing people, and there is no one who exemplifies these traits more than her. He finalizes this conclusion as he pays for the chicken nuggets at the drive through window and pulls off into an open parking space.

"Here. You're hungry, right?"

Death hands Emily the bag and her eyes light up.

"How did you know?"

"When you eat every day of your life you develop a habit. Even though you don't need to eat in your current state, you're still hungry. You have that look of someone who desperately wants food but doesn't want to ask for it. I was worried you were going to start complaining soon and I don't want any complaining."

Death stretches back into his seat and shuts his eyes. It's getting late and he'll have to do something soon if he's going to do anything at all. The workday is almost over and once his shift ends, he will officially be breaking company regulations. Harboring a fugitive soul. A fire-able offense. Death can still get out of it, he still has a few minutes to make the call. It's not his responsibility. It's not his head on the line yet.

Yet.

The smell of citrus. Death opens his eyes and for an instant he's there. The balcony, the inky black waves, the orange juice sky. Death can feel the breeze on his face as he hears a faint knocking sound behind him.

The sound nearly makes his heart stop. Death can hear the blood pounding in his ears as he whips around and his peripheral vision blurs.

Emily's sing song voice.

"What are you thinking about?"

Back in his car. The sun is just beginning to set and the sky has a prink, gradient tinge. Emily is looking at him with a kind of quizzic head tilt and, for the first time, Death notices her.

Emily. Emily. Emily.

Death tosses the name around in his head again and again. It doesn't fit. She doesn't look like an Emily. Perhaps a Daisy or even some weird hippie name like Rain or Meadow. Death works with countless people every day so he rarely chooses to pay attention to anything about them. It's not worth the time and energy involved considering how useless and forgettable almost every person is.

Seeing someone like Emily on the street is like being at a football game and seeing a balding white guy wearing the home team jersey with a watered-down beer in hand walk past you. So unsurprising and expected that you would not think twice even if that same man walked past you from the same direction five times in three seconds like some kind of time jumping warlock. Emily is just like one of these balding white guys if on their jersey was the name and number of the team's second-string kicker.

Nothing about Emily is special. Nothing horribly wrong looking about her either, just nothing especially unique. Average height. Slightly too skinny. Straight, shoulder length reddish hair tucked behind her ear which does nothing but accentuate her already mousey features. The only thing special about that reddish hair is that it's kind of uncommon. Though on a second glance, it's not even red, more like a brownish shade of auburn. However, like that balding white guy with his watered-down beer and strange jersey, upon closer inspection Emily is set apart by one small detail. Her eyes.

Emily's eyes are brown but it's a light, sunny kind of brown like caramel melting in the sun. Not that the color itself is anything groundbreaking, there is just something about them that Death cannot help but feel is worth remembering.

It's been some time since Death last saw anything worth remembering. There's a life in her eyes that one does not often see in the dead. A few things change about your personality when you die, especially in the short term. People tend to become more somber and pensive for a time. They have a lot to think over and it usually lasts for a couple months. Emily seems to have bridged that extremely fast, which reminds Death of something.

Death takes a deep breath as the numbers on the car's clock change and his fate is sealed.

Now it's his head on the line.

Not really knowing what to do with her, Death puts the car into gear and begins driving to the only place he can.

He considers calling Peter and chewing him out, this is all his fault after all, but he knows that Peter will find some way to pin this on him or worse, Michael. Peter and Michael have always had a bit of a rough relationship. Both are the supreme kiss-asses of Heaven, locked in an eternal battle to see who can get God to like them the most. Peter obviously still has some insecurity issues about the whole denying God's kid three times thing so he's always trying to make up for it. Michael was created as the head honcho archangel, but then the angels got replaced by the humans as God's favorites. Michael being the loyal dog he is, bless his heart, of course agreed with God that the humans should be His favorites. The only problem is that Michael is obviously very resentful even if he refuses to admit it to himself so the cognitive dissonance makes him a hot mess. But he's not a bad person, and certainly not bad enough to take the fall for one of Peter's multitude of stupid mistakes. Peter is always trying to cut good old Michael out of the game and Death will not give him the perfect opportunity he's looking for. A screw up of such a grand degree is more than reason for a certain angel to get fired. Life is hard for an angel that's been fired.

Now that Death really thinks about it, Peter probably wants his job. All the constant questions and need for updates, coupled with how hard he had fought to head the organizing of Death's day off...

That piece of shit is trying to be me. Fucking creep.

Death's initial anger is quickly replaced by something resembling fear. This could be it. Is this really how all these years of work and effort come to an end? Harboring some blathering human for absolutely no conceivable reason? Death doesn't even find the conversation interesting.

"They're really pretty."

Death turns to look at Emily, head leaned against the glass, gazing up at the tree line as they drive by.

"What's pretty?"

"The trees."

"I guess. They're just trees."

They had gotten off the highway a few minutes ago and are moving down the dirt roads towards Death's house. What better place to keep a fugitive soul? They are driving through a patch of especially grim trees when Emily turns to face him.

"So, did you kill me or something?"

"What?"

"Well, like, you're Death. I'm dead. Don't you reap souls and everything?"

"That's not at all how it works."

"How does it work then?"

Death sighs.

"Humans are bound to die eventually. It's your own fault with that forbidden fruit business. You're cursed because of it so eventually you die, and it's my job to make sure you're on the way to where you need to go whether that be Heaven or Hell. I don't do the killing. That's between your kind and God. I'm just the middleman."

"That makes sense."

Emily looks out the window for a time.

"So where exactly are we going? None of this really looks like Heaven or Hell."

"Does it matter?"

"Well, I suppose it doesn't really, but I'd still like to know."

Death sighs and continues driving without a word.

"We're going to my house."

Emily's face lights up.

"You have a house?"

"What kind of question is that? Of course I have a house."

How stupid can she get?

"Well, I mean, you're Death. I guess it's just odd…"

The two sit in silence for some time. Death focuses on driving, until Emily turns to face him again.

"So, did you grow up here?"

Oh my God stop asking me questions.

"What do you mean?"

"Well, like, you're Death..."

"You've noticed."

Emily pauses, deciding whether to say something back or just let it pass. She lets it pass.

"That must have been weird."

"My childhood was fine."

"You're so gloomy though, something must've happened."

This takes Death off guard.

Am I gloomy?

The statement is innocent enough, but that seems like a rude thing to suggest.

"I'm not gloomy."

"Yes, you are. It's funny."

Death scowls as Emily continues.

"Do you have parents?"

"A mother."

"Where's your dad?"

"No father."

"Was it always that way?"

"Yes. It was just my mother and I."

"Did you have any friends?"

"Not really. One, but things have been distant for a while. I had a dog once, but it died."

"Your dog died?"

"Yes. That's what dogs do."

"But you're Death, why wouldn't you just make your dog not die?"

Death doesn't answer.

"You drive a funny car. I would've expected more like a hearse or something. Did you ever drive a station wagon? Because I always thought those kinda looked like hearses."

Death remembers why he doesn't let people sit in the front seat as he pulls into the driveway. After a quick inventory of events, he is becoming quite certain that he has never wanted to go inside and be alone more in his entire existence.

"Is this your house?"

"Yes."

Death opens the car door and fumbles with his keys as he approaches the front door. As he opens the door, he turns around to call Emily from the car but she is one step ahead of him. More precisely, five inches behind him.

"Christ. Don't do that."

"Do what?"

"Come up behind people like that."

"I'm sorry I didn't..."

This grown woman looks legitimately hurt that he snapped at her. She's young, but not *that* young.

"Come on."

Death's home is simple because he likes to think he is a simple man. Two bedrooms, two bathrooms, one kitchen.

Death has put everything together to be as neat as possible. In the entryway, there is a coat rack next to a table with a bowl for storing one's keys and wallet. Beyond that, a recliner chair and surprisingly roomy couch are arranged around a wood coffee table. The second bedroom serves as his studio because he has yet to need a guest bedroom. Holidays are spent at his mother's house so she has never needed it, and Satan is always working, and those are two of the only people he would even consider letting through the front door, with the former being almost entirely out of obligation. This is Death's first time being a host.

Once they are both in the entryway, Death turns around to face Emily who is looking around as if she had never seen a home before, leaving the door wide open.

"First. Close the door."

Done.

"I am going to leave for a little while. You are going to stay here."

"At your house?"

Death moves into the living room.

"Yes. There's a bathroom over there. I think there's some food in the freezer. This is the TV remote. Good?"

Emily nods her head.

"Good. I'll be back in a while. Don't answer the phone no matter what."

Death snatches up the keys he stowed in the bowl for the combined thirty seconds he was in the house and makes it to the door before having second thoughts.

Death's head pops out from around the corner of the entryway to find Emily standing exactly where he left her and points at the studio door down the hall and says, "Don't go in there," then pops his head back and exits the house, locking the door on his way out.

I might as well have just given her an invitation to go in there.

If she goes in it's his own fault, really. In his mind's eye, Death can see Emily going about his house wreaking a path of destruction. Dirty dishes in the sink, lost TV remote, his toothbrush used and balancing precariously on the edge of the sink, the faucet turned off but not well enough so a barely audible drip feed of wasted water trickles out. After destroying the rest of his home, she would almost certainly make her way into the studio and do God-only-knows what. The scene is enough to send a chill up his spine.

Death takes a deep breath and lets out a heavy sigh.

No good deed goes unpunished.

He has time to process everything that has happened today on the drive, and after some serious thought and contemplation he comes a conclusion:

This is an awful situation that is only getting worse with every passing second.

Nothing too profound or original, but that's fine. Death is already on thin ice for what he asked God yesterday. Then today a human under his charge does not show up to their spot. Sure, it could be the soul's fault. But once the seventy-two hours are up and they track her down, someone will realize that she was never given paperwork. Whether or not she had a destination, it's Death's fault for not calling it in.

Death puts himself in God's shoes for a moment (size ten and a half men's, but he has a narrow foot so it can be hard to find comfortable shoes. For anyone wondering). You're Creator and Ruler of the universe. Trying to get things done. One employee asks for something they need but because you're an asshole you say no. Soon after, said employee has this thing they asked for. They say they were given faulty paperwork and it's not their fault. However, they never called anyone or tried to get help. If the problem was really one of faulty paperwork, they would have called in. You're God of the universe. You don't have to put up with bullshit from employees you don't like. Goodbye to said employee.

Death has done a stupid thing, but he is not stupid. If this gets to the wrong ears then he is done for.

This is what I get for picking up the phone.

CHAPTER TWENTY

The traffic getting into Hell is generally bad, and Death had gotten on the road just in time for rush hour. Every inch is a fight through lanes of tired and irritable demons who want nothing more than to get home, eat dinner, and watch some television. Upon arrival, Death tried the bar, but there were just demons there. A quick consultation with Jeff revealed that Satan was at his apartment, having left the bar a few hours earlier. Jeff did not seem happy to give Death this information, but there was no excuse he could use to withhold it.

Death strides through the sliding glass doors and into the apartment building lobby. A young female demon is seated behind the desk reading a book while Death makes his way to the counter. He stands there, waiting for her to look up.

She doesn't.

Death notices a small bell situated a few inches from his right hand, he taps it lightly.

Ding.

The young demon looks up and smiles in that insincere way that everyone in the service industry has mastered.

"What can I help you with today, sir?"

"I'd um, I'd like to go up to see him."

"Is he expecting you?"

"No."

Light exhale.

"Have a seat."

She gestures to the couches in the other corner of the lobby and Death takes a seat while she picks up a phone and pokes at the keypad, waits, waits, waits, then speaks to someone on the line. He cannot hear everything she is saying but he is able to make out a little bit here and there.

"I don't know…some guy…medium height, kinda sulky…ok."

She puts down the receiver and gestures to Death.

"He'll see you now. Go over to the elevator, I'll send you up."

Death rises from the couch and stands in front of the elevator. The demon presses a button on her desk and the doors slide open and he steps inside. She presses another button and the doors slide closed and the elevator starts moving up. He has a feeling Satan is not going to be ecstatic about his visit.

"This couldn't wait until tomorrow?"

The two are seated in the living room of Satan's penthouse suite. This room alone is decadent to the extreme and Death can't begin to imagine how expensive each respective piece of furniture is, let alone the art and decorations. A large wall mounted television is situated between two bookcases and the news is playing on a muted volume, but he could've sworn he'd seen some soap-opera-looking show onscreen for an instant when the elevator doors opened but Satan flipped the channel too fast to be sure.

Death is sitting on the couch across from Satan who is lounging in a silk kimono robe with a gold and crimson dragon embroidery on it. Death remembers when he got that robe. Satan had hinted around for months that he wanted it for Christmas and did so around Death because he was the only person gullible enough to buy it for him. Jeff never would have done it, and probably would have said something about him being a "pansy asshat" to boot. Death had felt no greater sense of self-loathing than purchasing that infernal robe with his hard-earned money, but it got Satan off his back.

"No. It really can't wait until tomorrow."

Satan sits up and retires his glass of scotch to the coffee table.

"Well? What is it?"

Death takes a deep breath.

"I found a human today."

"You do that every day. It's your job."

"Well today was different."

Death notices that Satan is not finding these responses amusing.

"There's a problem with her paperwork."

Satan gives Death the nod to continue speaking.

"She…I wish there was a better way to say it…"

"Death, buddy, I really need ya to spit it out. I've got a big meeting tomorrow and I could really use the time to-"

"She doesn't have any."

Satan's expression changes over the course of the next few moments. Moving from one of mild annoyance and distraction to shock and intense thought.

"No paperwork."

"No paperwork."

"What does that mean? You didn't give her any?"

"Well, no. But there was nothing on the list that Peter gave me."

"But what does that mean? It didn't include her entire life story? The street she grew up on? The name of her first puppy? Or there was nothing as in nothing?"

"Nothing but her name and the location of death. I determined the cause on the scene. But there was no destination listed."

"Are you sure? Are you absolutely sure there was nothing? I mean, there has to be missing stuff sometimes. But never a missing destination. That doesn't happen because He puts that in Himself. The Old Man is a pain in the ass but he's thorough with that stuff. Did you check the database? Did you call Peter? Wait, isn't today your day off? Why were you anywhere but your house?"

"I double checked the database from my phone when I got there and it was the same problem. I was working today because Peter, long story short, threatened to blame Michael for a staffing mistake if I didn't come in and do a route. I don't entirely know why. I didn't call him because I had a feeling he would use it as an excuse to get at Michael for no reason and now I'm starting to think that he may even be using it as an excuse to get me fired. It sounds crazy, but I think I might have been set up."

All of a sudden, Satan is up and pacing. Death knows of no one else who paces with as much fervor as the Devil. Satan goes back and forth across the room like a general preparing for war, Death a mere infantryman awaiting command. Satan is snapping his fingers all the while and muttering until he comes to a halt, picks his glass up off the table, looks it over like a prize cow, and downs the remaining contents in a single gulp. He then picks up the bottle on the end table, refills his glass and drains that one.

Satan puts the glass and the bottle down and opens the drawer of the end table, revealing an ashtray which he tosses carelessly onto the table, then sits down and rummages around in the pocket of his kimono, retrieving a lighter and pack of cigarettes.

"I hope you don't mind but I'm gonna need one."

Satan lights the end, holding the cigarette between his thumb and forefinger and taking a long, hard drag off of it. Death notices that his hand is shaking ever so slightly. Satan leans back in his seat and lets out the smoke in short puffs until he sits up and looks at Death for the first time in the past few minutes.

"I have a plan…of sorts."

"What is it?"

Satan inhales and exhales on his cigarette once more.

"Now, it's going to take a lot of work on your part, and there's no guarantees it'll work, and it definitely won't be easy even if it does."

"Again, what is it?"

Satan taps the corner of the ashtray and takes another puff.

"You're going to guess the right place to send her."

"If I was qualified to do that, wouldn't it be part of my job?"

"That doesn't mean you can't do it."

"Yes, but if any person other than God would be qualified to do it, that person would be me. And I'm not qualified to do it. If I was, then do you actually think He would do any more work himself than he has to?"

Satan ponders this, nodding his head as he puffs on his cigarette.

"True. But you're going to have to figure it out."

"I don't…"

"You're gonna have to. It's the only way."

"What about Peter? He's going to notice something is up soon. The guy is stupid but he knows it and therefore double checks everything. And then there's always Michael to worry about. The guy sticks his nose in everything."

Satan pauses and pours himself yet another drink and yet again drains it in one flip of a glass.

"I can handle that."

"That doesn't sound good."

"It'll be fine. I can handle Peter if it comes down to it. Also, aren't you friends with Michael? Isn't he the whole reason you're in this mess? Why would he be a problem?"

Huh. Is Michael my friend? I suppose he is. I never really thought of him that way.

"He's getting more desperate as time goes on all cooped up in that guard box."

Satan scoffs.

"Charon is in a guard box all day too, but you don't see him ratting out his friends."

"Michael isn't Charon. He's convinced he's made for greater things."

"Well that's stupid."

"Agreed."

While stupid, Death can see why the Archangel would think this.

Michael was once a winner of wars and slayer of fiends, and now he's the Heavenly equivalent to that fat guy you pay to get out of a parking garage. When the time for God's army to disband finally came around, God had tried to work Michael into His new army of office workers. Problems arose when Michael started asking questions and constantly demanding to know what they were doing and why they were doing it and how they could be doing it better. In any other context he would have been the model employee, but God did not need Michael's constant questions setting an example for the other angels. And so, Michael was "promoted".

There was a tasteful ceremony and Michael was presented with his uniform in front of all his fellow angels with a big grin on his face. They muttered amongst themselves about how lucky he was and what an honor it was and how unfair it was that they were not chosen to be the gatekeeper of heaven.

It took about a week before the white block text on Michael's uniform jacket went from reading "Gatekeeper" to "Wasted Potential". Therein lies the problem for Death and Satan. Ever since his "promotion", Michael has a lot more free time and a starving ego, a dangerous combination. Sort of like an old man who struggles to hold onto what little purpose he has left in life by reporting his neighbor's lawn infractions to the homeowner's association. If Michael gets a whiff of what Satan and Death are trying to pull off, he is sure to make problems.

Death holds his head in his hands.

Why didn't I just report it as soon as I found her. It's not like it's my fault. You could've reported it, there's always that.

But he had not reported it, and now he's sitting on Satan's couch thinking of ways to dig himself out of this hole. He should have just brought her in. Why didn't he? Death hasn't had much time to think about anything since he decided to bring her home or throughout the day. But now it's all coming out at once.

That was a seriously self destructive thing to do. Like a whole new level of self destructive. Lose your job and get sent to the Abyss kind of self destructive. Do I want to lose my job? Did I actually want to keep her? Oh my God did I actually want to keep her? I stole a soul. I actually took one and right after God said no. I'm screwed. There's nothing I can do. I'm done for, I can't do anything about this, I-

Satan is watching Death crumble into himself, slowly swishing the drink in his right hand until he brings it close to his face as if inspecting its contents. Apparently finding his search results satisfactory, Satan drains his glass once again and sets it down. The sound is enough to rouse Death from his mind and back to the present situation.

Satan looks him in the eyes and Death knows he needs to listen. This is not an expression he sees often. Satan looks serious.

"Alright, like I said before, this is going to be hard as balls but we can do it if we stick to the plan. I can help you, but I need you to promise me something. Can you do that?"

Death nods.

"Good. If this is going to work, you're going to need to cool it with that whole thing of yours."

"What whole thing of mine?"

Satan gives him a look and Death sighs.

"I know what you mean, ok. I'll try and be nice."

"I'm not talking about being nice. I'm talking about not shutting yourself up in that house of yours and leaving me out to dry at the first sign of trouble. This whole thing is going to be hairy beyond belief and there's no way I can do it by myself."

"Ok, that's valid."

"I know it is."

"So, what's this plan of yours?"

Satan takes a deep breath…

"Alright, so here's what we're gonna do…"

CHAPTER TWENTY-ONE

While Death and Satan are having their important planning conversation, Emily is having a lonely time of self-reflection back at the house. Death is having a long day, but so is Emily. The poor woman wakes up in the morning, expecting a Saturday of good, relaxing fun, but instead finds out that she is in fact dead. Not only is she dead but Death himself has been speaking to her and he's more awkward than she had expected. Emily is not entirely sure what she was expecting when it came to dying and the afterlife, but she didn't think there would be ordinary houses and awkward immortals, though it serves to reason that if people can be awkward then the immortal are entitled to a bit of it as well.

A ravenous growl rises from Emily's stomach and she begins to work her way through Death's pantry and fridge/freezer. Stumbling upon a solitary hot pocket, she rips it out of its wrapping and tosses it into the microwave. A slow and heavy humming filling the kitchen after she presses "Start".

Emily has a lot to consider as the pizza-filled dough rotates. What happened to her? Obviously, she died. But there are a lot of ways to die and Emily is having difficulty finding one that could apply to her. Although she has definitely been more physically fit in the past, she still goes to gym a few nights a week and does her best to eat well most of the time.

Emily keeps going in circles. Little to no alcohol, no drugs, no history of cancer, no history of heart attacks, no history of strokes, no history of ment…

That doesn't apply. I was asleep when it happened so there's no way it was that.

That's when it hits Emily.

He didn't want me to go in the room. The room's where the body is. He didn't want me to go in there because he didn't want me to see it but why? If it was something simple, then it's sad but it's not traumatizing. I just died in my sleep of something and that's not so big of a deal. That's easy to understand.

Emily's breathing quickens and she can feel her breath growing ever shallow.

He's more considerate than he lets on, but he's not that considerate. If even I think I could handle seeing my own corpse then he definitely wouldn't stop me from trying. But why did he? How would I have to die for him to demand that I not look in? I mean what would be the most distressing, terrifying, and confusing way to die?

Emily is hyperventilating as her realization sets in.

What could I have possibly done to someone? I don't have money, and even if I did, I would give it to them. I treat people well, there's nothing I've ever done, I just, I mean I'm sure I've done something to someone but maybe back when I was much younger, what did I do that would make someone do something like that? I try my best to treat people as good as I possibly can. Why would this ever happen-

Beep. Beep. Beep.

The hot pocket is finished.

Emily does not move from her position as the aggressive beeping stops.

Then resumes. Then stops.

Then resumes as Emily works to steady her breathing which has gone completely awry. Emily hasn't been this much of a mess since college. Nothing has been this bad since college. Emily gasps for air as the inky black tendrils spread through her veins like oily claws, finally grabbing hold of her brain and sinking themselves into every ridge and groove they can find. Emily snatches up a short blade from the knife block, the kind you would use to cut the tops off of strawberries or maybe slice some artisan cheese, and yanks her sleeve up to the elbow before flipping her left arm palm-upward and plunging the knife into her wrist. Emily lets out a pained gasp as she drags it up her forearm and the blood begins to flow. Emily feels the inky black tendrils leaving her body, mixed in with the warmth of her own blood. Emily feels nauseous, closing her eyes as she winces and gasps in pain.

And when she opens her eyes the wound is gone.

The pain is gone, the blood is gone, the inky black tendrils are still there.

Emily places the knife back in the block with a sober understanding of her situation.

Beep. Beep. Beep.

Emily opens the microwave and takes a bite out of the hot pocket.

It burns the roof of her mouth.

CHAPTER TWENTY-TWO

Death has a lot to think over on the ride back. The big thing being of course how he and Satan are going to deal with the situation they've gotten themselves in. Well, the situation that Death got himself into. Or, the situation that Death never should have been a part of, but stupid, good-for-nothing Peter got him into. Death feels anger welling up inside. Everything is on the line because of that selfish, insignificant little man. It's boiling now. This hatred inside him that's kept in the basement of his heart like an illegitimate, red-headed, cannibal stepchild is now banging on the door and demanding to be let out. The banging of his fists grow louder and the screaming becomes more shrill. Death can feel the pounding in his chest and the screaming in his ear. Suddenly there are big dents in the iron door. One more punch and then he will finally be free.

Death sighs.

I don't have the brain cells for this.

Death runs through the plan once more, recalling his conversation with Satan.

"Alright, so here's what we're going to do…we're going to buy time. Your part in this is key, Death. I can do a lot when it comes to distracting Peter, but no matter how well I can keep him off your back, in roughly forty-eight hours it will become your fault. It doesn't matter that her records are incomplete, it doesn't matter that he blackmailed you into working, the only thing that's going to matter to Him is that a soul you were in charge of didn't show up, and after your most recent visit to Heaven we both know what conclusions He's going to draw. This is do or die time, and every second is going to count because now I'm involved as well."

Satan squashed out his cigarette, downed another drink, and lit a new smoke.

"First thing's first. We need to make sure that Peter doesn't figure out what's going on. He's not bright, but he's a suspicious motherfucker and trusts his instincts. If he hasn't already, he'll figure out that something's up, and once he does we'll have to move even faster. Death, this is where you come in. Your job is to figure out where she should be. The key thing is not to let her realize that. It's the only way. Jeff is going to be busy covering for you and Peter has the master list. You have to figure out where she should be going and make sure she gets on a bus, all within the time limit. You know what happens if He finds out about this, right?"

Death nodded.

"Yeah. It won't be good. Just act like it's business as usual. Retrace her steps. If she was murdered, figuring out the details behind that will show her true character. You know the criteria. You've been doing this for a long time, Death and this is it. No safety net. You understand how serious this is, right? You held onto a soul, and not just any soul. A soul with missing fucking records. The one soul in all of human history with missing *fucking* records. But that's behind us and now we're working the solution."

Death avoided eye contact during the last part.

"While you're out and about, I'll be here holding down the fort and buying as much of Peter's time and attention, but you'll still have to move fast? Got it?"

Death nods.

"Good. Then go. You'll need to get an early start."

And so, Death left without a word. Looking back, he should have said thank you or something but none of it came out. There has just been something stuck in his head that was, and still is, eating away at his conscious thoughts.

Did I take her? I know I took her but did I mean to? I don't think I did, but I can't rule it out entirely.

Death has not considered his near crippling sense of loneliness in any detail in quite some time. Over the past few centuries, he's found himself more and more busy, leaving less time for activities such as painting which allowed him the unstructured time to consider such things. He has never come close to finding an answer for the origins of this feeling or a solution to it, but the pursuit has a therapeutic effect in and of himself. Just the time spent considering what is going on inside his head helps him a great deal.

It soothes Death's fear that everything he does is wrong and that he inconveniences the people around him and that he isn't as considerate as he believes himself to be and even worse, that he's actually quite rude and spiteful and maybe he's past the point of no return and that maybe his last chance at any sort of connection with anyone or anything has long since come and gone and maybe if he had been born with a larger heart or made more of an effort to be someone completely other than himself perhaps he might not have this thing just behind his lungs that eats away at his very self and maybe he wouldn't wake up every morning feeling just a little bit more tired than the day before and that he wouldn't take just a little bit longer to get out of bed than the day before until one day he gets to the point where there is no difference between sleeping and waking, between dreaming and existing, between dying and living.

Death is sitting in his car in the driveway of his home with keys in hand because this is what you do when you're unwell and the radio goes silent. Looking up, he sees movement in the windows.

She's probably wondering why I haven't come in yet.

Death sighs and exits the vehicle, making his way to the door, pushing through it and is immediately met with a nervous Emily who blurts words at him the moment he enters the house.

"I'm sorry about before."

"What?".

"About the dog. I'm sorry".

"What about the dog?"

Emily takes a deep breath.

"I asked why, if you're Death, you didn't just make your dog not dead. That was really rude and I'm sorry. I had a hamster once and when it died I cried for three days straight and even knowing that and having that happen to me I still asked you a question as inconsiderate as that and I'm so sorry. I hope I didn't bring back any bad memories, please forgive me, I'm really sorry. It was traumatic for me, and I know it must have been for you."

Death is dumbstruck.

Was the dog dying traumatic? What was its name? Roger? Rover? Something with an -er sound.

He gives up but his train of thought is still moving.

Was I traumatized? Did I have a traumatic experience?

Death considers the nameless mystery dog but can't think of any especially affecting moments regarding its death. His mother told him the dog had gone to live on a nice farm somewhere, but Death remembers knowing this was a lie because he had seen her through his window throwing its corpse into a garbage bag and leaving it out for the dump truck. She must've thought he had just been playing with his dolls, a hobby which he did not realize was odd until late Elementary school, and had not seen her covert operation. Death makes a mental note to ask his mother about this at some point.

"Oh…um…don't worry about it."

The silence is deafening.

Death glances around the room to see if anything is out of place. So far it looks like she actually kept things clean. Peering into the kitchen, he notices a few crumbs on the counter but all things considered, it's much better than he expected. It's not like he was expecting his house to be burned down anything, but he wouldn't have been surprised if it was.

Death points at the door to his studio.

"Did you go in there?"

Emily shakes her head.

"Are you lying?"

"No. You asked me not to go in there."

"I told you to stay in the car earlier as well."

Emily hangs her head.

Is she an adult woman or a child? It seems like everything I say makes her almost cry.

Death heads into the kitchen and sweeps the crumbs into his hand where he disposes of them in the trash can. Then he washes his hands and takes a seat in the living room.

"Take a seat."

Emily sits on the couch across from Death.

"There are some things we need to look into when it comes to your death. Without going into it too much, there have been some mix-ups with your paperwork."

"What do you mean by mix-ups?"

"I mean you have no paperwork."

"But what does paperwork do? Why do I need some?"

"Because I need paperwork to determine which bus to put you on so you get to the right place."

"By place do you mean, like, Heaven or Hell?"

"Yes."

Emily takes a second.

"Ok. So why do we need to look into my death to figure that out?"

Death momentarily considers telling her the truth. He may find her annoying and kind of petulant at times, but she doesn't deserve to be forced to prove herself to him. No one should have to do something like that. Death just wants to tell her so she can speak for herself and he can put her on a bus and be done with all of this. But if she lies and ends up on the wrong bus then Death is done before he's even had a chance to try and help himself.

"You have too much attachment to the world because of it. If we figure it out, then you'll gravitate to where you're meant to be. Wondering about your death has been eating you up inside, hasn't it?"

Emily hangs her head and considers a moment before nodding.

I hate myself. All this lying is disgusting.

"Someone will be here in the morning and he's going to take over for me for a bit while you and I figure this out."

The wall mounted phone next to the kitchen rings.

"Hello?"

"Death, this is Peter."

"What do you want?"

"I just wanted to call to make sure everything went well today."

"Fine. Goodbye."

Death goes to hang up.

"No, wait! Don't hang up."

"Why? You said you called to make sure everything went well. It was fine. Conversation over."

"It was really unfortunate that you had to do that today. The angel responsible will definitely be punished accordingly."

"Or you could just do your job, but sure."

"My job is not to collect souls. That's *yours*."

"Correct, but today was my day off."

"Well at least Michael doesn't need to be punished for anything. Really dodged a bullet there."

"And I wonder who pointed the gun at him."

Silence.

"I don't appreciate your attitude, Death. I called as a courtesy for what you did today. Just because you helped us out does not mean you can talk to me like that. I am your supervisor after all."

"We both know the only reason you have your job is because you happened to exist on that rock in the same place at the same time and in the same religion as the kid."

"He would not like it that you're speaking to me like that."

"I can speak to you any way that I damn well please. I'd be interested to see how you explain why we were talking on the phone at this hour."

"Who said anything about you? Michael's the one who would take the fall for this."

"You must feel clever right now. Well anyway, enjoy your tiny prick tonight."

Death hangs up.

Do I have a deathwish? Do I want my entire life to fall apart?

"Who was that?"

He looks up from the phone and over at Emily.

"Someone useless from work."

There is a flash of recognition in Emily's eyes as if she too has useless people from work.

"Once my affairs are in order tomorrow morning we're going to get started with figuring you out. Get some sleep because it's going to be a big day. Your room is that way."

Death points at his bedroom. It's impolite to ask your guest to sleep on the couch no matter how much you'd prefer it.

"Oh, ok. Thank you. I guess I'll, um, turn in."

Emily gets up and walks over to the bedroom and turns back upon passing through the doorframe.

"Goodnight, Death."

He hears the door shut and is alone in the room once more. Like usual.

"Goodnight, Death."

He gathers everything he can to make his couch more comfortable and as he attempts to sleep, he begins his ritual. Death creates constellations from the texture on the ceiling, quieting his mind down to a soft whisper until he can barely keep his eyes open and he begins to fade out. Then the gunning of an engine sounds in his mind and it comes rushing back. He is standing in a road as a car speeds down the road coming straight at him.

Death's eyes are starting to flutter, dozing off, almost there.

The car is picking up speed. It is going to hit him. Death can feel the dread in his sinking stomach. The tendrils shooting through his veins trying to reach his brain.

Almost asleep.

The car is so close he can smell fuel. The roaring of the engine moves to the background as Death's eyes finally close and he floats down to the ground, allowing the car pass right over him. As it's just about to do this, he hears a quiet voice in the background.

"Goodnight, Death."

Death's eyes open and he finds himself on a bed. The ceiling is different. Pure white. No constellations, just ceiling. As he sits up, Death finds himself in a four-poster bed with pale, almost translucent white drapes fluttering in a breeze. Looking through the drapes he makes out the shape of shuttered doors open wide and leading out to a balcony. The sound of crashing waves. The faint smell of citrus mixed with the salty ocean air. He turns his head to find a large mirror on the wall across from the bed where a television would normally go. The wind blows in from the balcony, causing the drapes to part for an instant, allowing Death to catch a glimpse of himself.

Back in his living room. Death stares at the ceiling, burning the image of what he just saw into his memory. Then he rises and enters his studio. Nothing had been touched or moved.

She really didn't snoop around.

He picks up his brush and begins to paint. Adding the mirror and the little details of the bed. The design of the four bed posts are simple but beautiful with seashells carved into the wood, yet each one is as different as a snowflake. Death cannot shake the image of himself in the mirror. He only saw it for an instant, but it was enough to notice. As Death completes the mirror and begins working on his reflection, he becomes utterly consumed in his work. So consumed in fact that he does not notice the figure stopped just outside the doorway.

Emily had been having trouble sleeping as people generally do the first night after they die and decided a glass of warm milk was just what she needed. As she was walking to the kitchen, she noticed Death's makeshift bed on the couch and was immediately filled with a deep feeling of guilt. This was his house after all, why was she sleeping in his bed? She had assumed the room he told her not to go into was his bedroom or something and that's why she was not allowed in. Emily does not like to impose on others.

It's was at this point that she noticed the door to the room was ajar and Death was nowhere to be seen. Emily decided it was best to go talk to him and make things right and offer him his room back. She had no idea, after all, and she would have been just as happy and comfortable sleeping on the couch. As she approached the door, Emily saw that he was at work on something in there. A painting. Death is so focused and invested in his work that he does not notice her standing there. She watches him work on it as she feels an immeasurable wave of guilt flood over her like a tsunami. Death had told her to stay out of here after all and even though she is not breaking the letter of the law, she is fairly certain that the intention was for her to not look at what is inside. Emily hurries back to her room, the glass of warm milk completely forgotten, but not the painting. That is seared into

Emily's mind and as she drifts off the sleep, gazing into the eternal spin of Death's ceiling fan, she feels that it seems like the kind of place she would like to go someday were it not somewhere that lived in a painting. Something about the image feels so real yet at the same time a fabrication of complete and utter fantasy.

"Almost like a dream," Emily whispers.

As the sun begins to rise, Death finishes his additions. The details of the bed, the drapes, the waist height dresser, the mirror, and his reflection in it. The latter being the most difficult and time intensive of all the additions. Death had to keep changing what he painted, forcing himself to forget how he knows he looks. As he gazes now at the finished addition Death is certain he has painted himself exactly as he saw it. The reflection he sees in the painted mirror has no bags under its eyes.

CHAPTER TWENTY-THREE

Satan sits in the darkness of his penthouse suite staring at where he knows a particularly unpleasant stain is. The stain is hidden behind the cabinet where Satan keeps his top of the line speaker system. The stain is an off red, almost purple, color which made its way onto Satan's wall one weekend during a house party when he had managed to get some of the more immature demons to try wine for the first time. They learned two things that night:

(1) Wine is actually pretty good. (2) Demons do not handle wine well.

While Satan was occupying some other group of guests, they began to fiddle with the wine glasses as if they were some high society fellows and of course one of them tipped over and spilled the contents onto the wall and nearby floor. Satan glanced over soon after it had happened and witnessed three pitifully drunk demons trying to lift, push, and walk a cabinet from nearby onto the stain to cover it. Satan had done everything in his power to contain his laughter and succeeded. They were trying so very hard to make up for their mistake, however poorly, and he just didn't have the heart to embarrass them any more than they were already embarrassing themselves. So now Satan has an ill placed cabinet and a hidden wine stain.

Something Satan has had to get used to over the years is how much the demons want to get to know him. At first, it kind of put Satan off. After all, when he first arrived in Hell, it was not under any kind of glorious circumstances, and not only that, he was the angelic foreigner now in charge of them all. Satan had actually been a little afraid that if he did in fact take them up on the invitation to "go get a drink" then he would be taken advantage of in some especially merciless fashion. It was not until an awkward, but very eye-opening conversation with Jeff did Satan realize the demons were actually just being friendly.

It happened when Satan had been across the hall at Jeff's apartment for dinner like he often did in those days. Usually under some pretense of bringing him a gift that he conveniently forgot in his apartment and would bring him the next day and then casually staying for dinner because it smelled delicious even though, in reality, it was because he simply had no groceries in his own kitchen. Jeff picked up on the scam almost immediately but made sure never to say anything and always pretend that he did in fact believe a present would come. Just not that day.

Jeff had been boiling pasta and Satan was fidgeting around with something on the counter while watching him cook.

"They asked me to go out with them again."

"And I assume you turned them down?"

Satan stopped fidgeting and looked up with an expression that almost felt like disappointment, but more in oneself than anything else.

"Yes."

"They'll keep asking."

"I know."

"Then you should take them up on it instead of having mediocre dinners with me every night. We both know you would prefer to be out doing something."

Satan opened his mouth to speak but Jeff interrupted him.

"And before you go on some obligatory tirade about how they are in fact above average dinners and that you're perfectly happy to keep having the same pasta dish with me every night for the rest of eternity, take a second and be honest with yourself. Can you remember the last time you got plastered and weren't alone in that shithole across the hall?"

Satan twisted his face as he thought back, trying his best to come up with something.

Satan sighed and shook his head.

"But I have a bad feeling about it. They should hate me, I'm the new guy and one that shouldn't even be here yet *I'm* the one in charge. Not one of them that's been here their entire lives and know how things work. Just me who has a fancy background and knows absolutely nothing. I know I would hate me."

"Well they're not you."

"Obviously not, they're demons. And demons that are probably going to haze and torture me into oblivion if I'm alone in a private place with them."

"The trouble is you're still thinking like yourself, Lucifer that is, and not thinking like yourself, Satan. Things are different down here. They're run differently. People behave differently. You're still stuck in the old ways of thinking instead of adapting to what's around you. Angels treat each other much differently than these demons. They're not the brightest, and I think that works to their advantage sometimes. All of this to say, I think you should take them up on the invite. You may find that you have a good time."

Satan had leaned against the counter in Jeff's apartment then as he does now in the lounge of his penthouse suite, considering his options as he turns his body into a sentient bundle of tightly wound, kneaded-but-never-broken bundle of stress. Satan allows it to wind and tighten around his muscles from its point of source at the low center of the point between his two shoulder blades. Once wound around his muscles the stress itself hardens and creates a second layer. An armor almost. And Satan picks up the phone.

It rings once.

"What's wrong?"

"Wow, Jeff, so quick to jump to conclusions."

"You would not be calling at this hour if there was not something wrong."

"You know, I have absolutely nothing to counter that with."

"What's the problem?"

"Oh, it's a doozy. Can you meet me here in, let's say, three hours? It'll be easier for me to explain in person. But long story short, I don't think I'll be getting any sleep tonight."

"I'll be there. Anything else?"

"Hmm. Bring some booze, I'm almost out."

"That red you've been enjoying lately?"

"No. Something a little more befitting the Devil. I'll leave it up to you to decide what exactly that is."

"Will do."

Jeff hangs up.

Satan takes a breather before downing the last of his drink and heading towards his dressing room.

The room is lined with suit after suit of impeccable quality. Satan browses for a bit, but finally settles on a classic. Pitch black coat and pants, spotless white shirt, and a crimson red tie with a simple, but very tasteful, floral pattern indented on it. Satan draws each item from their hangers and begins the process of getting dressed. Although he could, Satan has never hired people to help him dress. Something about it just felt too demeaning, both for the demons that would do the job and for himself. Satan has never been incapable of dressing himself, so why would he ever have others do it for him? Besides, Satan finds the task to be one of centering and readying. He has never exactly felt like the Devil, but as he meticulously assembles his suit, he can make the transformation. As Satan sets the cufflinks and adjusts the tie, his skin appears to become even redder and his horns that much sharper. The hellfire in his eyes grows more intense and his grin becomes especially wicked.

This is what he sees in the mirror, in reality there is no change whatsoever.

CHAPTER TWENTY-FOUR

Death wakes up in a not-so-comfortable position on the couch with a crick in his neck to boot. As he comes to consciousness, Death hears rummaging in the kitchen and looks over as his eyes begin to focus. Emily's head pops up from under the counter, giving him a damn near heart attack. Death moved out of his mother's house a little bit after the creation of time, so it's been a while since he's lived with someone. Death scans the room.

Nothing out of place. She hasn't destroyed anything. Yet.

Emily is currently making herself breakfast and, noticing that Death is awake, makes her best attempt at an awkward smile.

"Do you want some oatmeal?"

I forgot I had that. How did she even find it? And how did she make it? I don't think I have bowls...

"Um, no I'm good."

As rude as it is to turn down a meal someone has made for you, especially breakfast, Death is not ready to eat a stranger's oatmeal. That's a no go. Emily hangs her head a little bit as she places one thing of oatmeal to the side, revealing to Death that the oatmeal had been made inside a coffee mug. He hates when people do "quirky" things like that. They always do it to make themselves feel special, but they never are.

It's from a company anniversary party about a century or two back with a little design of an angel giving a thumbs up and the words "Happy Anniversary!" printed over his head.

It's not even the right shape for oatmeal, the lip isn't big enough.

The mug is poorly made and it feels brittle enough that you could break the handle off if you squeezed hard enough. God has a tendency to cheap out when it came to company gifts, after all, they give out the same cruddy nativity set every Christmas that no one except maybe Michael would ever use.

Emily gives him a kind of forlorn look as she slides the oatmeal away.

Why does she care so much? I hate sweet things, especially in the morning. I'm under no obligation to eat anything she offers me. Especially not in my own house.

Death feels a twinge of guilt. It was rude of her to make this food and put him in this kind of position without knowing the kinds of things he likes and dislikes. It's presumptuous to assume that everyone likes the same things as you. Death hates presumptuous people. Death also hates ungrateful people.

A knock sounds at the door. Simple and decisive, two wraps, not too quiet, not too urgent, but loud enough to hear anywhere in the house.

Death is at the door in an instant and the mug of oatmeal originally meant for him is now off the counter and in Emily's left hand.

It's Jeff. The demon must have been standing uncomfortably close to the door because it feels like he is right up in Death's face.

"Satan sent me here to help you with some things."

"Yes. Come in."

Death stands to the side to make space for Jeff, but it's an awkward amount of time before the demon enters. When Jeff steps inside the house, he looks like a GI deep in enemy territory. Stealing glances to the exit, making sure he knows where all the potential weapons are, and giving his host a menacing look whenever possible. Death has not changed out of the t-shirt and jeans from the day before while Jeff is dressed for business. When he's at the bar, Jeff wears a plaid button-down tucked into his blue jeans and tops it off with a simple black leather belt and some kind of old-man-shoe. Death has never seen Jeff out of his trademark upscale lumberjack style, but today he's wearing a shirt and tie, slacks, and a new pair of leather old man shoes. He also has a briefcase that Death can only guess is a loan from Satan. The demon with his bushy eyebrows, full beard, and close-cut hair reminds Death of those dogs you see on Halloween that are all dressed up by their owners. The little dogs often like it because they have no self-respect as it is, but big dogs are different. Even if it's all just an illusion, they feel they have some kind of control and power in their lives, but once you dress a St. Bernard up as a dinosaur and a small child tries to ride it, the dog will never look at itself the same way.

All of this to say, a tie does not suit Jeff.

"Laugh it up. I'm here to clean up your mess."

My face didn't change, how did he know?

Jeff stops in the entryway and gives Emily a good long look. She is still standing next to the couch, two mugs of cinnamon oatmeal in hand. Jeff doesn't say anything for a bit, though he rarely needs to with his wonderfully emotive eyebrows.

"Alright, so I'll need all your account passwords. I'm going to start following the paper trail and get to the bottom of this."

Death nods and snatches up a notebook and begins scribbling down any relevant account names and passwords. Emily looks at Jeff with a weak, hopeful smile.

"Would you like some oatmeal?"

"That would be wonderful, thank you."

Emily's smile doubles in size as she bounces up to Jeff with a skip in her step. He takes the mug and spoon with a thin, warm smile and the two begin chatting, Jeff giving the most concerted effort Death has ever seen to such an inane conversation. Emily is going on about something pointless like the weather or how she made the oatmeal and Jeff is just smiling and nodding along.

What the fuck?

Death is in shock. Jeff has never been so much as mildly polite to him and here the demon is, chatting away with some random woman about absolutely nothing. Death has never taken his rudeness personally, but now he's starting to wonder if he should.

Death sighs in silence and finishes his list of passwords. Once completed, Death folds it up and hands the note to Jeff.

"Well, Emily and I should be heading out. We have a lot of ground to cover. Thank you for your help, Jeff."

Jeff gives Death a condescending look before taking the paper and turning to Emily, taking her mug of oatmeal along with his to the kitchen and begins washing them out. Emily approaches to try and help but he brushes her off.

"It's the least I can do. Think of it as a thank you. Besides, you had best get ready to go."

Emily looks a little shocked, hesitating before she replies.

"Oh, um, you're welcome. I'm glad you liked it."

Death watches as Emily turns towards the front door.

"Do you have everything?"

Emily nods her head.

"I don't really have anything."

Death internally bangs his head against a wall.

Stupid question.

Heath knows that Jeff is thinking the same thing.

"Alright. We'll be heading out. Hopefully you'll be done by the time we get back."

That was subtle enough but still biting, right?

Jeff chuckles without looking up from the dishes and Death feels a deep indignation as he turns on his heel and passes through the front door. Emily follows but makes sure to turn around and wave to Jeff who replies with a smile.

Jeff watches as Death and Emily leave, waiting until their car has pulled out, left the driveway, and been gone for several minutes.

Once the coast is clear, Jeff dries the mugs and spoons with a dish rag and finds their proper places before pulling an old beaten up cell phone from his pocket, extends the antenna, flips it open, and presses it to his ear.

"Hello? Yeah. It's not a bad joke, he really has a human."

There is a loud sigh and then a voice on the other side of the call.

"We're fucked."

CHAPTER TWENTY-FIVE

Satan hangs up the phone and tosses it on his desk before rummaging around in his desk for booze. The Devil's hand shakes as he pours, spilling a drop. Satan brings the drink up to his lips and knocks his head back.

Pause.

Repeat.

Pause.

Repeat.

Pause.

Repeat.

Repeat.

Satan stashes the bottle and the glass back in his desk before picking up the phone...he pauses and decides to have a quick smoke first. A few minutes later, window closed, air freshener sprayed and ashtray returned to its hiding place, Satan picks up the phone again and began dialing.

Ringgggggggggg

Ringgggggggggg

Ringgggggggggg

"Hello?"

Satan gulps.

"H-Hey, Agnes, this is Satan."

"Oh, hello, how are you?"

"Well."

"If you're well, then why are you calling me on this fine morning?"

"There's something important I need to tell you...It's about Death."

There is a long pause. Ever since he was a kid, Satan has been terrified of Agnes. The woman has a way of controlling the conversation and getting in your head. Agnes is no fool, she's fully aware of how people view her and uses that to her advantage. Satan has always admired that, but it's never done anything to rest his fears. There is something dark and powerful inside that woman and Satan has no interest in angering it.

"Are you two dating? You know, I always knew this would happen. You were always very close and you're very good for him. If you've called to ask for my approval, you should know by now that I am a very open-minded person. When's the wedding? It had better be in June because I have the perfect dress for a June wedding. Not on a Thursday though, Thursdays are bad luck."

Satan is in shock for a moment. He was sure Agnes would be one step ahead of him. She must have softened out over the years. No. She hasn't. This is a ploy, or is it? No. Yes. Is she trying to get him to let something slip? Or is she actually ignorant? If he lies, she'll know.

Satan's brain is starting to hurt.

"No, we're not...I'm not...it's not that."

"Well then what's going on?"

"Death was on the job yesterday..."

"His name is Thomas, and yesterday was his day off. Continue."

"Yes."

"And?"

"He found someone."

"Someone?"

"Yes."

"Alright. That's his job, isn't it?"

"Yes."

"So why are we speaking about this?"

"Because, um, he still has her."

Silence. A menacing silence. The silence of the ocean as a shark swims straight towards you, opening its maw wide.

"Why am I being told about this now?"

"I know we should have told you immediately but-"

"Don't say 'but'. No excuses. Tell me."

"Dea-Thomas wouldn't want me to tell you."

"And?"

"Well, I wanted to respect his feelings."

"If a child wants to have six cookies before dinner, do you respect their feelings?"

"No."

"You're right. You don't. Because a child does not know what is best for them. Their mother knows what is best for them. I am his mother. The one who decides what is best for Thomas is me and *only* me. Is that clear?"

"Um, yes."

"Where is he now?"

"They're trying to figure out her destination. She doesn't have any paperwork in the system, so we have no idea where she needs to be placed and it's impossible to judge someone without getting to know them. He has to get to know her."

"Judgement is not your concern. Your job is to stay in your little prison in the underworld and fiddle around so as not to cause trouble for your God. Know your place. Who knows about this?"

"Me, Thomas, the girl, and Jeff."

"What in God's name is a *Jeff?*"

"He's an employee of mine and he's taking over Thomas's work while he's gone with the girl. He's also working to make sure Peter doesn't figure anything out. If Peter catches on to something then we're all fucked."

"Firstly, it is rude to use such vulgar language when speaking to a lady. Secondly, you will have much more to worry about than being 'fucked' if something happens to my boy."

"Yes ma'am."

"Do you fully understand how bad this is, Lucifer? No. You don't.

You can't. Because if you did then you would not have done something as horrifyingly stupid as sending them off together. Alone. So he can get to know her."

"Yes ma'am."

"I will deal with this. You will hear from me if I need something and you will give it to me if and when I ask. Are we clear?"

"Yes."

"It's good to see that we're on the same page."

Agnes hangs up.

Satan sits there with the phone in his hand, letting the sweat run down his face. There is movement in his stomach and he gags, rushing from his desk, Satan arrives at the attached restroom just in time to vomit into the toilet. He stays there for a time, breathing deeply and letting the blood come back to his face.

A knock on the office door.

"Sir! There's an important message for you, may I come in?"

"No," Satan snaps, "just give me a moment."

Satan rises, rinses out his mouth with water and pops a mint from his pocket. Satan returns to his desk, leans back in his chair and props his legs up on the table.

"Come in."

The door opens and a young demon enters. Small horns grow from his forehead and he has a bright red skin tone. His innocent features look nervous and his eyes keep flitting around, trying to be polite but also wanting to avoid eye contact. Satan doesn't recognize him, so the demon must be new and therefore has the job of bearing bad news.

"Sir, I hate to bring bad news but-"

"What's your name?"

The demon seems surprised.

"My name...my name is Grimtail, sir."

"Grimtail, nice to meet you. Take a seat. What is it you're here to talk to me about today?"

Grimtail sits down across from Satan with an air of hesitation that is only present in someone tasked with delivering bad news.

"Um, uh, sir. I was told to inform you that we need to," Grimtail removes a crumpled piece of paper from his pocket and reads it aloud, "get our asses into gear."

"What?"

"Word on the inside is that we're being audited. They'll be here in two hours."

CHAPTER TWENTY-SIX

Peter is neither superstitious nor intelligent, but he is intuitive. He can tell if something bad is about to happen, though he rarely knows what the thing is. He's also good at knowing when he is being lied to, but never knows what the lie is. Whenever something feels off, Peter gets an itch on the knuckle of his right hand forefinger. This has been the case ever since he was a child. His family and friends would employ this power of his when they sold their fish at the market because there was usually some shifty Samaritan who tried to rip them off, but Peter would just let someone know he had a bad feeling about it and one of his more intelligent friends would take care of it. That was how life had always been for Peter and there had been no real end in sight, but that was okay. Peter was content.

Then a guy named Jesus showed up one day and told him to drop everything and follow him. Regular looking guy, all in all nothing really special or interesting looking about him, though he did have one weirdly shaped freckle on the side of his neck, but that was it. There was a way about him though that just drew Peter in. When he tried to get a read on him there was nothing. An open book. Absolutely nothing to hide. Before he knew it, Peter was on a road trip with Jesus and a bunch of other guys as they went around the nation and did some politically questionable stuff. Peter had never been one to get involved in anything like that, but suddenly he was wrapped up in something akin to a revolution and he kind of liked it. He didn't like it as much as the other guys, but he did enjoy it. There's something nice about feeling like you're a part of something bigger.

Peter sometimes thinks that he was the only one who saw Jesus for what he really was. The others all tended to throw their own interpretations into the mix. Not on purpose of course, they all meant well, but they were always finishing his sentences so to speak. As it would turn out, Peter became guilty of this later on, but for the most part he assumed less. Most of them viewed him as a freedom fighter here to overthrow the Empire. Jesus had no such ambitions as far as Peter saw and that didn't bother him. Peter was content to wander around forever, really. Jesus was an empty and unassuming vessel and Peter liked that.

Then it all came crumbling down when they were betrayed and Jesus got offed. Peter was a bit distressed. He had given up his future for this. Peter had gone all in on a dead guy and he and his friends were fearing for their lives. This time in his life is where Peter gained his reputation as angry and hotheaded. None of this was exactly true and especially so considering none of it was written from his perspective. Sure, Peter had done some crazy things leading up to Jesus's death, but everything was coming to an end. It was the best time of his life and it was suddenly over. People always complained about no one choosing to understand them but they never give that understanding to others.

In the end, Jesus came back, forgave Peter for all the forsaking him three times business and it was all hunky dory. But Peter never really forgave himself. He had, after all, betrayed the person he thought mattered to him the most. That person was dead, he came back and was more forgiving than ever. Jesus was giving people cool jobs and new responsibilities and Peter ended up being the foundation the Church was built on.

So, Peter became an insufferable asshole.

Coincidentally, Peter wakes up in an especially insufferable and asshole-y mood the morning after Death's "day off" and immediately feels an itch on the knuckle of his right hand forefinger. Peter sits up, scratching it and pondering. If it were any other day, he wouldn't think much of it. Maybe that angel really had borrowed a company stapler without asking, or maybe he really had been taking a personal call during work hours. These are little things. Yesterday was not. Yesterday was, from a managerial perspective, one of the biggest days in history. Death's long awaited day off. That ungrateful brat had been pestering everyone about it for years and it had gotten to the point where he was calling the home office several times a week and sending a slew of passive aggressive emails to various department heads.

Death had always bothered Peter. At first, he had tried to get along with him but there's no getting along with someone who has that bad of an attitude. Nothing ever makes him happy and he's unbearably apathetic. Everything he touches seems to wither up and rot, every room he enters becomes that much worse. It's not so much that a rain cloud follows Death around, but rather that he chooses instead to *be* one. Peter plays it polite though. Now Peter knows he can manage Death's job without him.

If only Raphael hadn't called in. I'll deal with him soon enough.

Peter would prove himself. This is *his* century. He will cleanse the afterlife of all the traitorous, lazy, and useless. As Peter gets ready for the day, moving about his small mess of an apartment, he continues to think about the previous day and the itch on his knuckle gets worse.

Something must have happened yesterday. Whatever it is, Death will never tell me. I have to find out.

Whatever happened while Death was on the job is his fault. If he had just taken over instead of Death, none of this would be a problem. But he had to stay back and manage everything. How could he have done the work itself while also managing everyone else?

If only Raphael had not called in.

If only Death weren't so useless.

Peter finishes putting on his tie, moving plastic bags and jackets off his chair and onto the coffee table so he can sit. He stares at the weird yellow stain on the wall near the door that has been there since he moved in. He had been given the option of staying in an infinitely nicer complex near the outskirts of Heaven with the other apostles, but Peter refused. He prefers living downtown because, unlike the other eleven, he is the only one who still works. Who would want to spend eternity lazing around and being useless when you could spend it doing something of value?

Something is happening and Peter has no idea what it is, but he knows he has to stop it. Peter needs evidence, but the trouble is that he's not very smart. He has intuition after all, but no intelligence. That's when it hits him.

Michael.

Unlike Peter, Michael has no intuition whatsoever but he's smart and detail oriented. The closer he keeps Michael, the more he can use him as a threat against Death. Michael's high and mighty attitude is not conducive to a better Heaven so he needs to go at some point anyway. All Peter is doing is getting some use out of him before his inevitable demise. For some reason, Death has a soft spot for him. Or maybe it's not a soft spot, who knows. Either way, Michael's a useful tool and that is all that Peter needs.

Before he does anything hasty, Peter pulls out his phone and dials Death's number.

"What?"

"Hi, Death! I just wanted to call and wish you good luck today. So sorry again for yesterday. You're sure everything went well?"

"It was fine. I told you the same thing last night."

Peter's knuckle begins to tingle.

"Oh, ok. Good to know. Well anyway, keep up the good work!"

The line goes dead.

Peter frowns and scratches the itch.

Getting to Death will not be easy. He has a feeling that if Death is involved in something then the Devil is too.

They've always been too close for comfort.

The problem is that Satan is intuitive, smart, and well connected. Therefore by extension, so is Death. If they're in on something together then it'll be that much harder to get to Death. But not if Satan is distracted by something bigger. Peter will have to act fast.

Peter grabs his briefcase and rushes out the door. If he moves now, he can catch Michael on his way to work. Peter is already moving shifts around so someone can take over for him. Michael has to accept now. The tables are turning and Peter is causing it. This can work. If he finds something, he can get all of them removed in one fell swoop.

I forgot to eat breakfast again.

CHAPTER TWENTY-SEVEN

"Was that the same person from yesterday?"

Death turns to Emily with a look of confusion.

"Oh, I mean. The person who called last night. The one you don't like very much."

She's more observant than she seems. Could mean she's manipulative, I'll add it to the notes.

"Yes."

"I thought so. You talked to them the same way."

Awkward silence.

"So, what's our plan for the day?"

"Well, first we're going to try and figure some things out concerning your situation. And from there I think we'll just follow the trail."

"But don't you have other souls to deal with? I'd feel bad if I took up too much time away from your work…"

Selfless. An important quality, but she's kind of making a mopey face there, so is it really selflessness or just a mad grab for positive reinforcement? I'm not very good at telling the difference.

"So, what's our plan…Death?"

"Why the pause?"

"I don't know, Death just feels like, you know, a title more than a name, maybe? It feels kind of weird to call you Death when Death is something that happens, right? You've always been called Death?"

"What's the point in calling me anything other than Death?"

"Well you're not always Death, right? You even had a pet dog. I don't think Death would have a pet dog. Not that I know that much."

You don't.

"But if there's no point in calling me anything other than Death, why would having a pet dog matter? You're not making sense."

"I guess not."

The sound of the car engine is deafening against the awkward silence that follows.

"So, um, the plan…"

"Yes. First, we'll head back to your apartment and see what we find, then we can figure out where to go from there."

"Oh, ok…"

Death glances over at the woman in his passenger seat who is now gazing out the window with a forlorn look on her face.

Why do they need to have so many emotions? It just makes this whole process more difficult. I get it, you're dead, it happens to everyone. It's nothing special, you're not special, so take happiness from it.

Death glances over again. She's still forlorn and sulky.

She's probably going through a lot right now. Most people are settled in their places by now, but not her. It's not like it's been very long, and she's been busy, but I'm sure this is far from what she expected. There's usually a quick turnaround, they never have a chance to wonder...

"There are CDs in the center console if you'd like to pick one. I need music when I drive."

Death does not move his head, his eyes stay locked on the road ahead, and he says it as if it's the most clear, casual offer anyone could ever make. Death can tell that she's the type who would make things awkward if he were to ask if she wanted music. The type to respond with "oh no, I'm fine...unless you want to listen to something and then I'm good with whatever you want to listen to..." and he doesn't feel like dealing with a pointless conversation like that.

Emily turns towards Death, and even out of his peripheral vision he can tell that sulky look has vanished from her face.

"Sure. What are you in the mood for?"

"Anything is fine, just go through them and pick one you like."

Emily opens up the center console and begins to flip through the perfectly organized CD cases, selecting after a short time an unmarked green plastic clam shell case with the words "Thomas Favorites". Death feels a sinking in his chest, and before he can get the words out, the disc is out of the case and the car's CD player has eaten it up like a greedy ticket machine.

Oh god oh god oh god I thought that was gone. Why is it in there I could've sworn it was in my closet.

The piano line starts.

Death locks his gaze even further down the road, but he can sense the realization coming to Emily like some kind of building energy.

It's coming.

Oh no oh god please no, please tell me she's not-

"I'VE BEEN CHEATED-"

Death mourns internally.

"You like ABBA too?" Emily turns and asks with an excited, child-like look in her eyes.

Death closes his eyes and takes a deep breath.

If I say no she'll skip the song and get awkward and sulky again and then this was all for nothing.

"I, uh, I...yes...I like ABBA."

"That's so great! Oh, come on you have to sing along with me."

Emily breaks into verse and Death considers stepping out of the moving vehicle. It would take about one and a half seconds to be out onto the asphalt, rolling and tumbling as the car speeds forward. One and a half seconds.

Death opens his mouth slowly.

CHAPTER TWENTY-EIGHT

As he makes his way to the basement, passing through the other floors of the Tower of Hell, Satan realizes he has not been down here in a while. The top floor with his office is where all the paperwork is done while everything below, excluding reception, is designed for the punishment of souls. Satan is in the human suffering business and there's no way around it.

He's worked hard to make it as humane as possible. Everybody works their hours, a solid nine to five job and once they clock out, it's not uncommon to see humans and demons having a drink together. It's just business after all, there's nothing personal about it. Satan passes the gluttons being forced to eat deep fried foods, the sweetest candy imaginable, the fat of raw chicken, and sugary soda to wash it all down. Every time they falter they get ten lashes. There are ten souls and two demons to a room. The ratio works quite well. The screams are dreadful, and Satan withstands the urge to wince, but there will be a reprieve soon, it's nearly time for the lunch break.

The door is massive and made of iron with a large, ancient keyhole. At the bottom is a slat that looks like it can be raised and a tray slid through. This is the only door in the building that doesn't use key cards and no one has the key except for Satan. He loosens his tie and undoes the top button of his shirt, pulling out the rusty brass key which hangs at his neck, attached by a thin piece of cord.

Before he inserts the key, Satan presses his ear to the door and listens. The only sound is that of quiet breathing and the faint clink of metal on metal. Satan takes a deep breath and unlocks the door. The room is painted a simple white, a single light fixture is installed into the ceiling. There is an array of tools and items on a table to the right of the door, but many are scattered around the room.

Knives, hacksaws, planks of wood, hammers, a drill with several different bits, an iron maiden situated in the far left corner, a case of bottled water, a bucket, a box of matches, nails, a cooking thermometer, five wine glasses, four engagement rings, three boxes of lithium batteries, two alligator clips, and one portable generator among other things. In the center of the room is an obsidian pyramid on a tripod with a stepstool next to it and four straps hanging from the ceiling above it.

Sitting near the table is a ragged looking, pale man with stringy white hair, an unkempt beard, and no shirt. Scars and burns cover his body and he is currently biting his lip in focus as he holds a nail between two of his toes with one hand and a hammer poised to strike in the other. The man looks up as Satan walked in.

"Oh, hello. How are you?"

"Alright. You?"

"Pretty good. Going back to the basics. I haven't tried this in a while, but I think I can beat my record and do all eight. I don't know, I just have a good feeling. What brings you down here today?"

The man puts the hammer and nail down and crosses his legs as he speaks with Satan.

Satan has never been able to get used to what this man does. Satan oversees some miserable punishments, some really unspeakable shit, but this has always been a bit much for him.

"How would you like some vacation time? A break from the cell?", Satan tries to mimic a terrible Brooklyn accent, "I'll let ya out on good behavior."

No response. Just that straightforward stare with the knowing smile that always makes people feel uncomfortable. The inhuman amount of blood splattered around the room is various degrees of dryness is starting to make Satan a little sick. The man follows his eyes to the blood and immediately stands up and walks to the corner, gently taking a mop in his hand and wincing a bit. Satan notices an number of fresh cuts on his hands as the man begins mopping up some of the larger patches of blood.

"So sorry. If I had known I was having a guest I would have cleaned up a bit."

Satan waves him off.

"Don't worry about it. I'll have somebody else do it. Would you like to come out for a bit? I have a job for you."

The man's mopping became more intense as he stares straight down at the puddle of crimson water forming at his feet. Finally, he stopped and speaks softly without lifting his green eyes up from the reflective sheet of bloody water.

"I'm not allowed to leave."

He says it in such a way as if reminding himself of something. Satan raises his forefinger with a grin and retrieves a slip of paper from his pocket.

"Now that, is where I come in. When we did some reorganizing forever ago the Old Man had to sign the papers. Obviously, he never read them because in there I gave all of you fine human employees vacation time. It takes a while to rack up, but I made sure it was retroactive. Seeing as you've been here for roughly two-thousand odd years that gives you two weeks."

Satan gives an evil grin as he slips the paper back in his pocket.

"I need you for one. I have to sign off on the papers, but once you've done your work, you're free for a week. Seven days. One-hundred and sixty-eight hours. I can't help but imagine a man like yourself has some things he'd like to take care of. I don't know about you, but that sounds like a fantastic deal to me."

The man continued to gaze at the wet floor. Then he looks up at Satan with a difficult to read expression. The cool, confident, and polite veneer is shaved away. It's not quite excitement, but it's not quite apprehension. Almost like a child who goes to a theme park for the first time but is terrified of crowds.

"What exactly is it that you need me to do?"

Satan gestures for him to follow as he steps out the door.

"Come on. Let's get you cleaned up first."

CHAPTER TWENTY-NINE

Hell is not the best place for someone like Peter to be. Demons get touchy about their leader and even more so when anyone does something even mildly threatening towards him. It would seem that simply being in the underworld is threatening in and of itself as Peter pulls into the parking lot of the Tower of Hell, there is a steady stream of glares and sinister looks as demons return from their lunches and see an angel and an apostle driving by.

Can they be any more disagreeable?

Peter has a feeling the likelihood of him having a car to return to are slim to none so another is already on the way to pick him and his assistant, Afriel, up. The young angel is clutching his clipboard and bag to his chest as he looks around at all the demons.

"D-d-do you really think we'll be safe?"

"We'll be just fine. They can't do anything to us."

"Are you sure?"

"Yes."

Peter is not entirely sure, but that feels like the right thing to say here. Afriel is just a kid after all and this is his first time in the Underworld. Peter selected him to be his assistant during the audit because he has about as much common sense as Michael. If Peter tells him to do something, he'll do it immediately and without question. Not because he's especially easy to control, he simply trusts Peter and his knowledge implicitly. That also means he won't blab to anyone he doesn't need to.

Peter exits out of the car and begins making his way through the parking lot, calling back to Afriel as the angel gathers his things.

"Don't leave anything you ever want to see again."

***

Satan sits at his desk watching the door. Ready. Waiting.

The phone rings.

"Yes?"

"Sir, they are in the elevator and on their way up."

"Thank you."

Satan hangs up.

Ready. Waiting.

Satan stands and opens a window, lighting up a cigarette.

Death, buddy, you are really gonna owe me one after this.

***

The top floor. Satan's floor. Peter is deep in enemy territory now. The bullpen style office floor is bustling with demons going about their work, yelling, laughing, the sound of a breaking bottle, more shouts.

"Come on."

Peter begins walking to Satan's office, making sure to look straight ahead and not make eye contact with the demons. The pair are getting lots of stares and a few poorly veiled rude gestures. Then the laughs. Peter watches out of the corner of his eye as a demon sitting at a desk is smiling letting out a light-hearted chuckle as they march past.

Peter's knuckle begins to itch as he knocks on the door.

Something's wrong. What does he have up his sleeve?

"Come in!"

Peter opens the door and inside is Satan alone at his desk.

A smile on his face.

"Welcome! Take a seat. How was the drive down?"

"It was fine," Peter says absently as he glanced around the room, "You're in a fine mood today."

"Well why wouldn't I be? The weather's wonderful, business is booming, and, without being too gross, it seems I'm getting more popular with the ladies as the years go by. Aging has done me wonders, if it's not conceited to say."

"Sure."

"Anyway, take a seat. Please. We have a lot to talk about."

Peter and Afriel sit in the two massive leather armchairs across from Satan's desk. Afriel is nearly shaking which catches the Devil's eye.

"Well look what we have here. What's your name?"

"Um, uh, it's um, A-Afriel...sir."

"Afriel. What a beautiful name. You have very innocent features, has anyone ever told you that? I bet you're a sweet young man. You know...once this is all finished you should stop by my apartment for a drink, I have this-"

"We did not come here to talk about drinks. We're here for an audit, not an audition."

Afriel is visibly blushing.

"You're right, I had almost forgotten. Let me just call in my assistant," Satan looks over at the door and calls out, "You can come in now!"

The door opens and both Peter and Afriel turned around to look. Peter's eyes widen, his heartrate spikes, and his stomach drops. Afriel fumbled with the clipboard and nearly drops it.

Standing in the doorway is a man dressed in slacks and a button down with the top button undone and the sleeves loosely rolled up to just below his elbows, revealing bandages that cover his arms up past the sleeves. The man has a thin smile on his lips and a clean-shaven face, showing off his sharp features which are accented by his longer white hair. Those confident green eyes. Peter never thought he would ever see them again. A bead of sweat drips from his brow.

"Judas, welcome. This is Afriel and...well. You two already know each other."

Peter feels an impending sense of dread and the itching on his knuckle is almost unbearable.

Shit.

Judas had always been the smart one.

CHAPTER THIRTY

The look on Peter's face when Judas enters the room is enough to confirm for Satan that he made the right decision.

If you try to dance with the Devil you had best be ready to follow.

Satan is rather proud of that one. If he had said it out loud it probably would have sounded pretty stupid, but now is not the time for thinking out loud. Satan spreads his arms wide with a theatrical flourish.

"Now that the introductions are done with, we can get down and dirty with this audit."

Judas begins to walk past Peter's chair, taking his time, intentional, methodical, calculating. Nothing had changed. Their eyes meet briefly as he brushes past and Peter feels Judas's piercing gaze. Judas had always been good at that, making you feel like he was seeing through you.

Judas had been in charge of the money and together they always made sure no one ripped them off. Peter would just nudge him when he got a bad feeling, and Judas would take care of everything. Everyone trusted Judas and yet no one did. Peter's knuckle always itched around Judas. It was impossible to tell what it was about, but there was not a single time Peter could remember when his knuckle did not itch while speaking to Judas. That's just the kind of person he was. Or should he say, is.

Peter is starting to get the feeling that he's out of his depth. Satan has been doing this for a long time, a lot longer than Peter has been around, and he has the homefield advantage to boot. But this isn't about winning, this is about buying time.

"Yes. We've wasted enough time as it is. It's best that we get started."

Peter and Satan lock eyes. Satan is in power right now, but Peter has a plan. Peter is neither the smartest, nor the kindest, nor the wisest, but he does have a hunch and the only one with the drive to see it through.

Judas glances at Afriel and smiles. The young angel is already involved in more than he had ever imagined he would be. Today is the day he met Satan, the eternal enemy of his boss, as well as Judas, the betrayer of Jesus. His head is swimming. This is not what he signed up for. He didn't sign up for anything, actually, Peter just told him to come with him and so he did. Maybe that is something he needs to work on. He needs to learn how to say no.

Satan begins to withdraw documents from his desk. Peter motions to Afriel who undoes the latch on his bag and begins pulling out an array of complicated and one-hundred percent pointless papers.

"So, as you seem to have learned about this audit already, I will skip briefing you on its nature and move right into the details."

Peter draws his fountain pen and begins reading the script he prepared beforehand. Peter usually knows what to say but he has a bad habit of stuttering whenever pressure is on and Satan is not the type to let any weakness go unnoticed.

"Hell and its legions have gone unchecked for quite some time. Although you and Our Lord have had a successful business relationship for many years, the nature of your expulsion from Heaven always has, and always will, warrant suspicion on our part. We are not expecting to find anything, however with that said, we will need access to your complete collection of records from the time since your last audit on the twelfth day of March, two-hundred and fifty A.D. Although the audit may take some time..."

Peter looks up as Judas strides past him and out of the door. Peter's knuckle immediately begins to itch and he frantically scans for anything out of place. Satan's expression is unchanged and Afriel is trying to avoid eye contact with just about everyone in the room.

Poking just out of Satan's hand is a piece of paper. His hand is balled up into a fist and Peter can barely see it showing out the side. The itch on Peter's hand is nigh on unbearable now as is the stress and rage building inside of him.

Something is going on and I have no idea what it is. What are they planning? Dammit I need to stop him.

"What's wrong?"

Peter turns to meet the gaze of Satan whose expression is one of genuine concern and for an instant, he feels like answering.

If I'm being completely honest, no. I'm not doing very well. A mistake has been made which may well jeopardize my position in the afterlife. If it comes out, I am more than likely to lose everything I have and all the respect I've scraped together thus far. I will be nothing but a sellout who wasted every opportunity he was given and betrayed the people who trusted him the most. I'll be just like Judas.

Peter rises.

"I need to use the restroom."

"Huh?"

"You heard me. Afriel can brief you. I will be back in a few minutes."

As Peter turns, he notices Satan's expression shift from concern, to surprise, and finally to worry.

I've got him.

Before Satan can say anything, Peter is out the door and looking for Judas. The office bullpen is busy with demons bustling around and giving Peter sideways glances. Then he sees Judas round a corner on the opposite side of the room leading to the elevators. Peter sprints across the room, he has to catch him, he cannot let Judas get away and sabotage everything. Not this time, not again.

He bursts through the doors of the office and out into the hallway. The whole design of this place is too minimalist for Peter. There is a fine but significant line between removing clutter and making everything super awkward and pretentious. Satan lives on that tight rope doing a one-man samba across it.

If Peter had taken a moment to calm himself and look out the window, he might have noticed that the weather was quite nice in Hell today. The "sun" is shining and there is the odd bat out flying around and stretching his wings. From the top floor of the Tower of Hell you can see everything and you are also high enough to avoid the screams of pain below you. Looking out past the city you can see the outer wastes of Hell and you begin to feel like you are inside a beacon, an oasis in a horrifying and pain filled desert, a broken utopia, but a utopia nonetheless. Peter would also have thought that perhaps there is not much reason to hate this place and the people in it. That maybe there's something he is missing about it all.

But sadly, Peter did not stop and have a nice think on the machinations of his heart. As Peter bursts into the hallway, one of the two elevators is already closing and Judas is standing within it, a big grin on his face. Judas sees Peter and waves, the smile getting bigger. Peter gets to the door right as it closes and he slams his hand on the door with a yell and begins furiously tapping the down button on the second elevator.

"Comeoncomeoncomeoncomeoncomeon."

The display above the door lights up and displays "1".

Peter dives for the stairwell and shoots down like a rocket.

I can catch him I just have to move.

Faster.

Faster.

Faster.

Peter is hopping stairs now, sprinting as fast as his unworked body can go. He has not exerted himself this much since his days on earth as a fisherman two thousand years ago and he is breathing with great effort. He reaches the bottom and pushes through the door as Judas is exiting the building. Peter barrels past a group of demons, bumping into a few of them, their shouts and curses muffled barks in the background. The only thing Peter can hear is his own breathing and the blood pounding in his ears. He can see Judas through the clear glass doors as he makes a sharp left and vanishes from sight.

I can do this.

Peter opens the doors and makes the same sharp left, and almost crashes into Judas. The tall figure is leaning against the wall outside the Tower with a pack of cigarettes in one hand while the other digs around in his pocket.

"Whoa, watch where you're going, you might bump into someone."

Judas lights his cigarette and takes a drag.

"Oh, I'm so impolite. Smoke? It's been a while since I've done this around anyone."

Peter is wheezing, resting on his knees as he tried to catch his breath.

Dammit. Dammit. Goddammit.

Judas had always been the smart one.

CHAPTER THIRTY-ONE

Satan smiles to himself.

I knew I made the right decision.

Peter is a pain in the ass, but at least he's gullible.

"Afriel, if you don't mind, I have a call to make before we return to business. If you could just step out for a moment, please."

With Peter gone, Afriel is left in an awkward situation. The young angel is alone in a room with the worst of his kind. The Great Betrayer of God Himself. This is the being that angels are taught their entire lives to never be like, and both parties are well aware of this. Satan doesn't mind all that much because he likes knowing that people are thinking of him, whatever the context may be.

"Oh, um, I'm sorry but Peter told me that in case he had to leave, I'm not supposed to leave you alone. It's just protocol, I'm really sorry.

Satan sighs.

"It's a bit of a delicate situation and I really would like some privacy. But I understand. It's not your fault."

Satan pulls out his cell phone and dials a number and begins to speak.

"Hello...how is he?...dammit I am so sorry...no no, you're fine... a cleaning crew will be there soon so just make sure you're gone before then...alright...have a good day, I'll talk to you later...bye."

Satan hangs up the phone and sighs before looking at Afriel with the best pitiful expression that he can manage.

"Just between you and me, I don't like people knowing, but I love dogs and I just got a puppy recently. The dog sitter went out to get lunch and came back to everything chewed up and shit everywhere. You know how puppies are. The poor kid though, he was so panicked and offered to clean everything up for free. I just need to alert the cleaning crew."

Satan types on his phone and pretends to send a text.

"Perfect."

Afriel thinks back to a puppy he had as a child. She had done things like this but he had always loved her for it. They're sweet and innocent if not a little destructive.

Satan looks up from his phone and flashes the young angel a disarming, toothy smile.

Angels really aren't the brightest, are they?

CHAPTER THIRTY-TWO

Jeff closes his flip phone and slips it into his pocket. Looks like he'll have to finish up faster than expected. Since Death departed, Jeff has gone about making sure the place is clean and ready for any unwanted visitors that might stop by. Not a trace remains of anyone but Death being here, not that there was much to clean. Jeff would rather not cover for this guy. There are lots of people that float through life filled with discontent, they're troublesome that way, but not Jeff.

Jeff's always happy where he is and he can't think of a time where he wasn't. Not that he is an especially happy person, but he's fine doing just about anything and the "just about" to that "anything" is helping out Death.

Jeff has disliked him since the first time they met however many thousands of years ago. Death had come to visit Satan in the Underworld at one of his first house parties. Jeff took one look and decided that he was not a fan of Death. He was technically much younger than Death, but he couldn't help viewing the Reaper as nothing more than a petulant child. Jeff's biggest problem with Death is not his angsty behavior or that unbearable sighing but rather how unhappy he was. In Jeff's humble opinion, happiness does not mean that you have to actually *be* happy all the time. The important thing is that you try and Death never tries.

Jeff has always thought the best thing for Death is for him to go through some truly hard times or suffer a major loss so he can learn that all the moping and whining he does is really over nothing. Jeff is not a hateful person, being hateful is not conducive to being happy after all, so he wanted Death to learn from his mistakes and be a better person from there on out. If that happens, maybe they can even be friends.

Probably not.

Jeff has gone through everything, the bedroom, the living room, the bathroom, the kitchen, and even that room with all the dreadful paintings, but now he's on a timetable so he won't be able to double check anything.

There must be some issue back in Hell, meaning the Heavenly pains in the ass are on to something.

Not surprising, really. Who takes a soul? Who actually decides to bring a soul home with them?

Jeff has never understood Death's behavior and he probably never will. The girl is nice though. Much too good to be spending her time around someone like Death, but she doesn't have many choices at this point. The poor girl has no destination and, whether he likes it or not, Death's good at his job. Jeff does a quick re-scan of the main room and exits the house, making sure to lock the door.

After getting into his weathered two-seater pick-up truck, Jeff logs onto the database through Death's access point. His phone barely gets a connection, and he almost needs glasses to read on the poorly lit screen, but it's there, no denying it.

Wednesday, October 16th:

02:04-Emily Doe, 26, likes cats.

Murder, ---------------

So, he wasn't shitting us.

Jeff considers this as he starts up the truck and begins to drive to his first destination of the day.

Like clockwork, as Jeff's car rounds the corner and out onto the road, another car pulls off on the opposite side and into Death's driveway. Out steps the tall, thin figure of Michael. Unlike Jeff, Michael is actually having a pretty good day. Even if it's for Peter, he's doing something important and therefore something worth his time.

Michael's current job at the Gates of Heaven is important of course, and he knows this because God told him so, but it lacks the need for any special skills. Investigating Death's home does not necessarily require Michael to be able to level cities, but you never know what can happen on the job. There's a copy of Death's house key kept in Heaven, as are keys to all homes subsidized by God. Peter had given it to Michael, and he was told to use it to get in and out "without leaving any clues". Peter had specified as many times as he could that this is "just recon".

Even if it's "just recon", it sounds more interesting than what Michael had been on his way to do a few hours earlier when, on his way to work, Peter had stopped him in the street. Michael is a big believer in getting to work early, so he always tries to get there an hour or two before his shift starts. Almost all the world's problems can be solved by simply getting to work early. Michael has even heard of people whose sex lives improved after they started getting to work early, however, he has no personal experience to back this up.

Michael tried to avoid Peter at first, doing his best not to make eye contact. Run-ins with Peter generally result in something time consuming or irritating happening and Michael can only handle so much of that at a time. Peter is always trying to innovate, but he's just too stupid. Everything that comes out of his mouth is so incredibly banal that Michael often feels like jamming syringes into his ears to stop the pain. This would cause trouble for God on the health insurance front, so Michael has willfully refrained. Peter had harassed Michael for a little bit about an important job, but Michael refused because he was behind and only had an hour to make the rest of his fifteen-minute walk to work.

Peter, weighing the cost of spilling the beans, decided that this was a risky enough endeavor to warrant something as hazardous as telling the truth. Michael was informed of all the relevant information up until that point, only leaving out the subtle detail of how Peter managed to convince Death to forgo his day off with zero compensation. Michael had made a mental note to look into that later if the time allowed for it. Whatever the doubts, this was enough to make him call in sick, and team up with Peter. And now here he is using a key meant for official use only to break into an employee's house because the first pope has a "hunch".

Michael has never been in Death's house before, yet he's not surprised by what he finds. The whole layout and feeling of the place fits his personality: disordered but rather clean. However, after Michael takes the time to investigate and take in his surroundings, he notices that there is something deeply wrong about the house. Michael has to specify a "house" rather than a "home" because nothing about the place is very homelike. The feng shui is all off.

Many people are surprised to find out that Michael is in fact a huge mystery fan. Michael has a lot of spare time sitting in the guard booth and, though of course aware that in the grand scheme of things it is a job of grave importance, in the simple day to day it can feel so boring that he wishes to die. The solution, or at least a short-term cure, is reading. Michael consumes everything he can get his hands on and even though he often reads things he would never be able to wrap his head around with another ten-thousand years of trying, it's something to pass the time. It was not until the advent of the mystery novel that Michael really found his niche, especially in the realm of detective stories. There's something about that brilliant individual who always finds a pathway to truth that appeals to Michael, and now he has a chance to apply what he's learned from his novels to something of real importance: investigating Death.

Michael does not have any hard feelings towards Death, quite the opposite. Michael has always considered them to be good friends and Death asks polite and thoughtful questions. Michael had been writing his own mystery novel for a long time now and no one ever asks about it, except Death. In their defense he doesn't really talk about it either, but they could still ask.

Once upon a time in Heaven there was novel writers club. Since the whole deal with Jesus and the cross, the angels' jobs have been all but over. God's Son tidied up the human situation and now everyone can "speak directly to God" (automated voicemail message) so the angels don't have to be messengers anymore. The End of Days is still a good ways off so there's no call for any big celebration. They're also working with Hell now so there aren't any interesting wars on with the demons. Essentially, everything that once made an angel's life interesting is now gone. And what do people do when there's nothing interesting going on in their life and they feel like their "best of days" have already come and gone?

Write a novel.

Michael had founded the club because that's the kind of person he is, and he is still surprised at how popular it was. The club grew a bit and all of the angels were writing boring and unoriginal novels about God and how much they love Him. It was like reading an essay that a group of middle school kids plagiarized. Novels written by angels have a lot in common with porn, at least in the sense that they all end the same. None of the others took it as seriously as Michael, but that was alright, he just enjoyed having everyone around.

The club still exists, but Michael is the only member. The meetings were always at his house so it's no great inconvenience to keep holding the meetings. There was no big fight or anything that brought things to an end, it just happened. One by one, they all stopped coming until it was just Michael, alone with his story.

It's fine.

Michael has not finished his novel in about two-hundred years of writing it. Most of it is written, he's just stuck at the ending.

CHAPTER THIRTY-THREE

Pulling up at the apartment complex in the wee hours of the morning, Death remembers why he hates cities and everything to do with them. A ragged looking drunk is sleeping on the steps leading to the complex entrance while another, slightly less ragged looking drunk is slouched next to the sleeping one and mutters to himself an incoherent stream of consciousness and a stray cat with a hideous visage rests between them, glaring straight at Death.

Emily's eyes move from the cat, to Death, back to the cat, and then back to Death.

"Can it see you?"

"Yes."

Death has always had trouble with cats. It's not so much the fact that they can see him, and always have been able to, but more the fact that they tend to be so mean about it. Almost like they know what he's here for and they do not entirely approve.

"Does that mean they can see me too?"

"Yes and no. If it doesn't care to see you, cats are good at blocking things out. But if it has an interest, they're able to see things that other animals, especially humans, cannot."

Death feels that was a pretty smart explanation, so he gets out of the car and begins up the steps, passing the drunks as the stray cat hisses at him. Though annoyed by its needless aggressive behavior, Death feels a level of respect for the little feline. Cats are fearless, especially when it comes to those they love.

Don't worry, I'm not here for them.

Emily's feet hit the pavement as she jogs to catch up with Death after, he can only assume, being distracted by the cat.

She seems like the type.

As they make their way through the apartment building, Emily begins her next round of long winded questions.

"So. What exactly can I do as a…ghost? Am I a ghost? Or am I just a spirit? Is there a difference? But also, like, what can see me?"

Death sighs.

He has not needed to give this whole talk in a long time. Occasionally he'll get a flurry of questions about a specific cryptid or something, sometimes even a conspiracy theory but rarely things like this. People have lost interest in recent years because the idea of the afterlife is derivative and played out.

Death jams on the elevator button to no avail.

"It doesn't work, we have to take the stairs."

Emily points at the stairwell as she speaks.

"Come on, stairs are fun. It gives us more time to talk."

Emily pushes open the door to the stairwell and Death can almost see a cloud of stench escape it. City stairwells are always filled with stale air and ambient substance abuse. Emily grins and moves inside.

What other choice do I have?

The door slams itself shut, sending a resounding echo through the rank stairwell, and Emily resumes her inane questions.

"So, like, can I move through walls and stuff? Or can I haunt a TV or something like in the movies? And really, please give me a straight answer, who can and cannot see me?"

"It's a little complicated."

"That's ok. I like complicated things. Makes me think."

Emily punctuates her statement with a wink.

What's with temperament? She was serious, and even a little mopey earlier, but now she's utterly relentless.

"Sure, I guess. The key thing with souls after their bodies die, is they tend to linger. Most people leave some form of unfinished business. A task they couldn't complete, an old friend they never apologized to, a family member they never got to say goodbye to, the list goes on and on. But essentially, there's no one-size-fits-all answer for your questions. It is not so much yes or no as it is a probably, maybe, and well if...is this all making sense?"

Emily nods.

"Alright. So, if someone has no unfinished business, or at least nothing they think is worth finishing enough to carry into the afterlife, they just go right on their way and begin their eternity. Clean, easy, no problem. Now, if the soul has a level of emotional baggage weighing them down then it's my job to do what I can when I first interact with them. Humans have the perception that I'm some harbinger of doom, that I kill people, or that I escort you to your respective place. I did it back in the day when there were less of you but it's nearly impossible now with everything that goes on. But, before I move on to your questions, are you still with me?"

Emily nods.

"When it comes to interacting with the material world as an immaterial soul, the primary factor is that baggage. When I do the initial processing like you saw yesterday, I do what I can to lessen the load but it's rarely enough. In the end it's up to the person themselves to decide whether or not to get on the bus, because that's how it has to be. If they decide not to, then that's why this world has exorcists and paranormal investigators. We let them get their hands dirty because it saves us a good deal of time and energy. Everybody's different, and that remains the same after they die. Some can only make Ouija boards work, while some can even go so far as possession, so there's a bit of a range. It takes a lot of strain and energy for a soul to be seen after death, but it can happen. There are certain people or animals that are good at seeing souls though and can even see them without the other side making an effort. Cats for instance, and with less than acclimated personalities. Other than those exceptions, nobody can see you unless they're really trying or you want them to. Is this all making sense?"

Death notices the door and realizes they've been standing at the entrance to Emily's apartment for a couple minutes as he's gone on explaining. He feels nauseous with embarrassment.

How long have we been standing here? It can't have been long, right? She would have said something if I was wasting too much time blathering on, right?

As Death turns to apologize, he is met with an honest smile. Not the kind that is obviously forced and makes you feel horrible because you've wasted the person's time.

Rather, it's the kind of smile that encourages you to say more for no other reason than the person is really truly interested in what you're saying.

"Yep. That answers it pretty well, thank you."

"O-of course."

There's an awkward pause, at least from Death's perspective.

"Let's go inside."

Death opens the door and enters with Emily following. As he scans the room, nothing has been moved. No one has found the body.

Death hears hissing and looks over at the couch to find the meanest looking cat corpse he has ever seen in his entire existence and an equally mean looking cat soul resting just atop it, glaring at the Reaper with its teeth bared. An inhuman squeal rings from just behind him as Emily lurches forward and snatches up the spectral cat, showering it with kisses and words of adoration as it twists and squirms about.

"Is that thing yours?"

"This is Mr. Mustard. Mr. Mustard, say hello to Death."

She picks up one of his paws and waves it at Death as the orange-ish face frowns. Emily glances at the couch where Mr. Mustard was sitting and gasps, jumping to the side a bit.

Did she not notice that when she ran over?

Death approaches the couch where the overweight cat has made a permanent dent and begins examining the body as Emily begins another flurry of hugs and kisses.

"What happened to him? Who would do something like this to my cat? Did you see him yesterday? I didn't I was too distracted how could I have been so distracted that I missed him. He wasn't dead then...or was he? Oh my god this is just terrible I don't-"

Death snaps.

"Please just be quiet for a second. Let me look him over. Just go wait in the other room or something."

Death moves the body and confirms that the blood on the couch is dry. It all seems to have come from the head. He moves the fur aside and feels a little nauseous.

That is one nasty blow.

Someone with a fair amount of strength must have done this, and even then, it was more than one hit. Death is not a trained forensics expert, but he's done his job long enough to have a pretty good intuition about these things. The cat could not have been dead when he picked up Emily. The cat had to have been killed during the time she was gone, and Death assumes it's the same person. The first killer made sure to leave everything in order while they were in the apartment, almost eerily so. No drawers thrown open, none of the semi-nice-looking things missing or couch cushions turned over. No theft was involved. The plan from the start to finish was murder, pure and simple. Well, probably not pure, but definitely simple. Death rises from his crouched position and gives the room another once over and notices two more details.

First: The note is missing. The one that was on the counter with the atrocious handwriting.

Second: The door to Emily's bedroom is ajar and there is no Emily to be seen in the main room.

"Just go wait in the other room or something..."

Death sighs as he approaches the doorway.

A fidgeting cat, a spectral woman locked in place, a cold corpse gazing lazily at the eternal spiral of her ceiling fan.

CHAPTER THIRTY-FOUR

Smoke from the cigarette wisps about as it ascends to the Heavens.

Judas has always found that expression funny.

To the Heavens.

He understands that, yes, it means to the skies. Everyone always assumes that Heaven is upward, but Judas always suspected otherwise, and it was not until his death that he had his doubts confirmed. Heaven is really just the next door over, in universal terms that is. It's a whole process getting over and not just anyone can do it, but if a human were to try hard enough, they could find a pathway to Heaven simply by turning around.

At least, that's the conclusion Judas has come to. Everyone on Earth is just living in the shadow of Heaven. Going about their daily lives without any idea that if they get their heads out of the clouds and turn around then they'll find what they're looking for. Judas spent his entire life looking for Heaven and when he finally decided to turn around, he was terrified because what he found was a door smaller than the eye of a needle and a shadow stretching further than the firmament. Though covered by shade and shadow, Judas felt nothing but the heat of the sun and the weight of his body knowing he could never fit through the door. The weight grew heavier when he thought about how few he knew who could actually fit through it. Though told he could do it his entire life, it was not until Judas saw it for himself that he knew deep down in that little spot just behind his lungs that this was false.

Judas had to find his own salvation so he found a field with a tree and decided he would rest in the shade of that instead. Speaking of which, it's about that time. Satan will want him back soon and instead of doing what he said he would do he's just sitting in this bathroom stall smoking a cigarette.

Judas unlaces his left shoe and removes it, placing it and his sock on the toilet paper dispenser, then rummages in his pocket and produces a sizable pocket knife. As he brings his foot up to begin work on his toenails, the phone in his right pocket buzzes.

Judas speaks into the receiver.

"Hello?"

"It's been a while."

"It really has. If you don't mind my asking, how did you get this number?"

"I heard you were given a phone for the job and it's not difficult to find a number in this business."

"Fair. As much as I'd like to talk, this is not the best time. Can I give you a ring later?"

"This won't take long. I just wanted to let you know that this is it. I confirmed it all. So, there can be no mistakes on either of our parts. We can't let him down."

"I'm not sure your boss would be too happy that you're involved with something like this behind his back."

"That's true, but he won't find out. Clear?"

"Loud."

"Perfect. Keep me updated on your end. It's good to have you back."

"You too, Jeff."

"Oh, before you go…"

"Yes?"

"On a scale of one to ten, exactly how much did you and Satan fuck with Peter's head?"

CHAPTER THIRTY-FIVE

Peter is in what one might call a "tizzy". Michael has never liked Yam of God, but it's what everyone likes in Heaven, so he finds himself eating here constantly. The place is chintzy with a pseudo-diner aesthetic complete with booths, counter service, and cheap prices. Why anyone would like this kind of thing is confusing in and of itself, but what really confuses Michael about the place is the presence of so much borderline blasphemous iconography. The baked yams all come out with a brand of the Christ himself burned onto the skin, the kids' meals all come with a creepy paper Jesus mask, and the menu items all have horrific puns for names included, but not limited to, the jehashova sandwich, the king of spuds basket, and the high priest hasselback. It feels disingenuous to Michael, like they're missing the point and getting further from it with every t-shirt sale. They don't even close on Sunday, and that's quite clear judging from Peter's weight.

The rock on which the church was built is wolfing down an order of yam fritters which he said they should split the cost of and then proceeded to eat the entire thing himself.

Michael doesn't fight it because Peter is stress eating.

"Why is he like that?"

"Who?"

Peter looks to his left and right as if making sure no one is listening and once satisfied leans in for a whisper.

"Satan."

"Ah."

"What do you mean, 'ah'?"

"I mean, 'ah. You weren't here when it all happened'."

Peter glares.

"What does that have to do with anything?"

"Nothing. Just that you would understand more if you were."

"But I know exactly what happened. How would I understand more?"

"You just would. It's something you had to be there for to understand. At least, when it comes to why he acts the way he does."

"But he has a fantastic job. He has no excuse to be so rude and disruptive. All while I'm down there on official business trying to weed out a mistake."

"I agree, but he doesn't see it that way."

Peter grumbles as he finishes up the yam fritters.

He's too young for his own good. Too hungry in more ways than one.

Michael knows that people have a false perception of him. They view him as a delusional, neurotic waste of potential and as someone who would do anything to get back to the place he once was. This is accurate, to an extent, but it falls through on a key aspect. Michael is the first to admit he's a waste of potential. Working the gatehouse of Heaven is far from a fitting use of his talent and experience and this is not where the perception falls through but rather, in regards to the lengths he would go to get what he wants.

He's much happier with his job than he likes to admit. Even though there is the looming sense that Michael is wasting every second of training and experience he ever had, there is something indescribably peaceful about the gatehouse. Michael goes there in the morning, does his work, and goes home in the evening. Day in day out, the same routine, back and forth. It's a rhythm and a comfortable one at that. Michael wants to love his work, but that looming feeling persists. Its source a small spot just behind his lungs which leaks a poison which seeps into his veins until it settles in the dread center of his stomach where all guilt and fear comes to rest.

If Michael the Archangel wastes his potential, it gives a bad impression not just of himself but also to his Boss. God made him for great things yet here is in the guardhouse puttering away. It would be selfish not to strive for better and jump at every opportunity that comes his way to get out and onto bigger things. God may have assigned him this job, but Michael knows deep down that it was meant as a proving ground. A test of the Archangel's resolve and his resilience to complacency.

It is a difficult test to say the least, but Michael knows he'll succeed. He must. If he fails, then he lets down the God who gave him everything. Michael has never felt he deserves the title of Archangel, but he will do whatever he can to earn it one day.

The irritated Peter slides the empty food basket out of the way and leans forward. There are crumbs around his lips.

Disgusting.

"We need to come up with a plan for tomorrow. What did you find at his house?"

"Nothing."

"Not even a little bit? Absolutely nothing?"

"Absolutely nothing."

"But there has to be something there."

"If there was, then I didn't find it. And if I didn't find it then, and I'm sorry, I really doubt you will."

Peter scowls at Michael as he scratches his knuckle and descends deep into thought.

"He's probably sitting out there with a grin on his face, happy as can be that he tricked me. Well, that's when we know we can get him. We're gonna wipe that arrogant little smile right off his face."

CHAPTER THIRTY-SIX

Strawberry ice cream drips from its cone and onto the park bench Emily is sitting on. The spectral Mr. Mustard laps it up. Death watches her every movement while taking a spoonful of vanilla from his bowl. Under any other circumstances, Death would have tried to lead her away from using a cone. They're impractical and messy, but these are the circumstances that necessitate the phrase "under any other circumstances". Emily not only saw her corpse but figured out how she became one.

The whole seeing-your-own-corpse thing often bothers people, but when you're separated from your body in the way that she was, it can get a bit sketchy on the emotions side of things. Some people mourn their death, some people rage against what they consider an unbefitting end, some even scoff and laugh in the face of Death. The latter is pretty obnoxious in Death's personal opinion.

Emily is not playing by the standard rules of post-mortem psychosis. From where he's standing, it seems as if she's just shut down. After leading her back to the car, Death decided she needed some comfort food to try and get her out of her own head for a bit, so he took a shot and pulled up to an ice cream stand, Emily had mumbled something about strawberry in a cone, and here they are on a park bench a short walk from the stand. Emily is working on her cone at a snail's pace while Death waits for the slightest hint of movement, recognition, or any sign of willingness to exit the void she is currently in.

Emily won't respond if he tries anything so the most Death can do in order to cut his losses is sit here, nurse a cup of ice cream, and wait. Sometimes that's the most you can do with people: give them sugar and wait. Humans are strange. Death would like to get moving because as of now, he still knows nothing. They have made virtually no progress on solving the mystery of who killed her, and more importantly, Death doesn't know enough about her to make the call.

Heaven or Hell?

It's impossible to figure out that kind of decision off first impressions. Death forms his own opinions from first impressions, but those are for him and him alone. In the grand scheme of things Death's opinion of someone does not particularly matter and he is fully aware of this. But in this instance, it does. He cannot afford to be biased but all he feels is bias and opinion. She's annoying. So painfully annoying and inconsiderate and impulsive and imposing, but that's not enough. This is the first real reaction to anything that Death has seen and he needs to be attentive, he needs to take notes, and he needs to remember every detail and compare it against every other one. But he also needs to continue with their task and they're running out of time.

Emily looks up at Death as the ice cream continues to drip from the cone and down onto her hand in thin, pink trails that Mr. Mustard works to catch. The feeling her eyes give off is not the usual tentative, if not a bit shy, awkwardness. Rather, this is the determination he saw burning when Emily spoke to the little boy who died falling down the stairs.

"Why didn't you tell me?"

"That you were murdered?"

"No. That you have an ABBA CD in your car. Of course that I was murdered."

"There's no need to be rude. It's because you didn't need to know."

"Why wouldn't I need to know that?"

"Because I didn't think it would do you any good, and as we can see, I was right."

Emily takes a lick of her nearly liquified ice cream cone.

"You don't get to make that decision for me. You have no right to choose what I can and can't handle."

"If I say sorry can we get back to solving this?"

"No. This is not just a say-sorry-and-be-done-with-it kind of thing. This is real. This is serious, and you know what? I'm starting to have it up to *here* with your attitude."

"My attitude?"

"Yes, your attitude. Don't pretend like you have no idea what I'm talking about because you know full well."

"Care to elaborate?"

Emily huffs and takes another lick of her ice cream cone, looks at Death and opens her mouth, then closes it, then takes another lick of ice cream before turning back to him.

"I'm talking about your constant better-than-you mindset. You like to think you keep it secret and hidden and no one can see it, but you don't do nearly as good a job of that as you think you do. All this being considerate, following the rules, hiding yourself from the world around you thing makes you feel like you're a good person. Newsflash: it doesn't."

"Are you done?"

"No. I'm not done. Stop treating me like I'm some kind of child or lost puppy. I can handle things, and I really don't appreciate being treated like I'm some kind of burden. Even if I am, you don't get to treat me like that. You don't get to treat me like some stupid, idiotic, childish person just because I process things like an actual human being. Which is something you would never understand."

"What does my way of 'processing things' have to do with any of this?"

"It has everything to do with this. When was the last time you actually did something for another person? When was the last time you, really truly, out of the goodness of your heart if you even have one, did something for someone else because you wanted to do it? Not for something you wanted from them, but simply because you wanted to?"

Death feels something welling inside him as he replies with ice.

"You know nothing about me, so stop pretending like you do. I have met more people in my time than you have ever seen in your flash-in-the-pan life. I know how you work and I apply that knowledge from observations to improve our interactions."

"I will pretend to know everything about you as long as you keep pretending that you know everything about me."

"Sure. That's fine."

"But it isn't fine. You go on thinking you're the center of the universe. Because whether you like it or not that's what you think you are. You may not believe that but it's how you behave. You're such a sad person and all you do is treat others like less than you because somewhere deep inside it makes you more capable of walking through each day having to live in that husk of yours. You stay up painting in that room of yours hiding from the truth, which is that you-"

"You went inside my studio?"

"No, but I saw you working last night."

"What gave you the right? I told you not to go in there for a reason. That's extremely private and I don't like others seeing what I have in there. You were in my house, staying in my room and you still did that? Where are you coming from being so rude and confrontational to me when you're just as bad?"

"Oh, so treating me like an idiot is just as bad as peeking in on your painting? That's how this works?"

"You know what? That *is* how this works. I kept that from you because I honestly did not want you to get hurt. Would you have preferred if I sat there and told you, 'hey, how's it going? So, you were strangled to death. It was brutal. You probably woke up and fought back. You definitely saw the killer's face, but you don't remember it because the memory is just that traumatic. Here, how about we go take a field trip to check out the body and give it a good long look?' Yeah, that would've made you feel so much better."

Emily opens her mouth to shoot back at Death but stops mid syllable.

"Did you say strangled?"

"Yes? You saw the body, didn't you?"

"Sorry, I was a little too distracted by seeing my own corpse to really process the specifics. But strangling..."

"Ok. What about it?"

"I mean, there's no way..."

"What?"

"...oh my god..."

"What is it?"

"When I was a kid, there was a little boy in the house next to me.

We could see into each other's rooms from our windows so we would always wave at together and play little games. He was so tiny. I was supposed to start babysitting him when I turned twelve..."

"What about him? Emily, you're not making any sense."

"He was murdered one night. But not just murdered, he was strangled. I didn't find out until later, but he was strangled in his bed in the night. They never found the killer."

A drop of strawberry ice cream falls onto Mr. Mustard's face and he meows with an air of irritation.

CHAPTER THIRTY-SEVEN

Ring ring ring ring ring.

Satan answers his cell.

"Hello?"

"It's Death."

"I gathered that. How's it going?"

"Alright. Can you talk?"

"I can, they left for the day. It looks like Peter will be alone from now on as well, I think I scared his assistant off big time."

"Great. We have a lead. It took a little...coaxing, but we're onto something."

"That's good news. Why do you sound so disappointed?"

Silence.

"That's a bit of a long story, but it's fine. Anything on Jeff's end?"

"I hated to do it because he's done such a stellar job so far, but I sent Judas along with Jeff to help him out. It'll be cutting it close, but I think they'll have something tomorrow. Keep on with what you're doing though."

"Judas?"

"Yep. I called him in to do some work in exchange for some vacation time. It's pretty easy to mess with Peter if you pull in the right people."

"You're not worried about him trying to pull something bigger?"

"Nah, he'll be fine. The guy can only think about punishing himself, he won't try anything fancy."

"Alright, just keep an eye on him. He's different from the rest. Judas is one of the only ones who didn't react when I did his paperwork. If anything, he was friendly."

"Sure, sure. Jeff will keep a close eye on him."

"Alright. I should be heading out then."

"Oh wait, wait. I forgot. Now don't get mad."

"Mad about what?"

"I called your mother."

"You what?"

"I called your mother. Gave her the rundown on what's happening. I just wanted to give you the heads up in case she calls you."

"Satan, why would you-"

"Because you know full well she can help. Looks like they're coming back, good luck, keep me updated."

The line goes dead.

Satan sighs.

They've got to work out their own issues.

CHAPTER THIRTY-EIGHT

Judas strolls through the commuter gate of Heaven and into the jam-packed parking garage. The front gate with all the gold and pearls is for the new arrivals. The back entrance is a rusty tubed fence like the kind you use on a ranch and at night it is held closed by an array of chains and a singular padlock. The garage will be crowded with angels soon as the work-day winds down. That gives him enough time to get in and get out before it becomes too difficult to walk around.

Glancing around, there does not appear to be anyone around. That makes this easier. Judas is not exactly well liked in this corner of the afterlife and making it around without being noticed will make everything much easier. Judas checks his cell phone and heads for the address Jeff has sent him.

If travelling around Israel with him was enough of an indicator, Peter is probably a slob. They had always fought about things like that. Judas has always been meticulous about the way things are organized and stored, especially when it comes to food. Peter is just glad to have a meal most of the time since he almost always forgets to cook. The others, the Apostles that is, were alright but even for his faults Judas had always liked Peter the most.

There was just something earnest in his behavior that made Judas able to respect him more than the rest. Besides, Peter is the only one who even made an attempt at understanding after the big falling out. You know, his betraying-the-Messiah-for-some-silver kind of big falling out. Peter would never admit to it, but he tracked down Judas the next day. Naturally, Judas told him lies because that's what he does. He told him that it was all a lie because the "Messiah" was dead, that Judas betrayed him for no other reason than he just wanted to, and that the whole Jesus thing was a big hoax and they had all been tricked.

Peter refused to believe that his friend could do something like that. All the evidence pointed to it, but he had gotten an itch on that knuckle of his and decided something was up. Judas convinced him otherwise because he's stupid, but the faith was encouraging. None of the others had the courage to do what Peter did.

It's been good to see him again, because at the end of the day, he was one of the best friends that Judas could have ever asked for.

That's what makes this so hard.

Judas jams the miniature screwdriver into the keyhole and fiddles with it until he hears a click. Crime is non-existent in Heaven so there's no need for quality locks, which makes things a bit easier for sinners like Judas. Closing the door behind him, Judas scans the room for any sort of access point. It serves to reason that Peter would be dreadful with technology, so he's looking for something simple and likely old.

You're kidding me.

Judas approaches the desk and takes a seat in front of the monitor with a monolithic computer hooked up to it. Judas presses the power button and watches the machine sputter to life and the fans begin to blast while an out of date operating system boots up on screen.

Password:

Hm.

Password: God

The home screen opens up.

Judas chuckles.

Alright, let's get started.

Judas sets to work going through all the local files on the computer before moving onto Peter's online access point. The local files are nothing of interest, just meager grocery lists he likely prints out and the occasional diary entry. Judas decides not to read those because even though he has broken into Peter's home there are some privacies which should not be invaded.

From Peter's access point, the password is "Je$us", Judas is able to work through the files on every soul destined for one place or another. Judas searches "Emily" and then filters by day and time of death.

There.

The file is there, full and complete. Peter made a simple mistake but it is one with great repercussions, and one he was destined to make. Judas sighs as he deletes the file.

Sorry, buddy. Hopefully Death guesses right.

Now that Judas has done what he was sent to do, he can get to what he really came out of his cell for. Judas sets the right filters in place and searches. The file is hidden towards the back in an inconspicuous folder. The best hiding place is in plain sight. It requires a password.

Here we go.

Judas knows for a fact that it is set to allow a single try before locking the user out, so he'll have to guess correctly. And Peter doesn't have access to this one so Judas can be sure it's at least marginally complex.

Think. If you're God, and you don't want anyone else to see this but also need to make sure you remember it. What would you set as the password? Something from the inside. Something you think only you know…

Of course. The song...their song.

Judas types, presses enter, and the password is accepted.

Judas scans the folder until he finds the file that reads "Thomas (Death)" and downloads it to a thumb drive before logging out of everything, deleting the access history, and shutting off the computer.

All done.

CHAPTER THIRTY-NINE

"Can we talk about before?"

"What is there to talk about?"

Emily sighs.

"I'm trying to be the grown up here."

"Do grown-ups get so lonely that they can't stay in a car for five minutes?"

"That's what I was talking about. That. Why do you have to be so vicious?"

"I'm not vicious. I'm stating a fact."

"You are unbelievable."

Emily huffs and slumps down in her seat, shifting her weight to the right side facing the window, setting in to watch the passing of flora and fauna.

Death thinks of himself as the type to always take the high road. Be the bigger man, apologize and get it over with because then it just makes everything easier from then on out. None of the drawn-out pointless passive aggression. It's a waste of time and he knows it deep down but something about the situation just keeps him from letting go.

She looked inside my studio. The one thing I asked her not to do. Sure, I asked her not to go IN my studio, but she knew what I meant. She had no right. No right whatsoever but she still did it and I just can't let that slide. There's just something about her...No nope no, she doesn't get the satisfaction of being in the right. I won't let her.

Death feels a deep, insatiable need for an apology. This is what he deserves. Death keeps his eyes straight ahead with a rare determination...

...which dissipates like a balloon letting out air at the sound of a meek voice from the slouching lump in the passenger seat.

"What do you think we'll find there?"

"At your old home?"

The slouching lump nods.

"Hopefully something that brings us closer to figuring out what happened to you."

"We already know what happened. I was murdered. A detail you felt was perfectly fine to leave out."

"Are we back to this again?"

The slouching lump whips around and scowls at him.

"So, what if we are back to this again? You thought it was a good idea not to tell me I was murdered. I'd say that warrants a coming back to."

"What else is there to say? It happened. I didn't tell you. Now you know. It's over and done with."

"But it isn't because you're still being snippy."

"You're arguing in circles, Emily."

Those intent caramel-brown eyes burn into the right side of

Death's head.

Emily bursts out laughing.

"That's the first time you've actually used my name."

Emily is bent over with laughter now, cackling, wheezing, tears forming in her eyes. It's an ugly laugh, loud and sharp, the kind that everyone always hates because it's too much of an attention grab. But the thing with this one is it's real and Death knows because he's well versed in fake laughs. Every dinner party he and his mother were ever invited to at God's place, every joke Jesus made, Death and his mother replied with the same molded-plastic-laugh.

Now that Death thinks about it, that's when he started to hate Jesus. Not when everyone made a big deal of him going down to be with "the common man" like a politician grasping for relevancy, not when it was announced that Death and Satan would be out of a job once the kid eventually takes charge, and not when the kid started doing nothing but tip tap away at his phone.

No.

Death started hating Jesus at one of those many dinner parties when he had to laugh like a sitcom audience for the kid's terrible jokes, as did everyone. Yet there was nothing but contempt in the eyes of young Jesus. Contempt for the guests, contempt for his Father, and contempt for Death. Contempt for everyone with an aluminum-Christmas-tree laugh.

Emily's laugh is akin to kettle corn at a county fair. Popping, crackling, growing and rising, sweet but not too sweet and, unlike aluminum Christmas trees, real.

Death can't help but smile.

Emily gasps.

"Oh my god you just smiled."

Back to a frown.

"I did not."

"Oh. My. God. You so did. You just smiled ha!"

"You're seeing things, stop."

"Sure. I'll stop. But you know you smiled. You like me, you just don't want to admit it."

Death remains silent.

"Death..."

"Mm?"

"I'm sorry. For looking in at your studio. I shouldn't have done that. I could try and say I was just curious or something but there's no excuse. You asked me not to and I should have listened, it wasn't right for me to do and I hope you can forgive me."

It feels as if a weight is lifted.

"I'm, uh, I'm sorry for not informing you about the circumstances of your death. I realize why that would be important to you and it would have been better if I asked you whether you wanted to know or not instead of assuming. I realize that must have hurt you to find out."

Emily nods.

"Apology accepted."

Death glances to his right to find a serious and expectant face.

Death takes a deep breath and lets it out as a sigh.

"Apology accepted."

Emily grins.

"Alright, we're good now. I don't know if it's still open, but there's a great bagel place near my old house that's open into the evening. We should go there if we have the time it's so good."

Death nods along for the rest of the drive, nodding along to all of Emily's inane conversation starters and comments, nodding along to it all while he rests within his mind playing over those words again and again and again and again.

I'm sorry.

After all, no one has ever apologized to Death and meant it.

CHAPTER FORTY

Agnes rocks in her chair and knits. The act of knitting has served as a great comfort throughout her life. A simple task that requires a good deal of concentration and time, something which she has much to spare since her son moved out. Agnes cooks for one now, though she has yet to truly master the sizing and tends towards making too much. There is just something about single portion sizes that feels strange to Agnes, almost like it betrays the integrity of food, betraying the wordless pact a person makes when they step into a kitchen and whip up something with their own two hands. Food is not meant for one person, it's just wrong.

Needless to say, Agnes owns a catalog's supply of Tupperware. If she used them slightly less, Agnes feels it would constitute a collection. A tupperware collector.

Agnes lets out a silent laugh.

One hobby at a time.

For now, Agnes's garden is her pride and joy. Those little living things that grow from the ground, it just fills her heart with excitement. Tending to them day after day with their simple needs. Water, sunlight, some proper soil, and maybe a trim or a stake if they're especially needy. But no matter how needy they are, each day her little agrarian children are overjoyed to see her. The way their leaves and stalks and petals flutter in the breeze it feels like they are waving at her.

Oftentimes, Agnes thinks about having a bigger garden like the one she used to have. It was massive and brilliant and wonderful, but she's not sure if she misses it. Tending to a small garden gives her a much greater sense of meaning. The same plants every day, no risk of getting lost, no worrying about whether she can get to each and every one to spend quality time. If you don't keep a close enough eye on plants, they can get into trouble.

Speaking of which, Agnes feels like she should call her son. His friend had called her earlier today and she is still deciding how best to deal with it. God may be too scared of her to do anything to Thomas without just cause, but if what Lucifer told her is true then this could give Him the reason He's been looking for.

Agnes shakes her head.

Always trying to get rid of Your mistakes. You haven't changed one bit.

Thomas is just a child, but he's no idiot. There has to be a reason why he would do something as self-destructive and irresponsible as this. Agnes was not some absentee parent. There should be nothing wrong with him. But that's just how it goes sometimes.

Agnes sets down her knitting needles. The bright orange blanket will have to wait.

I suppose I'll need all the information before I can do anything. No son of mine will be destroying his career while I have anything to say about it.

CHAPTER FORTY-ONE

Somehow, the house is not what Death expected. He was anticipating "quirky" colors, a white picket fence, pinwheels or some other fantastical element. Instead it is a rather forgettable, well-maintained two-story suburban home. The grass is cut, the gutter is clean, the shrubs are trimmed, and the plants next to the front porch are healthy.

"New people have moved in, but it still looks mostly the same. The plants are a little different."

Emily looks at the house with less emotion than Death expected. Usually when returning to your childhood home you get a bit nostalgic. Even if there are mostly bad memories, there are usually some formative good ones as well. There's some level of nostalgia whether you like it or not, but Emily is treating this like it's any other place and she couldn't care less. At least, that's what she's projecting, but Death finds it hard to believe coming from a person like her.

"Can we really leave Mr. Mustard in the car? Will he be okay?"

"Yes, he will be just fine. He's already a spirit. Come on, we'll have a little bit before people start getting home for the night. It's this one, right?"

Death points at the house directly to the left of Emily's. It's the same model so it feels uncanny to walk up to it after Emily nods her head. The only difference is that the grass is longer here. Not by much, barely noticeable to someone without a personality such as his. The pair approach the door and Death makes to enter but Emily hesitates.

"What?"

"I just...it feels kind of rude, doesn't it?"

"You've done this before."

"Yeah, but..."

"But what?"

"I know these people. They're the same couple that lived here when I did. It feels kind of worse when I know them, I didn't know any of the others we visited."

Death sighs internally. Sure, he doesn't particularly enjoy breaking into people's homes on a daily basis, but he doesn't go around making a big deal of it.

"It'll be fine. They're not home and it's not as if we're stealing anything. Besides, like you said, you know them. That should make it less awkward."

Emily still hesitates, the corner of her mouth twitches ever so slightly.

"Would you rather wait in the car?"

She shakes her head.

"Then let's go."

She's hiding something.

There's something behind those eyes that she doesn't want him to see. Emily knows more than she's letting on and Death gets the feeling that she's had a lot of practice honing this technique. Even Peter's magic knuckle might be fooled, but not Death. This lead came at a perfect time because he was starting to give up. They had gone through most of the day without finding anything and Death is not known for being tenacious. The situation still feels desperate, but now there's something of a light at the end of the tunnel.

"You should go look around over there, I need to reply to a message and then I'll be over."

"Alright."

Emily goes on ahead and Death pulls out his phone only after she has completely rounded the corner and is out of sight.

Death opens up the file Jeff sent him and begins to scroll.

Interesting.

Death glances up and around to make sure Emily hasn't snuck up on him or something before returning to the file.

Bryson Russel.

Before getting to the things that pertain to his current situation, Death has to sift through several pages on details about the Bryson's life. All the times he said "no" to his parents or bit another child at daycare. Sins are expunged until a child is "of age" and then counted against them at death should they never repent. Death always thinks this is a rather stupid system because it ends up just being better for everyone to die as a child if you're considered pure and automatically get into Heaven.

God instituted it early on and made sure it went down the line so the humans became aware. They love it of course but honestly Death thinks it's a cop out, something set up to ease the conscience of an absentee God and make the mourning process easier for those left behind. It takes the responsibility of judgement away from God who lets whatever befalls the child happen and dissipates it in the air as if nothing but vapor.

Responsibility doesn't work like that. Some problems need answers, some blame needs to be taken. At least, that's what Death thinks.

The kid was four when he was murdered. It was late at night and it seems as if the killer entered through the back door which was open because no one locks their doors in this town. At least, they didn't until this happened. It was a rather short and simple event all in all. Enter, strangle kid in bed, leave. Police were unable to trace any of it back to those in their records, and they were unable to make any of it stick on the few suspects they managed to round up. Case closed and a sadly common thing at that.

There's just something about the record that Death finds so odd and he cannot quite place his finger on it.

Kid murdered. Person leaves. End of story. But there's something missing...what is it?

Death's head begins to swim, going around in circles. He's almost there, he can feel it.

Emily enters the room and shakes her head.

"Nothing, sorry."

"Alright. Let's head up then."

Death looks at Emily.

"It'll be ok. He's not here. Bryson, or the murderer."

Emily nods more than once as if agreeing while also convincing herself.

This'll be a big one.

Death doesn't need to be a powerful demigod to feel the immense guilt seeping out of Emily. Everyone has some level of guilt in their life that weighs them down like a lead ball that rests in the lower part of their stomach. In theory, when people die this weight should be lifted because there is nothing left that you can do. For better or for worse, your responsibility is gone. But some people hold onto that guilt because their baggage is just that heavy. Emily's guilt is strong. Stronger than it should be.

What did she do?

Death considers it as they head up the stairs and the family photos grow older. None with the child yet.

I guess you wouldn't want those out depressing the guests.

Death turns to Emily once they get to the top.

"You'll have to lead the way. I don't know where it is."

Emily turns the corner as if she's in a haunted house, which in a sense she is, and makes her way down the hall with caution.

Nothing is going to jump out at you.

She reaches the end and points at a white painted door with a chalkboard side on the door. In big block letters that look faded and absorbed into the board from time: BRYSON.

The door handle has a thin layer of dust on it.

Death enters as he can feel the pressure of time beginning to set in. They don't have much time left in the day and if Peter is on to them as much as Satan seems to think, then Death will need to be back home by a normal hour. All Peter needs is the slightest bit of evidence that something is amiss and he'll call it in. Anything that gives him a reason without making him look like more of a paranoid idiot than everyone already thinks he is.

Death sighs as he enters the room.

I'll have to find somewhere for her to stay tonight won't I? If Peter were to make some random awkward visit to my house and she were there, then I'm totally screwed.

It doesn't look as if the family has changed the room since their son's demise. It makes sense, he was really young. It feels like a four year old boy's room from twelve years ago, the only major difference is how organized it is. The toys are lined up in a sensical fashion, the bed is made, the nick-knacks are all the bookshelf. It feels like a soundstage or a museum display.

Death waits for Emily to pass through the door and as she does, a soft gasp escapes her lips. Without needing to be prompted, Emily begins to wander about the room at a slow but methodical pace. Running her spectral fingertips over every toy and every surface before ending at the covered window on the far side of the bedroom.

Death watches with anticipation as Emily grasps the blinds and draws them with care, revealing a simple view of the side yard, the dividing fence, and the adjacent home with a clear line of sight into the opposite window. Emily's eyes grow distant.

Come on. Give a rise. Something, give me something to work with. I only have one more day until it's too late.

Emily's breathing becomes more labored like she's thinking about every breath. Telling her body to take in the air, bring it down to the lungs, now lungs do your job alright good now send it back up, alright now back out and through the blood and discard the rest, deep breath out, good now repeat. Emily's subconscious is operating all on its own now, her spectral form running on manual.

Emily nods and does not stop nodding as she steps away from the window.

"I, uh..."

"Yes?"

"I uh, I remembered something."

"Ok. Did the cops ask you some questions? Any details that might tell us something to go off of in figuring out what happened to you?"

Emily continues to nod in that mindless, self-assuring way.

"I don't know why I've never remembered this until now. No wonder they were so weird about it. No wonder they sent me to live with grandma. It all makes sense, I just never knew why didn't why tell me."

"Emily, what are you babbling about?"

"I saw it."

"You saw it? The murder?"

"I saw it. I watched the whole thing happen..."

At this point Emily looks up at Death and he sees tears streaming down her face.

"And I didn't do a thing to stop it."

CHAPTER FORTY-TWO

Jeff sighs.

"Ma'am. I just need you to sign here."

"I don't want to. Kyle's gonna be at my house to pick me up in like, thirty minutes. I need to get back."

"Ma'am, you can't go back. Just sign here so I can go on with my day."

"No."

"Then we'll just have to stand here until you sign."

Jeff taps his foot, not breaking eye contact while the Ford Fiesta smokes and burns to his left. The girl glares at him.

"You're not going to give me a ride back home?"

"No."

"You have a car."

The blonde teenage girl with the haughty expression points to Jeff's pick-up parked a few hundred feet back off the freeway.

"I do, and you're not riding in it."

"Hmph."

"Still not going to sign?"

The girl shakes her head.

Jeff shakes his head, withdraws a pen from his pocket and writes her name on the document, fills out the card, stamps it and hands it to her.

"Be where it says within forty-eight hours or they'll send someone for you. Also, Kyle has a fun night without you. When you see him in a few days, make sure to ask him about Suzanna."

Jeff turns on his heels and strides back to the truck as the realization hits young Kayleigh and she begins to wail. Jeff tries to be a good person, and he's far from malicious, but he's still a demon.

As he turns the keys and the engine spits and sputters to life, Jeff sighs.

This job sucks.

CHAPTER FORTY-THREE

"Because you'll get mad if I go without saying anything, I'm speaking with Bryson tonight."

Emily nods, all of her attention on the purring Mr. Mustard in her lap.

"I know you would like to as well, it's just not possible. It's far too risky because if anyone from Heaven finds you then we'll both get in trouble."

Emily continues to nod without question.

Death takes a deep breath.

I hate this kind of thing.

"Do you want to talk about what happened back there."

She shakes her head.

"Are you sure? Because it seems like you do."

She shakes her head.

"I'll ask one more time. Are you sure?"

Emily starts to nod but stops herself.

"I just. Why didn't I remember it?"

I honestly thought this was the simple part.

"You blocked it out. Lots of kids do it."

"And why didn't my parents tell me?"

"They wanted to protect you from having to deal with it."

"But they sent me to live with my grandma not long after. And then they left."

"They left?"

Deep breath on manual.

"They um, they pulled the station wagon into our garage, stuffed the exhaust and put on a jazz CD."

"They killed themselves?"

"Yeah. About three weeks after they sent me to live with my grandmother. Everything seemed fine leading up to it. They lied to everyone and said they were going on a month-long tour of Europe. That's why it took so long for people the find them. I lived with my grandma until I left for college and if I'm being honest, I've avoided coming back here since."

They committed suicide almost immediately after the murder. They sent their daughter away and lied to everyone. Why?

"How was your family doing?"

"I thought we were doing well. I don't remember my parents being especially stressed until after the whole thing with Bryson. They never argued except for this one time when I was about eight they blew up at each other during a road trip when our car ran out of gas because dad wouldn't ask for directions."

Emily smiles as she brings up the last part.

"I don't talk about them very much. It feels like so long ago that it happened that I kind of just try to pretend it didn't. My friend Anita is the only person besides my grandmother who knows about it. She's great...oh crap!"

The exclamation startles Death.

"What?"

"I was supposed to call her when I woke up but...yeah."

Emily is scratching behind Mr. Mustard's ears when Death's phone rings.

"Can you check that for me?"

She picks up the cell phone and reads with a puzzled expression forming into an incredulous grin.

"It says, 'Mom'."

Death's heart sinks into his stomach.

No. Please not right now. But if I don't answer she'll call again. And again. And again. And then she'll show up at my house under the guise that she thought something was wrong. Why today of all days?

Death sighs.

"Hold it up to my ear. I want to keep both hands on the wheel."

Emily grins and answers the call, holding the phone up to Death's head.

"Hello?"

"Hello, Thomas."

"Hello, mother. May I ask why you're calling me?"

"You may, even though it is quite rude."

Silence.

"So why are you calling me?"

"I received some very interesting news from the devil friend of yours. What's his name? Larry? Louis? Oh, please don't tell me it's Lucius. I tell you, parents have no idea how to name a child I just cannot imagine giving someone such a-"

"Lucifer. He gave you a call? What about?"

"Oh, nothing serious. Just some interesting information about your day-off escapades. He tells me you took a soul."

I was hoping I wouldn't get this call.

"That still doesn't explain why you're calling me."

"You're in a snippy mood today, Thomas. I can get to the point if you're going to be like that: You need somewhere to stash the girl tonight, correct?"

"...yes."

"Good. I figured you wouldn't want anything to happen in case of an emergency, because I'm sure someone will be looking for her soon enough. You can drop her off any time but sooner is better."

"Alright."

"Can I get a thank you?"

"Thank you, mother."

"You are very welcome, Thomas. I'll see you soon."

Agnes hangs up.

"You can take the phone away now."

"I-"

"No."

"What?"

"No."

"I don't get to ask any questions?"

"No."

Everything just keeps getting worse.

CHAPTER FORTY-FOUR

"What a good little team we have here."

Judas and Jeff glance at one another before turning their attention back to Satan sitting on the sofa across from them.

"It's more secure to talk at my place so we'll be using it to do our catching up and planning. First up, Jeff."

"This job is horrible."

"Great input, I'm glad to hear your thoughts. Anything constructive to add?"

Jeff sighs.

"I cleaned the house so there's no trace of the woman ever being there. All of Death's assigned souls were taken care of for the day, however there are a few that took longer than others. They were more unruly than I expected."

"That's immortal souls for you. Try and be as fast as you can, Death has an exceptional work rate and we need this to run without a hitch. Understand?"

Jeff nods.

"Great work. Next up, Judas."

Satan behaves differently when he's had a few glasses of wine.

Judas leans back into the couch cushion and crosses his legs at the knees.

"Her file is missing. It looks like Peter is covering his tracks."

"It really does rest on Death then, doesn't it?"

Judas and Jeff remain silent.

"Alright. Jeff, keep up the good work. Judas, report to me first thing. I'm still deciding what you'll need to do. It all depends on what Peter does. Good job today, both of you, get some rest."

Once the two are in the elevator, Satan mutters to himself.

"I'm not as gullible as you think."

Inside their stainless-steel box, Judas and Jeff stare as the floor numbers slowly tick down.

"I have the file on the drive, along with Death's."

"Good. And you deleted Emily's?"

"Of course."

"Perfect. That should allow for enough precedent."

"That's the plan."

"Do you have the drive? I can deliver it when all of this blows over."

Judas shakes his head.

"I think I'll do that myself. I have the week off after this."

"Are you sure you can do it?"

"To be completely honest, no. I just feel like I should."

Jeff shrugs.

"Suit yourself. I'm sure the boss will be happy to see you."

Judas's thin smile almost looks like a grimace.

"Perhaps."

The elevator comes to a stop with a ding and the doors slide open.

CHAPTER FORTY-FIVE

As he rolls into his mother's dirt drive, Death eases on the brakes, coming to a stop. Her car, a two-door bug, is parked in front.

Death sighs.

"Why did you sigh?"

"Because we're visiting my mother."

"Don't you like your mother?"

Death turns to Emily with a blank expression.

"I don't dislike my mother. But she's my mother."

"What do you mean?"

Pulling the keys out of the ignition and opening the door, Death steps out and leaves her to formulate her own answer. The cottage is small but cozy. A white picket fence with a little gate blocks off the cobblestone path within. The path leads to the three steps that bring you up onto the porch.

Death always knew his mother felt like a failure as a parent because when he was a kid she was relentless in her offer of homemade kale chips. They were vile and they both knew it, but he ate them anyway.

As he knocks on the door, Death strains his ears to listen for movement. All he hears is the muffled sound of voices and a slight creaking on the hardwood floor within. The creaking stops and he hears some rustling within. He steps back from the door and bumps into Emily standing behind him.

"Dammit! Why are you so close?"

"I wanted to see what you were listening to…"

Death shakes his head and turns back to the door as it opens. The old red door reveals his mother. A little old woman with a full head of gray hair which she wears in a tight bun. She wears a pair of delicate half-moon spectacles far forward on her nose which draw attention to her gray eyes. They are the same, forlorn color as Death's, yet they don't move the way his do. Smiling, she spreads out her arms.

"Give your mother a hug, Thomas."

Death hunches down, his mother's head barely reaches his shoulders, and does as he's told.

Throughout this entire interaction, Emily's face is the definition of shock.

After embracing her son, Death's mother looks over at Emily and then back at her son.

"Now why didn't you tell me you were bringing a *girl's* soul over? I would've made cookies."

"I didn't tell you because I knew you would."

"Well, introduce us already, Thomas. It's rude to keep a woman waiting."

Before Death can speak, Emily thrusts her hand forward.

"I'm Emily, it's nice to meet you, Mrs. Death. I love your dress."

Death's mother stares at Emily then turns back to her son.

"What's wrong with her?"

"I'm not entirely sure. I only met her yesterday."

"She's far too nice for you. And you've been spending time together?"

"Yes, I've got no choice, I didn't receive any paperwork and I'm trying to determine the proper course of action."

Death gives his mother a look as he says the last part.

"I see. How long will she be staying here? And why does she have a cat in her hands?"

"Until tomorrow morning. I have to speak to some people tonight and then I'll be back to pick her up. Also, his name is Mr. Mustard and she likes him."

"That's a terrible name for a cat."

"Agreed."

"So, are you watching her or not?"

Agnes mulls over the question.

"Fine."

Death's mother wheels on Emily with a smile.

"No one calls me Mrs. Death. I usually make strangers call me Ma'am, however, I like you so you can call me Agnes. Also, thank you for saying that earlier, I love this dress too."

She turns towards Death once more.

"What are you still doing here? I said I would watch her, now get going. Shoo."

Death trudges back to his car, gets in, and drives away but not before giving a quick wave in Emily's direction. Emily waves back and watches him go and when she turns around, Agnes is already through the doorway.

"Come! My show is almost over."

Emily looks around, holds Mr. Mustard close, and enters the home, closing the door behind her.

The first thing Emily notices as she moves through the entryway is how similar everything is to Death's home. The décor is more tasteful, consistent with a farmhouse theme complimented by paintings and miscellaneous decorations. However, the little basket on the table by the door, the coat rack with a singular coat, the sparseness of anything deemed unnecessary. This is certainly the home that Death grew up in and it makes Emily feel like she knows him a little better in a wordless way.

A call from the living room.

"Why are you standing in the entryway like a tax collector? I said come in, didn't I?"

Emily hurries to the living room, the wood floor creaking beneath her feet, to find Agnes seated in a rocking chair knitting while the TV plays some kind of soap opera. Without looking up she gestures to a small couch to her left. Agnes does not say a word.

Normally, Emily would try and make conversation as she takes a seat but there is something about Agnes which keeps her from trying to break the silence. The woman isn't speaking because she doesn't want to, and Emily gets the impression that no nicety or politeness would change her mind. So, she decides to watch her knit, and there is something about Agnes's knitting that is almost magical.

Agnes knits with an unmatched confidence and deftness which

shouts that she does not even know what a mistake is. There is no concept of backtracking because she is not accustomed to ever needing to. The same movements again and again and again, perfect, flawless without faltering for so much as an instant. Emily has never been one to knit because she's bad at anything which requires precision, but she's certain that if Agnes taught her she would be able to do it.

Sound bites from the soap opera accent the background:

"Allan! How dare you...what kind of woman do you think I am?"

The click-clacking of the knitting needles. The quiet squeak of the rocking chair.

"Cynthia, my darling, I meant nothing by it I just-BANG"

Click-clack squeak.

"Cynthia, oh god it hurts, why?"

Click-clack squeak.

"Because I loved you, Allan."

Click-clack squeak.

"Witness the conclusion of the tragic arc, next week on-"

Agnes turns the TV off and wraps up her knitting gear before stowing it in a small end table next to her rocker. Agnes crosses her legs at the knees and turns to Emily.

Her posture is perfect.

"Emily."

"Yes?"

"There are a few things you need to know about me before we

move forward. First, I love gardening, so maybe we have a hobby in common. Second, I love my son very much. Third, I would do anything to protect my son no matter the cost to myself or to others. He is the most important thing in this world because I deem it to be so. Do you understand?"

Emily nods. Nothing about Agnes's face or tone has changed, but she feels a fear rising deep from within. This is not some old woman.

"Good. I hope that gives some context for what I am about to say and as I've already mentioned, I like you so I hope there are no 'hard feelings'."

Emily nods.

I don't like where this is going.

Mr. Mustard retreats further into Emily's arms.

"We are going to have a conversation. I will ask you some questions, but there is only one question and one answer that truly matters. I am a powerful woman. More powerful than you can even begin to comprehend with that mind of yours. My son is not. My son is beholden to the power of others and right now you pose a threat to his standing, and if I'm quite honest, his existence. You must explain to me why I should not destroy you to such an extent that no one knew you ever existed. If you go 'poof' the problem disappears."

"I-um, uh, I don't-"

"I know you don't, but please try."

"Isn't that against the rules or something? Wouldn't God be mad with you or something?"

Agnes smiles for the first time since Emily met her.

"Oh, sweetie, I am so much worse than God."

CHAPTER FORTY-SIX

Knock-knock.

Please don't be annoying.

The door opens a crack and a young man peeks out and sees Death, his eyes go wide and the door slams shut. Death hears the sliding of locks and the rattling of chains.

Death sighs as the door swings open.

I have a bad feeling about this.

"Mr. Death, it's you!"

Death forces a smile.

"It is."

"I thought you would never come to visit me, please come in, come in."

Bryson pulls the door wide open and gestures for Death to enter. The boy has grown a lot since his passing. It would be disingenuous for Death to pretend he remembers much about the kid besides the fact that he was young. After all, he was just one of the countless child murders Death has dealt with.

Death enters and stands on the cusp of the kitchen adjacent the entryway as Bryson scurries about, assembling some array of supermarket cheese slices and Ritz crackers. Bryson is a young man now with sandy blonde hair and a spark of innocence still left in his eye. That spark will likely be preserved forever, burning on past the end of time in a ratty apartment tucked away in a building on an off street in Heaven.

It's clear that Bryson never learned how to live on his own from the state of the apartment. Clothes everywhere, crumbs on the counter, nothing but junk food, the TV on in the background playing something loud and obnoxious. This is rather common with kids like him. There are certain life skills they never learn, and then they're put in an environment where they cannot sin, get sick or die. Combine that with a youthful state of absent impulse control and you get the man child that is Bryson. Doomed to never reach their full potential. That's the part that Death finds most tragic about the demise of a child. The thing itself is sad but not more than any other passing. What makes them so tragic is the loss of potential. The potential of what that child could do not only for themselves but also the people around them and the world at large.

This kid could've cured cancer and here he is making Death a plate of rubbery orange cheese and salty crackers in a ratty apartment with children's programming blaring through the television.

"I wish you had let me know you were coming. I would've gotten something better to eat."

"It's fine. I won't be long I just have a few questions for you."

"Oh, cool. What kind of questions?"

"Let's just take a seat."

Bryson finishes preparing his "cheese plate" and carries it into the living room, tossing it onto the round glass table between his two couches, the resulting sound causing Death to cringe.

I'm surprised he hasn't broken that by now.

Death takes a seat on the couch opposite Bryson, moving an empty bag of barbecue chips in order to make space. Bryson watches Death with bated breath, awaiting the questions. Death glances at the TV with its blasting audio then back at Bryson. He doesn't get the hint.

"Can you turn down the TV down a bit? It'll make it easier to talk."

"I can hear you just fine."

"Ok, but could you please turn it down a bit anyway?"

"Sure, don't see why not."

Bryson hunts about for the remote, checking behind cushions and under loose trash. Death has seen him walk past it four times now.

"It's um, it's on the TV stand."

Bryson laughs and picks up the remote, bringing the volume down to the point just above where Death wanted it before putting it back and down and returning to the couch.

It'll have to do.

"So, what did you want to ask me about?"

Death takes a deep breath.

"I want to ask you about the night you died."

Bryson freezes mid bite on a cheese covered cracker.

He chews and places the other half back onto the plate as he swallows.

"The night I died?"

"Yes. I know it's not something you want to think about, but I need to know some things about what happened."

Bryson gulps.

"Um. What do you want to know?"

"Really, it's just one thing, but if you find you're able to tell me more then I am happy to hear it. Do you understand?"

Bryson nods.

"Alright, it's simple. Did you see the face of the person that did this to you?"

"Did I see their face?"

"Yes."

"Yeah. I did..."

Death feels a fluttering in his stomach.

"...but I don't know what they looked like."

A sinking weight.

"How did you see them but not know what they looked like?"

Bryson is avoiding eye contact now and his breathing becomes more shallow.

"It was really dark because it was like, you know, it was night so I couldn't really see and it all happened so fast and I had just been asleep you know so I wasn't even sure what was happening until it was too late. But um..."

"Yes?"

"Afterwards. When I was, you know, like..."

"I understand."

"Well I was standing there, and I saw them again as they left. It was still dark and stuff and even if I could see them it was the eyes. The eyes were scary."

"What do you mean by scary, Bryson?"

"They were evil. They were really evil. And they shouldn't have been able to see me, right? Living people aren't supposed to see dead people, right? But when they looked back at me they didn't look at me in the bed they looked at me standing. Right here."

Bryson points at his eyes.

"Then they smiled. Big white teeth. Everything was dark except for the eyes and the teeth. That was all I saw. Those evil eyes and that big white smile. It was so scary, Mr. Death, I don't like thinking about it."

"What was scary about it, Bryson?"

"I mean, the eyes were bad enough, but those teeth…it was like they were hungry for something."

CHAPTER FORTY-SEVEN

Emily sits frozen in fear.

She's kidding, right? It's just her sense of humor, right?

"You're probably wondering if this is just my sense of humor or something. It is not. I prefer knock-knock jokes or something with a little substance. Present your opening statement so I can begin asking questions."

"I, how am I a danger to Death?"

"So he hasn't told you, that's interesting. I suppose it's the best way for him to figure out the decision."

"Figure out the decision about what?"

Agnes tilts her head.

"What is your destination?"

"Destination for what?"

"Are you going to Heaven or Hell?"

Emily's mind begins to work overtime. Crunching and grinding as it spits smoke and analyzes everything she has experienced thus far. She has never been told.

Why wouldn't I ask about something like that? Isn't it important? Why did I forget? Why wasn't I told?

"I see you're considering it all now. I don't like going behind my son's back but I must in this situation."

Emily can feel her breathing grow fast and shallow. Both confused about and fully aware of what Agnes is talking about.

Please don't say it.

"It is Thomas's job to figure out where you will spend your eternity, though it kind of feels like it's his job to *decide*. Apparently, there was a paperwork issue and you have no pre-determined resting place. Thomas has been watching everything you do and making notes as to where you should be sent. I think this is a waste of time and puts my boy in danger. He should have called in the second he found you because then you would be someone else's problem. Is this all making sense?"

Emily pauses before nodding her head.

"Good. If you're found, then Thomas is incriminated in wrongdoing and will be fired immediately. I can assume you understand that being fired from a position such as his does not mean the same thing as in your human world?"

Emily, still pre-occupied with her own thoughts and processes, nods absentmindedly.

"Because you do not appear to be paying proper attention, which is forgivable considering the circumstances, I will explain to you what happens when someone like Thomas loses his job. There is no other job for him so he would be without work or purpose for all of eternity. That is the best case scenario. The worst case, and more likely, scenario is that Thomas will be cast into the Abyss. In the eyes of God, Hell is too kind a fate for some. Thomas will cease to exist and spend eternity in the black, soundless silence of the Abyss. No one is entirely sure what happens when someone is sent there. The Abyss is beyond Creation and it doesn't play by the same rules as the world we live in. I don't want my son there. However, I am not without a heart. Do you understand?"

Emily nods.

Why is this happening to me? I just died. That's it. I didn't ask for any of this. None of this should be on me. I'm just supposed to be dead and over with it all. Nothing should be mine anymore. I just want to go home.

"Excellent. So, I will decide whether or not to erase you from both existence and memory. I still need your opening statement. Why should I abstain from destroying you?"

It's happening again. The little spot just behind Emily's lungs begins to leak out those inky black tendrils. They creep through her veins, spreading throughout the body and making their way to the brain. Emily's eyes shoot around trying to find something to stop it. Something with which to purge the blood. Nothing. The tendrils reach the brain, filling each and every groove with their inky blackness until the thing that was once Emily's mind is now a black orb hidden inside an armor of bone and flesh.

"You have no reason not to. I am a threat to your son, and there is nothing I can promise you to make that any better. In fact, it would be better if I were forgotten. It saves you the trouble, it saves him the trouble, and honestly it saves everyone the trouble. These have been a long two days for me. I was murdered. I've also had to walk around and eat food but not really eat food. My taste is starting to go away. So is my touch. I can hear but sometimes it feels like I'm listening from under water. The colors are starting to fade from my sight, they're old and rotten and they bleed into each other. To top things off, I died with a marriage that wasn't doing too hot. I think I was probably with him because he's the only one who ever gave me the attention I wanted because I am just that contemptable. I am a piece of complete and utter human garbage who deserves everything that happened to her. All I do is make the people close to me worry, I don't help other people enough, it's always about me. Even now. Death is out on a limb to help me and all I can talk about is how bad things are for me and how sad I am. There's something wrong with him, you know that, right? He is deeply broken and alone and you all just let it happen. Just let him sit there and exist like that without the slightest hand raised to help and that seriously pisses me off. He is not the kindest, he is not the most brilliant, and he is far from the best. But he is *good.* Somewhere inside that shell he is good, and he desperately wants you to see it, but none of you do. Death does nothing for himself, not one thing. Not out of any great love for those around him he simply does not see himself as being worth the energy. Deep down he thinks of himself as so lowly and unworthy that he can barely open a door without knocking, he is physically unable to take right of way in traffic, he cannot take what he wants and be the person he wants to be. I don't know what you all need from him, but he is worth more than that. You're despicable and you should be ashamed of yourself not only as a person but also as a mother for allowing your son to live such a miserable life and still be able to sleep at night."

Well, that's it for me.

It all just happened. The words came out of Emily's mouth like an unstopped dam. Once she started her feelings took over from there. Oddly enough, even with the fate of complete and utter destruction upon her, Emily would do it again. It feels good to say what she means.

Agnes smiles.

"Perfect. This should be an easy decision for Thomas. It's obvious where you belong."

Agnes rises from her rocker and moves into the kitchen. Emily hears the sound of pots hitting against one another, running water, and a stove turning on.

I'm still here. What did I say that changed her mind?

Agnes returns and takes a seat once more in the rocker and smiles at Emily once more.

"Stay out of trouble, because nothing must happen to my boy. You've proven you understand him, and that is enough reason for me to keep you around. Not many do, and perhaps spending some more time with you will be good for him. You must not tell him what has transpired between us or else I will end you as I see fit. Are we clear?"

Emily nods. Mr. Mustard begins to purr once again.

"Good. I'm making cookies right now and they'll be done soon if you would like some, but while we wait, can I trust you with some information? This is something you must keep from Death, but it will help you understand his importance more. Can you do that?"

On instinct, Emily nods and Agnes looks at her with those static gray eyes. The same shade as Death's except they remain stalwart and refuse to move and shift like his do. Agnes leans in.

"Death's father is-"

The flowers in the garden sway in the breeze.

CHAPTER FORTY-EIGHT

Music plays from Death's bedside table. Quiet jazz. It's not that the music makes Death feel less alone, it has a way of making him feel as if being alone were not so bad a thing.

"It's not like it'll kill him," the man says to his friend in a matter of fact way as they drive past an overturned car covered in flames, the animal sounds of a burning man shrieking from within.

Emily is much more aware of others than Death initially thought. She just shows this understanding differently than him and that's why it took so long to notice.

Death is not the only one spending their evening in quiet. The world is peaceful at night, whether or not people sleep, they rest.

Peter is seated at his desk, reading and re-reading files and going back through his notes when he finally finds it. The mistake he is looking for.

Jeff sits up in bed, nursing a glass of whisky in silence.

Michael reads, occasionally flipping a page or adjusting his position in bed.

Judas lies prostrate on the cold floor of his cell, gazing at the smooth ceiling from an ever-growing pool of blood, letting the pain spark and shoot through his body. A jolt to get him through the night.

Agnes soundlessly rocks in her chair, flipping through a photo album, a melancholy smile on her face.

God types away at his desk, stopping to sign some papers then returning to the document that will never get read by the one who needs it most.

Anita compulsively checks her phone. Five calls and still no answer.

Emily is curled up on the right side of the bed, taking up as little space as possible out of habit, trying and failing to sleep.

Jesus stands by the window of his bedroom, watching the souls of Heaven mull about below.

Death finds sleep at last as the sound of Davis' trumpet takes over and he is greeted by the sound of crashing waves, the smell of citrus, and a reflection absent of worry or fear.

CHAPTER FORTY-NINE

Knock-knock

The door opens to reveal Agnes with a pleasant smile on her face.

"Good morning, Thomas. Come in."

Death enters the home with a hesitancy.

I don't like this friendliness.

"Did you sleep well?"

"Well enough."

Agnes tuts.

"You need to make sure you're getting enough sleep. If you don't sleep enough then your brain gets a little skewey."

"Thanks for the advice. Where's Emily?"

"She's here. I think she just went back to your room to tidy up."

"My room?"

"Yes. She stayed in your room last night, and do not start complaining to me. You know we have no guest room here. Where was she supposed to sleep? The couch? Don't be grouchy, Thomas. I'll go get her."

Agnes makes to walk towards Death's old bedroom but he pushes past and strides down the hallway.

"No, I'll do it."

Agnes smiles as Death presses wide the door which was already ajar and he finds Emily making the bed. Death's childhood bedroom has not changed much since he left it, a little like Bryson's. Everything is still there, his old art supplies sitting at his desk below the corkboard where he used to pin his most treasured works. Death's bookshelf with poetry collections and art reference books, even one with the planets and all of their descriptions which he had been especially fond of.

The window had always been Death's favorite part of his room. When the blinds are drawn it allows for an unimpeded view of the garden. He would often stand by the open window, drawing plants and chatting with his mother while she worked in the garden. Death had never been much of an outdoors kid, but this allowed them to have quality bonding time, and he feels the lead weight of that bond as he stands here taking in the same view he once cherished.

"Good morning, Death. Did you sleep well? Oh, and your mom said she'd keep Mr. Mustard while we're off tracking down clues. Isn't that nice?"

There's something off about her smile.

As Emily stands with a pillow in her hands beaming at Death, he can tell that something is wrong. Her authentic, warm smile is now knowing and cold. The kind of smile his mother gives. The kind which Death has always found easy to read.

"We're leaving in a minute. Meet me out at the car."

Death turns on his heels and leaves. The spot just behind his lungs hissing and whining, his blood growing cold.

I have to get out. I have to get out.

Agnes smiles at Death. Not in response to seeing her son, not because the weather is nice, and certainly not because she's in a good mood. Agnes is smiling *at* Death. "At" as in to do something towards as a means of harming. Death begins to feel something he has not felt in a long time. The combination of animosity, devotion, venom, admiration, and malice coupled with a sense of complete and utter attachment and need which is reserved exclusively for a parent.

Death looks her straight in the eyes and speaks.

"Thank you."

"You are very welcome."

Death exits the home and fumbles with the keys as he takes the driver's seat and sits in the silent vehicle, watching the front door for Emily's departure. It would have been better to stay inside with them and make sure nothing important is exchanged, but he needed to leave. The house and his mother remain unvisited for a reason. But as he thinks about what his mother could have done to Emily, Death feels a twisting in his stomach.

Why does she always do this?

CHAPTER FIFTY

I found it. I finally found it.

Peter now has proof that something is amiss within the eternal bureaucracy. Since returning from his day of work in Hell, all of Peter's time has been spent going through his notes with a fine-tooth comb. No stone left unturned. Peter feels an itch on his knuckle every few minutes and he is determined to figure out why. It is not until he cross-checked every soul that was collected during Death's day off that he noticed there are several missing. Now, this happens quite often and exorcists will be sent in the next day if they have still not arrived, but Peter finds something curious upon checking those few souls one time over.

Emily.

Things were missing.

I must have just gotten distracted by something when I was putting her information down. Whoever was processing her could have just double checked through their access point.

Peter had typed her name into the database to no avail. The itch on his knuckle grew almost unbearable. Peter typed her name in again, last name first. No results.

This is it. This is bad. If no one processed her then...

Peter starts to feel nauseous. A missing file is a big deal, a fireable-

A missing file?

God inputs those files himself. Manually. He types out every line, copying them over from the Book of the Lamb that he himself wrote, all so that there are no mistakes. This is no mistake.

The itch subsides as Peter scratches it and finds himself getting closer to the truth he always knew was there. Just one thing needed to be checked, but to do so he would have to call in someone else. The most tech savvy person he knows.

Michael.

Which is why the archangel is now knocking on Peter's apartment door, only to have it shoot open before he can even get the second rap off.

"Come in, come in."

Peter is sure he looks like a mess, having not slept in almost two days, but this is important. Michael gives a puzzled look with his eyebrows and enters as Peter slams the door behind him and locks it. The stout saint with the square, pudgy face hurries over to his ancient desktop computer and gestures to the seat.

"So, what is it you need me to do? You were vague over the phone."

"I had to be. They might be listening."

"Who?"

"Them."

"Ok? And what is it you need me to do on your computer that's so important 'they' cannot hear about it?"

"Is there any way to check if a file has been deleted from the database?"

"I mean, I suppose. You have an administrator status, correct?"

Peter nods, not entirely sure what administrator means but certain that he has it.

"Then, yes, it should be possible. I've never checked something like that before so it may take me a few minutes to figure it out."

"That's fine. I expected it to take longer than that."

"Why did you call me again?"

"You're the best with computers that I know."

"Not someone in IT?"

"They can't be trusted. We don't know how big this is yet. The conspiracy could go deep."

Michael nods his head, pretending to understand.

"Well, alright. Let me try and figure it out."

In reality, Michael is not good with computers. Michael is below average in terms of tech savvy. Something about the mechanics and machinery of it all just puts him off. All of this stuff about cloud saves and incorporeal data just makes his head spin. However, what sets Michael apart from Peter is patience. When Michael encounters something technological that he does not understand, he usually reads through all the settings, maybe searches his issue online, or asks someone in IT to fix the problem and explain how they do it so he can do it himself the next time.

Michael plays around in the administrator settings and menus until he finds what he is looking for. Michael opens up the "change history" and to his surprise, actually finds something.

"Peter, come look at this."

Peter is behind him in an instant.

"What is it? What did you find?"

"An administrator account is the only one that can delete files and change history, correct?"

"I think so?"

"And who has an administrator account?"

"Me. God and Jesus have administrator accounts of sorts, but IT has said in the past that they have different permissions and accesses than me."

"So, you're the only person with an administrator account. Essentially, the only person who could have deleted anything?"

"...yes?"

Peter's knuckle begins to itch.

Michael takes a deep breath.

"Alright, because there is no change history. It's been wiped. Whoever did it was probably hiding something, and I am assuming you know what it is considering you asked me to do this."

Peter gulps and nods his head. He is starting to figure out where this is heading.

"The system shows you having deleted the history, so-"

"They're trying to frame me."

"For lack of a better word, sure. 'They' are trying to frame you."

Peter shakes his head as the itch gets worse and he scratches it, leaving marks all over his knuckles.

"This is bad. This is really bad."

CHAPTER FIFTY-ONE

"You wanted to talk?"

"Yes. Have a seat."

Judas lowers himself into one of the two chairs in front of Satan's desk. The Tower of Hell was quieter than usual when Judas made his way up to Satan's office. It's before office hours which Judas feels has something to do with the timing of their meeting.

"So. What did you want to talk about?"

"Well, first thing's first."

Satan reaches out his hand palm up.

"Give me the flash drive."

Judas does not move a muscle, his eyes stay locked on Satan's, his lips do not twitch, no sign of emotion or reaction.

"What flash drive?"

"You know which one. But if you need a reminder then how about the one with the file you took from Peter's computer. Death's file."

Judas tilts his head.

"Death has a file? That feels like confidential information, are you sure you should be talking to me about that?"

Satan grins.

"You're right. I shouldn't be talking to you about it. So how about you give me the file and we can move on to more pleasant conversation."

"If I had something as important as that, which I don't, why would I give it to you?"

"Because if you don't, I will ensure that time off of yours goes bye bye in an instant."

Satan snaps his fingers.

"And beyond just losing the only thing that's ever been able to draw you out of that torture pit of yours, I will personally guarantee that you are back to a more, 'guerilla' method of punishment. No props, no sharp edges, certainly no batteries which I've noticed you using quite a lot lately. You'll have to get a little more creative without those, and you know, I've also been considering putting in padded walls. I think that would certainly make it a bit more interesting for you. Do you? You've gotten used to this pain, so I think it's gotten too easy. Yeah. With some padded walls you'll have to use those nails of yours. That would be quite fun actually. You're obviously a smart guy so I think you could do it. Just might hurt a bit along the way."

Judas remains rigid. No emotion. No reaction. A thin smile on his face.

Judas's bandaged hand reaches into his pants pocket and retrieves a small flash drive and places it in Satan's hand.

The Devil smiles as his fingers close around it and he stows it on the corner of his desk.

"Excellent. Now we can get to the fun things. Peter has almost certainly figured out what you did yesterday by now. It bought us time, but it also puts down a safety net. Put everything in place to get Peter in an uncomfortable position, and then focus all your efforts back here with me to fake out him and Michael. Understood?"

"Absolutely."

"Excellent. Now leave. And know that I don't trust you, however I respect the quality of your work. I don't know what you planned to do with that file, and honestly, I don't need to. You have your own plans going on and I am fully aware of that. But this interferes. This is a problem. I don't want to see anything about this linked to you again or we can institute that fun hypothetical we were just discussing."

"That sounds fair."

"It's more than fair. Good luck today, and excellent work so far."

"Thanks, you as well."

CHAPTER FIFTY-TWO

Death never leaves the car running if he's not using it. There's too much waste involved. Why use something if you aren't actually going to get anything out of it? Death always saw this kind of behavior from humans, angels, and devils alike. This wastefulness. Not just a wastefulness of resource, but more so that of a mental, emotional, and spiritual kind. Death hates waste more than anything else in this world. Not so much the waste itself but more just the wasteful mindset that comes along with it. Death firmly believes that's what is destroying everything. It's why the Earth is dying. It's why Heaven is run by fools, why Hell is slowly losing what little freedom it ever had, and it's why nothing matters anymore and when people really truly believe that deep down in their very heart of hearts, there's nothing anyone can do to help them. It's why so much of Death's job is picking up after people who firmly believe that false truth. Death hates picking up after people.

This trend never ceases to surprise Death. He had always thought people had so much to add meaning to. There's so much about the life of your average person that is just wonderful, but most of all, everyone, everywhere has someone that cares about them. Death cannot help but think sometimes that everyone in the world has something to love, and that love defines them through and through. This also applies to the angels and demons nowadays. If you were to go back, it was just a human problem, but then the humans stopped liking the divine. The divine is too far away after all, and that distance only grows the farther you go looking for it. How can God compete with that much progress? The simple answer is, He can't.

No one could compete with that, including God. Everyone has more and more connections, never alone, never in solitude, never feeling like they need anything divine. Nothing is sacred when you feel happy and connected. Nothing is holy when you haven't had to sit alone for a long time and feel and worry and let those feelings and that worry wash over and through you until the saltwater seeps into your soul and muddies it up making it brackish and inedible. Then you're left with this loathing deep down. You don't feel the way you're supposed to anymore. You feel dark and separate and weird. But then you find, and quite fast, that the separateness is addicting and the darkness begins to eat away. It is not their separateness from God but rather their separateness from the Divine. From anything outside of and wholly Other than themselves. Something bigger and greater and more kind. Something or someone that says "Go, and sin no more".

Death differs in opinion with the angels and God on this. The general consensus is that, if given a choice, all humans would choose to be God. It's just in their sinful nature. Death is not so sure. Just from what he has seen of humans, and he's seen a good bit more than God, the only thing people hate more than Gods ruling over them is being a God themselves. Maybe back in the day people would've wanted to be God in their zeal and arrogance. Nowadays, your average Joe Schmuck is too numb to do anything but watch The Game and fuck a wife that wishes him dead on the daily. Death should know, death-wishes go straight to his PO box. This numbness is not some revolutionary new fad or some dark reality that snuck up on everyone. It's simply the logical end of things. The logical end of progress. The logical end of life itself.

Death is knocked out of his reverie by a whispering in his ear. Death turns to see Emily with a comical amount of plastic bags in her hands. She even has one clamped between her teeth while also appearing to smile, transforming her face into an absurd smile. Death hides his face in his hands for a moment and sighs.

We stopped to get gas and now I'm inside, loitering in a back aisle so as not to freak out customers with floating snacks?

"So. These were buy three get one so I figured, why not? We've got a stakeout, right? We'll need snacks and drinks and music and, crap, I didn't get pillows or blankets or anything do you think we might need, crap, I'm sorry I'm really sorry maybe we can pick those up later? They don't sell anything besides neck pillows here so if we want to be comfortable and stuff then there's nothing but the headrests, will that be ok?"

Death stares at her.

"I thought you said we were getting a few snacks."

"I did."

Emily looks at Death confused and then, following his eyeline, seems to notice the array of snacks scattered around her for the first time.

"Oh. Yeah, I know it's a lot, but I mean, we've got a long day ahead of us and just in case we don't have time to stop for lunch we can have something to munch on. Anyway, what kind of chips do you like? I've got regular, barbecue, salt and vinegar, I also got these lightly salted diet type ones but-"

"I'm fine. I don't eat very much."

"Do you just not like chips and are being polite? Cuz I have more than that I also bought some candy and other stuff. Do you like granola bars?"

"No, I'm fine."

"My grandmother always told me never to buy fruit from a gas station no matter what. I would've wanted to buy some apples but they probably tasted gross. We should pick up something you like though, it's not even dark yet."

"I'm fine."

Death takes the items from her, filled with an embarrassment as he walks over to the register that does not subside until he's seated in the driver's seat. Convenience store bags of food tumble to the floor as Emily rifles through the selection, one poor bag of salt and vinegar chips even being crushed under foot. Death hates crushed chips. Like, what's even the point? If the chips are crushed then you have to rummage around in the bag and crunch together all the little flecks and flakes in-between your now slick and greasy fingertips and then try to eat that disaster which inevitably results in crumbs all over your shirt and lap which, even if you brush them off they get all over the floor and next thing you know there are roaches living in your car. The last thing Death needs right now are roaches in his car.

"It's hot in here. Or is it just me? I always think places are hotter than they are...oh! Haha, the car's not on."

Death turns the key in the ignition and Emily frowns.

"Your windshield is so dirty. We need to clean that."

"It'll be fine. Let's just get back to business. We need to follow up and see if we can-"

"Death, it'll take five minutes. I'll do it, see?"

Before he can say anything else, Emily has already opened the passenger door, leaving behind her snacks, and is circling around behind the car. Death watches as she grabs the squeegee and sets to work on the windshield.

It was pretty gross.

Death manages to keep the interior of his car next to spotless because he makes sure never to eat inside, clean up if he ever tracks mud, and most of all never have passengers. However, the exterior has a tendency to get ignored. Death just finds that getting out a bucket of soapy water and setting to the task of cleaning the car takes a lot of energy which is something he does not have. The task is not especially difficult and he could probably do it in several minutes if he worked hard at it, but is it really worth the energy? It would only be for other people. Death cannot see the exterior while he drives. The interior is Death's domain so he takes care of it, but the exterior? What does it matter to anyone if there was dirt and dust and hard water stains? It's a nice car but they're not dents or anything.

Whatever. We just need to get going soon.

Emily finishes up, leaving Death with a crystal-clear windshield and anxiety about how long it took to get it. Death watches Emily through the rear-view mirror as she stows the squeegee back in its slot near the gas pump and turns, her eyeline pointing downwards as she does. She stops, inspecting Death's driver side rear tire with confusion on her face.

Oh no.

Emily looks up from the tire and into the driver's side mirror, making eye contact with Death before looping back around and climbing into the passenger seat.

"Why are you driving on a spare?"

"What does it matter?"

"How long have you been using it?"

"A couple days. Someone slashed it, besides, it's not a big deal."

"Death, you're driving on a spare tire. You're supposed to use that to get somewhere to get a replacement."

"It has worked just fine."

"Sure, but it won't work forever. We need to get that fixed."

"We have much bigger priorities right now than dealing with a spare tire. It will work for now and that's what matters. Now we really need to focus on finding whoever killed Bryson. I was able to speak to him last night and-"

"We can talk about that on the way to somewhere we can get the tire changed. If the tire blows out then we're stuck and we definitely won't find what we need. If you're not running at one-hundred percent, Death, what's the point?"

Death sighs and puts the keys in the ignition.

"I guess we're getting the tire changed."

Death pulls up to the stop sign at the edge of the lot, waiting for the Mazda down the road to pass before pulling out. A Suburban pulls up behind Death and just starts wailing on its horn.

It's a lot safer to just let the car go. They're going quite fast and there's not a single car behind. Just let them go and then everyone is guaranteed to make it through safe.

The Suburban continues to wail on the horn. The Mazda passes and before Death has even completely pulled out, the Suburban roars past nearly taking the rear lights of Death's car with it. The driver, a pudgy woman with a hateful, botox-cured face flaps her fattened arms at Death as she passes, cutting in front of him the moment it is feasible. Death slows down to let her in front and then accelerates to speed limit once she is a safe distance ahead.

Emily is trying to look at Death and gauge his reaction without making it obvious. Staring at him through her peripheral vision and looking away whenever he checks the passenger side mirror.

Why is she being like this? She's different now.

"So how did the conversation with Bryson go? I mean, how is he doing?"

"He's, um, alright. Very courteous host, and he seemed very

happy."

Death can tell that Emily appreciates the last part.

"Besides that, he doesn't remember much about what happened that night. Bryson definitely saw who killed him, however I think the fact that it was night, coupled with his age and the severe trauma of it all have caused him to forget or misremember the details. He does remember one thing though. He spoke in great detail about the eyes of the killer."

"The eyes?"

"Yes."

"What were they like?"

"He described them as being 'evil'. He did his best to go into detail but that was as much as he could come up with. They stood out to him so it looks like we need to look out for evil eyes. A stellar lead."

Death shakes his head.

Emily smiles.

"It'll be fine."

And there it is again: that cold, false smile. Looking down on Death from atop a high tower keeping the piece of him that continues to go missing. Not even sure what that piece is, Death always knew his mother was hiding something, and now Emily is too.

Is it bad to feel betrayed?

Death feels it whether it's bad or not. It surprises him. Why does he care in the slightest what Emily does? She's just a human who he happened to find and make the biggest mistake of his existence with. Yet here he is with that person in his passenger seat feeling bad about something they hypothetically did.

It's ridiculous.

"Oh, Death turn here. This place apparently has good prices."

Death turns into the lot and pulls up to an employee that flags him down. Putting on his best human face, Death rolls down the window.

"How can I help you, sir?"

"Oh, I've just got a tire that needs replacing on the driver side rear over here. On a spare right now, but I need to get a fresh wheel put on."

"No problem. Just park right over there and come inside, we can get you all sorted."

The employee points Death to an empty parking space. Death smiles, waves, rolls up the window and parks.

"I hate doing that."

"Pretending to be a person?"

"There's just so many customs and social hoops you have to jump through. It makes everything a pain."

The two exit the car and make their way inside. Death converses with the person working the counter and pays for a new tire to be put on, but they will have to wait so the pair takes a seat in the waiting area with the sweaty older men reading magazines.

The two sit and wait, talking to pass the time and making a plan for the rest of the day and what they need to find and check up on.

A man enters the building.

Death's words suddenly seem to pass right through Emily as if she were now nothing more than a cloud of vapor. Her entire being and attention focused elsewhere.

"Emily? Hey, are you alright?"

No response.

Death follows her gaze to an irritable pony-tailed man with a hideous-but-not-in-an-ugly-way face leaning against the counter. The same irritable pony-tailed man with a hideous-but-not-in-an-ugly-way face that slashed Death's tire, putting them in this situation in the first place.

"Do you know him?"

Emily nods.

"Emily-"

The man looks around the counter and into the garage where the mechanics are working. The man waves until one of them makes eye contact with him and he throws his hands up and shouts through the glass in the same bothered tone he shouted at passerby when Death first encountered him.

"Hey! Some help over here? I'm in a bit of a hurry, got a date in a bit."

Death turns his attention to Emily once more, the shocked expression still on her face.

"Emily, who is that? How do you know him?"

"That's um, that's-"

The man slams the bell on the counter several times.

"Come on, guys. Let's move it a little bit. Jesus H Christ, hustle."

"That's my husband. Eric."

Death slumps back in his seat and groans internally.

Why am I not surprised?

CHAPTER FIFTY-THREE

Jeff checks his notes for the day while he sits in his car. He had copied them down that morning and is taking a brief break from the hustle and bustle to make sure he knows his schedule for the rest of the day. Right now there is a small lull in the consistent demise of human lives and Jeff is using it to have a coffee and rest.

It's all about the little things with Jeff. It always has been, and he suspects it always will be. This was one of the many things that set him apart from his peers growing up in Hell. Demons are often obsessed with visions of grandeur concerning their future and potential wealth. Jeff considers these visions to fall more in the realm of delusions. Jeff knew from a young age that he would amount to nothing. Not in any particularly depressing or tragic way, there's no deep, dark backstory as far as he's concerned, rather he just woke up one day as a boy and sat down for breakfast and realized he would do this same thing every day.

And it made him very happy.

The main problem with demons is that they are not content to do this. To sit down each and every day and have the same meal. For Jeff, that meal is two scrambled eggs with one slice of wheat toast and half a glass of orange juice. It puts him through until he gets back home and the evening and can cook dinner. Most of his fellow demons would turn their noses up at this level of routine and order. They fail to find the excitement and joy in completing the same task day in and day out. Jeff loves it. There is a simplicity in scrambling the eggs, sliding the bread in the toaster, and pouring just the right amount of orange juice that carries through each action and gives Jeff a feeling of place and centeredness for the day.

Jeff works directly for Satan. He's his right-hand demon. The person he trusts most. Jeff's life and work all revolve around another, and this is why he has loathed Death since the first time they spoke. Death's attitude is repulsive and there is no reason for him to be the way he is.

At least, that's what Jeff had always thought before doing Death's job for the past day and a half. For the first time in Jeff's life, he was wrong about something. He has also discovered a newfound hatred for teenaged humans. Having to talk to these dead people every day would destroy Jeff. They are just some of the most pitiful and downright unlikeable things he has ever had the displeasure of having to spend time with. And Death has to do this every single day without complaint. Not to mention having a mother like his...Jeff shudders at the thought. That coupled with God not listening to anything you have to say, Satan helping as much as he can but also being exceptionally busy and unable to give the attention and care that he used to when they were growing up, and finally the knowledge that he will one day become obsolete. Tossed away like an old toy when Jesus comes into control and the curse on the Earth is lifted and Death is no more.

Jeff became accustomed with that little spot just behind his lungs at a young age. The one that seeps inky black tendrils of burning ice into your veins and makes for your brain like a ravenous beast. Jeff found it easy to block it off and remove the tendrils like picking those weird strings from a banana. A simple task, but as Jeff is learning, likely not a simple task for others. Jeff is realizing how little he really understands, but also how much others understand. Specifically, the one he has been working with to make things better for Death and hopefully, by extension, everyone.

Jeff sighs.

He'll have to consider these changing perceptions when he's off the clock, for now he has a new soul to process. Jeff reads through her notes and grimaces.

It's bullshit when they can do the whole deathbed confession thing. You can't do what she did and somehow make it into Heaven.

Jeff shrugs.

I don't make the rules.

CHAPTER FIFTY-FOUR

"I'm not even angry."

Death turns to Emily as she continues to speak.

"I'm serious, I'm not. It's a little confusing actually because I really should be, shouldn't I?"

"Maybe. Although..."

"What?"

"Can I be honest in a way that may hurt?"

Emily takes a moment to consider it and Death pulls a right to stay behind Eric's vehicle. It seems like they are heading out of the city. This would usually make the trip somewhat pleasant in Death's mind, but Eric drives like a madman which puts the Reaper in an unwilling installment of *The Fast and the Furious.*

"Yeah. You can be honest."

"Unless I'm mistaken, you're beginning to fade rather fast. Correct?"

Emily pauses before nodding.

"You're growing tired of this. Whether that's a choice or not, I don't know, but you're ready to move on. It makes sense seeing as you've been lingering for too long. We set the deadline for souls at seventy-two hours for a reason. If you fade completely then you lose sight of things. It's why they send you to purgatory. You need some time to sort of re-assemble before you can be counted ready for eternity."

Silence.

"What I'm trying to say is we don't have to follow him. We can turn around right now."

"But will you be able to send me off if you don't see how I react to what we find at wherever Eric is going?"

Death's heart drops down into his stomach.

"Wh-who told you about that? It was her, wasn't it?"

"Yes, it was your mother. She told me that you're trying to determine whether I'm going to Heaven or Hell because my fate was missing from my paperwork. It has nothing to do with figuring out who killed me. Is that true?"

"She had no right-"

"Well I know either way, right or not."

I can't believe her. Does she have no sense of boundaries? Or even right from wrong at this point? She had no right to do that, and now that she knows them it makes things harder. There's a conflict of interests. Emily can pretend to be good in order to get where she wants. I have to be so careful. I have to scrutinize everything. Every little detail needs to be watched.

"So, have you figured out the decision yet?"

"Why do you ask?"

Emily rolls her eyes.

"I'm not looking for your stock answer, Death."

"No, I haven't."

"Alright. So everything I say can and will be used against me?"

Emily laughs as she says the last part.

Death does not respond.

"You thought I would be angry, didn't you?"

Death nods.

"Yeah. I might have been, but I know why you didn't tell me. You needed me to act natural, right?"

"I haven't had to do this kind of thing before. There isn't a pre-determined operations guide or anything."

"I see. Well, anyway, I just wanted to tell you that I'm not mad and I understand if the final decision isn't a good one."

"Ok."

The sound of the engine as Death speeds along is all that remains.

Once out of the city, Eric makes another right and pulls into the driveway of a small if not slightly dilapidated house. One story, front door, no defining plants out front, the yard cared for but not stunning. Completely and utterly forgettable. Death parks down the street and watches as Eric starts to get out of his car before promptly getting back in, shutting the door, and reversing out of the drive. Death makes to change gears but Emily puts her hand on his arm to stop him.

"Look."

Death looks up and sees Eric parking three houses down, getting out and walking at a rapid pace down the sidewalk with a bundle of flowers in his hand. The guy looks nervous, almost like he knows he's being watched. Emily watches him go in disbelief, yet Death gets the impression that her disbelief stems not from his walking or the flowers, but rather from the house itself.

"Emily…do you know that house?"

No response as Emily continues to watch every movement Eric makes as he approaches the home and strides up the drive in that quick, nervous manner.

She has to know the house. There's no way she doesn't. But how? What is going on?

Eric arrives at the door and knocks, continuing to look over his shoulder like a hunted man.

There is an uncomfortable pause with no response at the door. Eric knocks again, faster this time and starts to tap his foot.

No response. The tapping increases. Even from this distance, Death can see the sweat rolling down his face.

Another series of knocks, this time the door opening before he gets through the second rap. An irritated looking woman sticks her head out, scowling at him and opening the door all the way before grabbing Eric and pulling him inside, shutting the door behind them.

Emily inhales deeply and lets it all out in a long, heavy sigh.

"Who is that? How do you know this house?"

"That's my best friend. That's Anita."

CHAPTER FIFTY-FIVE

It doesn't take Peter and Michael long to determine on whose route the discrepancy was made.

"Death."

They both look at one another as everything comes into place. Satan's resistance to an audit, the presence of Judas, and the radio silence from Death. Actually, the last part is pretty normal as things go, but still. It adds to the level of suspicious behavior going on behind the scenes.

At this point, even Michael is convinced. Michael is not one to jump on any bandwagons, especially when conspiracies are involved. It has just never suited his personality. Michael has such an implicit trust of authority that he finds the idea of any sort of not-entirely-factual, or even factual if we're being honest, criticism to border on absurd. But this is something wholly other. This is something big.

This is an opportunity.

An opportunity for both Michael and Peter to prove themselves.

This is what shoots through their minds as they drive through the main gate and into the streets of Hell. This is no longer just a place they dislike visiting, the Tower of Hell is no longer simply a job-site, it is all a proving ground. And they are determined to make the best of it.

"So, here's the course of action. We go in and meet with Satan to touch base for the morning and go over the documents and numbers I have with me. From there, you pretend to go to the bathroom or something and I'll get Satan out of the office for a walkthrough spot-check or something. Search his office while I'm gone and there's no way you won't find something. All we need is physical proof that something shady is happening and we're good to go. We'll be heroes, Michael."

"It would seem so."

Michael is doing his best to restrain himself. The image of the gatehouse haunts and invites him as Peter parks and the two exit the vehicle. This opportunity is exciting but it also means his time working at the gate may be over and he is feeling a pre-emptive nostalgia. A nostalgia for those quiet hours spent reading and thinking about writing. Processing souls while always doing what he wanted in the back of his mind. The work is easy and it demands almost nothing from him.

But Michael is supposed to be the Archangel, not cooped up in a guardhouse on the edge of eternity fiddling around with a magazine, stamping papers and recording data. That's not who he was meant to be but Michael wishes it was. By virtue of not wanting to be who he is meant to be, perhaps Michael has inherently lost the right to be that person.

A cellphone beep cuts through Michael's excited, self-loathing stupor. Peter is blathering on about what he would do with more authority as they walk through the parking lot and Michael opens the notification.

An email from an unfamiliar address with a file attached and no subject line.

Michael knows it's probably spam, but his curiosity overcomes him.

A short message reads: You may find this interesting. Do what you will, just looking out for your best interests.

Below the message, Michael sees an audio file so he presses it and brings the phone's speaker up to his ear.

Death's voice, then Peter's.

"It's my day off. Why are you calling me about an emergency? Isn't it your job to take care of those?"

"It doesn't matter what happened, what matters is there are a good number of souls with no one to process them. I'll send you the list, but you need to come in."

"Absolutely not. This is my one day off. I'm going to spend it the way I want to, and believe it or not, that does not involve swooping in to save your ass. Goodbye."

"W-wait, wait, wait! If you don't come in-"

Michael's eyes widen and he looks up at Peter who is slightly ahead of him. Peter, almost as if he knew on instinct that something has happened turns around and looks at Michael. Upon catching his expression Peter speaks to Michael with a tone of such genuine concern that it is frankly annoying.

"Is everything alright?"

CHAPTER FIFTY-SIX

"Thank you, this'll be a huge help. Satan will remember this."

Judas winks at the demon sitting across from him as he stows his cellphone in his pocket and strides out of the office. The division in charge of phones in Hell is exceptionally cooperative if you happen to have mandates from Satan. All of them are filled with ambition, behaving like little insects crawling over one another in a mad grab at any kind of recognition or possible promotion. Judas finds it kind of funny.

He probably shouldn't. The demon is so sincere as he calls after Judas, making sure he got his name. Judas had not, nor would he be able to remember. Remembering names was always a job left for Peter because he wasn't good for much else. This was the general consensus of the other Apostles, and although Judas disagreed, he had never felt the need to speak up. Peter was the only one of the group that he respected besides...him.

Peter had a spark. He was dumb and abrasive and rash beyond belief, but he cared. He cared so much more than the others about every little thing. Peter was the only one willing to ask the stupid questions, to make the stupid mistakes, and most importantly to learn from those questions and fix those mistakes. Judas may have never felt home in the group, but Peter was always fun to watch. Maybe that's why he feels a twinge of guilt at what he just sent to Michael.

This really is Peter's own fault, but it's difficult to blame him. Ever since he denied Jesus, that nagging voice demanding he atone for his failures to try and make his own redemption. It's foolish to try and earn your salvation.

Not that Judas is one to talk.

As he exits through the back and ducks into an alley, Judas opens up his recent calls and dials.

"Hello?"

"Hey, Jeff, how's it going?"

"Well enough. Did you send the audio files?"

"Mhm. They're set to arrive soon as well which will just make things that much more interesting."

"Good. Do whatever you can to throw them off Satan and Death. There's not much time left, but it's all still going as scheduled. I just hope those two are at the house when I get there."

"They will be. Death is much smarter than he lets on."

"Are you sure about it?"

"He's her son, isn't he? There's no way someone like her would raise a gullard. I mean, with a name like-"

"She goes by Agnes now."

"Does she...and why are you so scared to say who she really is? She's not here, you know."

"Because I know what she's capable of."

"I suppose that's valid enough, but you surprise me, Jeff. I never took you to be the scared type. Especially not of old women."

"Do not try to poke at me. I have a healthy fear of Agnes and I also know it's necessary to be on her good side."

"Or at least not on her bad side."

"Mm."

"Well, I'm sure it goes without saying but both of us will be on that bad side once this is over."

"She won't find out who it was. This is just a fault of the system. God's system, yes, but the system nonetheless."

"You know full well she won't accept that."

"Well, she's just going to have to accept it. She may not like it, but her son has proven himself to be a hazard time and time again. This is the logical end of things, even if we pushed things along a bit."

"You see, that's the little detail I'm not sure she'll be too happy about. And what if it gets back to him? What do we do then?"

"That does not happen. If any of this gets traced back to him then all of our work has been wasted. Both our life's work flushed down the train in one fell swoop. Are you having second thoughts?"

"Not at all. I'm just raising concerns."

"Well, Judas, keep those concerns to yourself. It makes you seem like a traitor."

"You know, I get that quite a lot. My apologies though, I've always been best at finding faults."

"That's why he wanted you to be a part of this."

"I suppose. The verdict is still out on me."

"There's no point in arguing with you, is there?"

"Probably not."

Jeff sighs.

"Well. I'm almost there so I'm going to hang up. Make sure your tracks are supremely covered. No trace. Agnes can find nothing."

"Yep. I've taken all the proper measures. S–I mean, Agnes, will have her work cut out for her."

"...I know you think this is funny but you really shouldn't say her name."

"Yeah, yeah. I know. Good luck."

CHAPTER FIFTY-SEVEN

Her best friend and her husband. Eeeks.

Death feels a sense of awkwardness, almost like he is an invader in a very personal conversation. The person stumbling in at the least opportune time, asking where he can find the restroom. Emily has not shown the slightest of reactions yet. Her poker face is in full effect. He can understand why, and it's what anyone would do when put in her situation, but Death cannot help feeling a bit hurt.

Death had hoped that through the time they had spent together she would trust him a bit more. It's not as if he's expecting anything from her. It's not as if he is expecting her to trust him. It's not as if they're friends or anything.

Are we friends?

He is unsure when it comes to the fine print of both having and being a friend. Death was never very good at it as a child. The whole process kind of confused him and still does to an extent. Young children walk up to another child, or perhaps a harmless-looking adult and ask if they would like to be their friend. They get either a yes or a no (usually a yes) and move on with their respective little lives.

Adults, or in Death's case, immortal demi-god-like beings are a bit different. Everything is divided up into groups. When you're a child everything is divided into family, friends, and people you don't know yet with the occasional person you dislike thrown into the mix. Everything gets more complicated as an adult, because now you've got to deal with a whole array of different people and there are an exceptionally large group of folks that you just damn well have to get on with whether you like it or not. You soon find that you have different groups of people for almost every social circle you have, with everything divided up once more into subgroups of family, friends, people you don't know yet, people you don't want to know, people you hate, people you are friends with but not close enough to hang out with, people you hate but still hang out with, people you find funny, people you work well with, people you wish you knew better, people you want to fuck, people who want to fuck you, and people you feel like you should know more about but can't for the life of you remember their name or the slightest detail about them so you avoid their presence and passing gaze out of fear that your ignorance be found out.

Death is unsure where exactly he and Emily stand. Their relationship is strictly business, especially considering they've only known one another for a couple days now, but he can't help but feel there's something more. Death is unsure whether it's his own projection or if there really is anything in the slightest going on. Not that Death projects all that often, but if he did that would present a bit of an awkward situation. Even if there is nothing, and even if she is one of the most irksome and exhausting people he's ever interacted with, Death cannot help but feel like he has enjoyed their time together. But why?

This isn't the time.

Emily is already in the home, making her way through the halls and doors towards the voices of people she should have known better. Death can only follow as he always does. The only difference being the force and purpose with which Emily strides forth. There is something not entirely natural about taking your fate into your own hands. Humans are not exactly supposed to do that. Everything is already written, nothing anyone does is out of what has already been foreordained.

Yet, Emily moves forward as if this were not the case. A resolute fire burning her eyes. A flame not of anger, not of hatred, not of rage, but one of determination pure and simple.

Eric and Anita are fighting when Death and Emily enter the

kitchen. They could hear the shouts from the entryway. Eric shouting and Anita shushing him.

Death and Emily exchange a look as they enter the kitchen. The flowers which Eric carried into the house are strewn across the kitchen island.

Never a good sign.

"Eric, seriously, you need to leave. Now."

"I'm not going anywhere. We were supposed to meet today."

"But things have changed. You need to get out of here, for the good of both of us.

"Why would that be good for both of us? Come on let's just go, Anita. If we hurry we can still make it. We'll just miss the opening credits."

Anita is glancing around the room as if deciding the best way out and it is then that Death sees it.

An instant.

Death looks at Emily to gauge her reaction.

Nothing.

Maybe I just imagined it.

That's the only explanation. After all, that would be just about impossible. But Death is certain he saw it even if only for an instant...

"Because, Eric, I know what you did."

Eric who has been fidgeting to an almost childish degree, halts.

"I'm not going to turn you in. You just need to leave. I don't need to know why you did it. I just need you to go. Please, Eric."

The halted man's expression shifts to confusion. But not the unsure-about-a-detail kind of confusion. Eric's expression reveals the confusion of someone who is realizing he placed a bad bet. The kind that changes like lightning from a simple misunderstanding to something violent and frightening. Death dislikes domestic disputes as it is, too messy, and he has a bad feeling as to where this is going.

"You know what I did, do you?"

Now it is Anita's turn at confusion.

"Yes?"

"You say it like you didn't already know. Like you weren't the one who told me to do it..."

"Tell you to do it? Why would I ever tell you to do that?"

"Are you really going to make me say it?"

"What do you think I told you to do?"

"I killed her cat. Mr. Mustard. You're allergic, remember? His hair was on my clothes so you kept sneezing so you told me to get rid of him."

Anita gasps and reaches at the island for support.

Eric rushes for her to help but is met with a hand outstretched in the gesture of "stop". Anita steadies herself.

"Are you alright? Should I go get you some medicine?"

"No. No, I'm fine. I just...what are you even talking about? You killed her cat?"

Eric nods. The suspense is consuming Emily, that much is clear.

Anita begins to mutter.

"I just, I can't, this was never supposed to happen. Nothing like this oh God it was just a mistake..."

"Anita, what are you-"

As Eric reaches in to hold her, Anita shoves him back and screams. Emily jumps as if startled in a haunted house which, to an extent, this is.

This all must be quite surreal for her, isn't it?

Emily is watching as if none of it were exactly real. Sort of the way in which Death's mother watches her daytime soap operas. Watching with the intensity of someone who has yet to feel the social and emotional repercussions of what is happening on-screen. It is all so far away for Emily right now. It affects her but not yet. Emily does not have to feel any of it yet. What she is watching is not really happening.

Yet.

"Anita, what's-"

"You killed her, Eric. You killed your wife. You killed Emily."

"What the fuck are you talking about? Emily's not dead. I killed the cat, sure, but you told me to. It was right here. We were eating takeout from that Chinese place in the shopping mall down the street. We were sitting right there. Don't you remember? You even told me how to-"

"Eric, that never happened."

"What never happened?"

"We've never had takeout here. There's not even a Chinese place in that shopping center. We were only together once. It was a mistake, Eric, you need to leave. Now."

"What are you talking about? Of course there's a Chinese place there. We've had it so many times. It was only just the other night..."

Eric is descending further and further into confusion.

"Eric, please just leave. The cops are already looking for you. I got the call this morning and they've placed you at the scene. Now, why you would do it I have no idea but you need to leave. Please."

Eric slams his fist onto the counter. Sweat is beginning to drip from his brow."

"I didn't kill Emily and I'm not leaving. You invited me here. You told me-"

"I told you to come here because we needed to talk. Because what we did was a mistake and I needed to tell you in person that it can never happen again. But then Emily stopped answering my calls...and then I started remembering things you said that night, and then it all started to make sense. And then on the news..."

Anita shakes her head as if trying to confuse herself. As if she could shake the memories and the guilt from her mind like shaking water from your ear.

Eric is watching and considering. Absolutely stupefied. None of this had gone through his mind. None of this was part of his plan.

This was not supposed to happen.

And why doesn't she remember? Is she lying? Am I crazy? Death can almost see the thoughts flying about in Eric's mind as he is trying to come to terms with his surroundings. That is, until he comes to the final realization.

"I killed my wife...I killed her with my own two hands..."

Anita nods. Continues to nod as the tears begin to stream down her face. She steadies herself on the counter and reaches for an open book resting next to a bowl of fake fruit.

Apples and pears to be precise.

Anita takes the book and clutches it as she begins to mutter.

"Oh, dearest Lord forgive us our trespasses..."

The reading seems to knock something loose in Eric's focus.

"What the fuck are you reading? Is that the Bible?"

"We did a bad thing, Eric. You did a bad thing. We need to ask for forgiveness. You need to repent."

Anita stretches out her hand to Eric, but it's his turn to recoil.

"What are you even...no. No, no."

Anita nods.

"Yes, Eric. You did something horrible and now you need to ask God to forgive you. I've done it. That guilt eating you up inside will only quiet down if you do."

"But if anything you made me do this. You started all of it that night, who's to say you didn't start all of it this time?"

"You're unwell. You need to get help."

"Unwell what are-"

"The image in your mind. You talked in your sleep, you wouldn't stop. You kept twitching and muttering."

Anita reaches out once more, this time Eric does not smack her away.

"The evil eyes can't hurt you here, Eric. You looked in the mirror and saw them, didn't you? You kept talking about it. How the eyes were inside your brain and eating you alive. I don't know what it means, but I do know that you need help. The evil eyes can't make you do anything you don't already want to do. That's why you need to repent. God can help you, but you need to ask."

There it is again.

Death is not entirely sure how to describe it, but when Anita mentioned the evil eyes he caught it again. An instant of that something. But Death cannot focus on that right now. The eyes are what's important.

This guy killed Emily but did he kill Bryson? Did he kill that little boy? Death just can't believe it. The evidence is there, and Death can even attest to unhinged behavior with what he saw when it came to his car. But why would he kill the boy? Why would he kill a little kid? And he had to be about as young as Emily then. To be able to pull off something like that at that age and then kill Emily later on you'd have to be cold, manipulative, and most of all smart. Eric is red hot, blunt as a club and dumb as a rock. The guy's a dumb shit, but is he a psychotic murderer?

It just doesn't sit right with Death.

Eric does not seem to be listening much to what Anita is saying. Lost in his own little world, addressing his surroundings, considering his own place, giving a little self-diagnostic on his current mental health situation.

Anita leans in.

"Eric-"

Hands grip her throat.

"You bitch. The eyes started after. You did do this. I didn't do anything. You made me do it. I would never do it. I would never kill Emily. I would never do that I would never kill Emily. You killed her. You killed her I didn't kill her you did now shut up. Shut up shut up shut up and *die*."

The hands tighten and Anita writhes as she reaches about, trying to grasp at something, anything to aid her. Her fingertips brush against a knife but Eric pulls her to the left and bashes her against the refrigerator. Death can see the stars in Anita's eyes as her consciousness fades.

"You should probably look away."

Emily doesn't reply.

Death is rarely there for these parts. Even with large scale deaths and the like where being on-site early makes the job easier, it's just always felt wrong. Not that there's anything unnatural or morally gray about it. Death has just always worried he would get desensitized. Death may not like the people he works with but being able to watch something like this without feeling anything is horrifying to imagine. It happened once a while back, but Death remembers it like it were yesterday.

A group of teenagers, five of them, college aged, men. Boys really. It was late, roundabout midnight when they were walking back from a bar they never should have been at, having drank more than their bodies ever should have let them when an older homeless man asked them for some change. He was curled up with a blanket due to the winter cold and through clattering teeth he asked the boys a simple question.

Could they spare him some change for a beer? It was awfully cold after all and the man needed something to warm him up if only for a little while.

The group being the intoxicated, college men they were, promptly told him to fuck off.

It was cold enough to freeze your balls off, this man had been curled up, shivering for hours now and beer was not expensive back then. They certainly had the money and he had nothing. Just one simple desire and that is to feel a bit of warmth for an hour or two while he nursed a shitty beer inside a shitty bar in the dead of night.

This man was not always homeless. So few are. He had been just like those boys, except his luck and impulse control poor. And now he was here on a street corner roundabout midnight letting his balls that didn't work anymore freeze, wanting nothing more than a little pocket change to buy a cheap beer and get an hour or two of warmth, and here were these kids, no different than he was except with better luck and...well. Their impulse control proved itself to be just as bad as this old man's because when he replied with a fuck you as just about anyone would do when told to fuck off after making a simple and quite reasonable request, something lit inside of them.

Death has spent a lot of time considering the events that followed, and the details are not something he prefers to relive, but needless to say the old man was a little more than dead by the time those five intoxicated, college aged men, boys really, were done with him. The battered, bruised, and beaten corpse of the old man who wanted nothing more than an hour or two of warmth and maybe a working set of balls lay face-down and cruciform on the ground, his hole-ridden trousers tossed to the side and the three pennies to his name absent. The men, boys really, lived good long lives and never gave the event much thought.

Death stopped showing up early after that because watching what those boys did bored him and nothing has scared the Reaper more in his entire existence.

As Eric slams the gasping Anita into the fridge once more, Death looks away. Emily's gaze is still locked onto the conflict. No emotion, no feeling, but soon. She knows that the time of moral decision making is fast approaching as life slips away from Anita with every passing second.

The writhing and fighting and Eric's sobbing continue until Anita's corpse falls to the ground, released from Eric's grasp, and at the same time Death hears movement from the doorway. Turning his head, Death comes face to face with Jeff who gives him a quizzic look.

"Looks like I got here right on time."

CHAPTER FIFTY-EIGHT

"Well, if it isn't my two favorite people in all of Heaven. What happened to Afriel?"

Peter and Michael are seated across from Satan desk in that accursed and legendary office, legs facing out from one another. Peter responds.

"He had other work to take care of back at the home office."

"And Michael didn't? He's the gate keeper after all. Very important job."

"I-um..."

"I volunteered."

"Wow, he speaks. And how are you today, Michael? And why did you decide to volunteer for such a specific and boring job as this? Random auditing doesn't really feel like your style."

"Anything that threatens the Kingdom of God is my 'style'."

Silence.

Satan continues to hold eye contact with Michael until the Devil can't hold it in any longer. Satan snorts and begins to giggle in an ever-ascending rise of laughter until the room is filled to the brim with auditory mockery.

Peter, uncomfortable with the tone in the room, tries to join in with an awkward half-laugh coupled with a glance over in Michael's direction. The latter is not amused.

Satan finishes off his laughter and wipes a tear from his eye.

"Ahhh, whew that was funny. I know you weren't joking, Michael, don't worry. I'd just forgotten that you actually say shit like that. Damn. We don't talk anymore. We should talk."

"I'm alright, thank you."

"What? Too good to hang with the Devil? We've known each other *literally* forever. That's not even an exaggeration. Come on, let's get something to eat sometime. I'm free tonight, you can tell me all about gatekeeping."

"I'd rather not."

Peter does his best to pipe in.

"We do have some work to do so I think it would be best if we-"

"Come on, Michael. What happened? We used to be sort of friends. I mean nothing crazy close or anything, but we knew each other. We got a meal once or twice."

"If we could get started for today then maybe-"

"Is Yam of God any good? I got the boot before those opened up, but a few of the demons here who've gone up to deliver papers and such have stopped in and said it's better than they expected. Just tell me straight out: is it worth the trip?"

Michael is still completely and utterly unamused.

"I need to use the bathroom."

"Do you know where-"

"I'll ask."

The door slams shut.

"Did you do something to piss him off?"

Peter looks startled.

"What?"

"Michael. Did you do something to piss him off? He seems kind of on edge. More than usual that is."

"Oh, um, no. He's just a bit tired."

"You're a terrible liar, Peter."

Peter gulps.

"Um, so this paperwork..."

"Yes, we do need to get to that, don't we."

As Peter rustles about in his bag with inky black tendrils of guilt seeping through his veins and taking hold of the grooves in his brain, Michael is sitting in a bathroom stall stewing.

That prick. That little fucking prick. He's been using me like a hostage this entire time. Keeping me close so he could make sure I never got the wrong idea, and flat out using me to do his dirty work. All of this to get rid of Death. I can't be a part of this.

The trouble is that Michael wants to be a part of this. He wants to let things go with Peter and go along with it all. With this proof of Peter's behavior in his inbox, no matter what he tries to pull, Michael can turn it around as a net positive for himself. If Peter doesn't try to pull anything then Michael gets the glory he's been wanting for so long.

But at the cost of Death.

Michael has never been all that fond of Death. There's no bad blood between the two of them, but they've never been friends per say. Or maybe they were. Not really though. No one was really friends with Death besides Satan. The three of them spent time together growing up, but it had more to do with forced proximity than any sort of shared interests or camaraderie. But just because they're not close doesn't mean that Death somehow inherently deserves to take the fall for anything.

He's an insufferable, whiny, ungrateful, entitled, pain-in-the-ass, but he also has an odd morality of his own design. Michael is not one for personal moralities because they tend to get a little weird along the way. He believes you can't have any true morality without it coming from a place outside of your own locus of control. But Death manages it pretty well with his whole "don't affect other people thing" even if it devours him from the inside out like a swarm of emotional termites.

Death doesn't deserve this, but neither does Michael.

I don't deserve to be stuck in a gatehouse. I don't deserve to have my God-given potential squandered day and day out for eternity. I don't deserve to be a waste.

But neither does Death.

Michael checks his watch and sighs. Peter and Satan are most likely on their tour now, and the former has almost certainly transformed into the most nervous and awkward thing on two legs. The fat bastard is probably stressed out of his gourd about whether he's actually going to search Satan's office. Peter has been scratching his knuckles ever since Michael had put his phone back in his pocket and brushed concerns off by saying that, "No, nothing is at all wrong." Peter's intuition refuses to let him believe that, and he has a sinking suspicion of what might be wrong, but he is also worried that it is in fact nothing but his own worry and that it will strike back at him if he tries to remedy anything about the situation with Michael, the party he has wronged but also very much needs in this situation.

Michael is not some sadistic monster who enjoys the internal suffering of others, but he feels that he can wait to soothe Peter's conscience. It only feels fair.

Without realizing it, Michael has made his way from the bathroom down the hall all the way to the entrance of Satan's office. Michael's body moved without his even thinking about it. The decision has not yet been made. Michael does not yet know what he wants even as he opens to the door, making sure to do it in an inconspicuous enough way to avoid the prying eyes of other demons.

And what a surprise for Michael as he opens the door to reveal a figure leaning against Satan's desk. A human man of a little above average height, inexplicably white hair, business clothes which he has somehow managed to make casual, and green eyes of an almost unearthly hue.

Michael is certain he should know who this man is, it's just on the tip of his tongue but he can't manage to place it.

"Oh, good. I've been waiting for you. We haven't met before but I know who you are. I'm Judas, and I'm sure you know a bit about me from that."

Michael looks at Judas with suspicion.

Judas raises his hands in surrender and puts on a wry smile.

"I surrender, I surrender alright? I'm not here to cause any problems or eat your brains or something. I don't know what they say about me up in Heaven but I'm sure it's nothing too kind. Did you get the audio file?"

"So that was you."

"Yep, it was me. I figured you deserve to know what Peter's been doing behind the scenes. Don't hold it against him though, trust me. I know him really well and he's not a bad guy deep down, just a little emotionally skewed."

"You've been waiting in this office to tell me that?"

"Not exactly. You're here to find incriminating evidence about the shady things that Death and Satan are up to with that woman's soul, right?"

Not a twitch from Michael.

Judas's wry smile forms into an almost evil grin.

"You're good. If I'm being honest, and I promise I'm not trying to be rude here, I wasn't expecting much. You've been in the gatehouse for so long I figured you would've worn down a bit but you're still as good as ever. As a sidebar, huge fan. I heard about you all the time growing up. Protector of Israel and the like. So really, it's quite an honor to meet you."

Silence.

"Alright then. Guess I'll get straight to the point. You're the only one we can trust right now. This whole business you've gotten yourself involved in is a whole lot bigger than you realize. You won't find anything incriminating in here because Satan is smart, unlike Peter. However, I can give you what you need under two conditions. One, you will listen to what I have to say which will bring all of this into a much clearer perspective, and two, you will not whisper a word of anything I tell you under condition one. Is that clear? I'm assuming you're still on the fence about this whole, throwing Death to the wolves thing, but I think you'll have a change of heart once I give everything a backdrop for you. What do you say?"

Without hesitation Michael nods in assent.

He's not entirely sure why he does it. It's probably a bad decision. After all, trusting Judas has never gotten anyone very far, but something about it just feels right to Michael. Somehow it feels like the right thing to do as if he were always meant to be here in the entryway of Satan's office in the pits of Hell having a cordial conversation with perhaps the most hated figure in all of Heaven.

Destiny is strange.

"Wonderful. Now shut the door, would you? We can't have any

prying ears for this."

CHAPTER FIFTY-NINE

Movies with those scenes where the female trophy character changes into some Mission Costume in front of the beef-cake action hero before they depart on their last-ditch effort to save The Ship really fail to capture the awkwardness of real life. Usually the scene is played for laughs and the ogling eyes of the pubescent and/or sexually dissatisfied male audience, but the part that's especially important is not the softcore pornography inherent in close up shots of a woman changing, but rather in the awkwardness inherent in the male character pretending they did not in fact watch every single ounce of movement and skin he could get his eyes on.

That's a little bit of what it's like to watch someone die and then commune with their spirit. There's an immediate feeling of violation, and the sense that you really should not have been watching. Dying is a rather personal matter and you rarely look your best and the reasons are often a bit embarrassing which is the case with Anita's spirit now standing above her corpse watching a bumbling, bellowing, bawling Eric on the kitchen floor. She turns her head to the three standing in the entryway who immediately look in different directions. Emily at the ceiling, Death at the floor, Jeff at an unknown something-interesting out the kitchen window above the sink far to Anita's right.

"You saw all that, didn't you?"

Emily: No, nope we just got here.

Jeff: Saw what?

Death: I, uh...

Anita sighs.

"You're all terrible liars. Except you in the back, the tall one."

Jeff is pleased.

"Well, it looks like I got myself killed. Somehow I never thought it would end up like this."

Jeff begins to fiddle about in his bag in the same fashion that Death has done day after day. It's those innocuous sounds that do it for Emily. It's finally time to take it all in.

Anita turns to face Emily, the pleasantries with the others taken care of, and strides toward her. Death and Jeff get the impression that they should leave but considering how pivotal this is, they simply cannot. They resort to watching Eric in his slapstick attempt to clean up amid the tears and blood dripping from the refrigerator.

"So..."

"I suppose an apology is up first, isn't it?"

Emily nods.

"I'm sorry. I know that doesn't make up for much, but it's about all I can do for the time being seeing as..."

Anita gestures to her spectral form and Emily nods in reply.

"Do you have any questions? Anything I can answer to make this easier for you? I have a feeling we don't have much time before I'm sent off somewhere."

Anita nods her head towards Death and Jeff. The former piping in.

"You know who I am?"

"Who else would you be?"

Death shrugs.

Anita turns her head back towards Emily.

"So. What do you want to know?"

Emily is not sure she wants to ask any questions. At this point, she kind of just wants to curl up in a ball and disappear. She would do that sometimes when she was growing up. When it became too much and those feelings of dread consumed her from the inside out she would crawl under her bed, curl up into a ball, close her eyes and wish the world away. If you can't see it, it can't see you. The problem is that Emily has remained under that bed for years. Since the perpetual Hell her life has been since that day. It sowed something inside of her just beneath the surface. A little something in the spot just behind her lungs, and it continues to rot away at her blood and brain. Slurping up all the good things and all the moments worth treasuring.

No amount of therapists, exercise, healthy eating, or God managed to cure the rot. It just stayed there in that same spot doing as it pleased, occasionally making a grab for her very consciousness.

College was a bitch.

Emily had hoped with near desperation that it would get better if she was away. That if she just changed her environment and got to be her own person then maybe it would stop. And it did for a while, but then that string of bad luck managed to track her all the way from the suburbs, out to college, and right into the bedside drawer of her roommate. Without a roommate, Emily was left once more to the lonely nights with that not-so-great-feeling in the spot just behind her lungs.

She exhales softly.

"I don't need to know anything. It's just good to have you back."

Anita looks relieved. As if a weight has been lifted from her shoulders which has been wearing her down for some time. This has all the makings for a heartfelt reunion were it not for Jeff inserting himself into the conversation as soon as the sentimental forgiveness moment is over.

"Alright we've made up, very cute. Death make a decision while I do this one's paperwork. There's not much time left."

Oh. So that's how it is.

Emily feels somewhat hurt. It's not the fact that a decision must be made concerning her eternal fate, but rather that Death is the one who has to make it. Emily would have preferred someone a bit more nameless. Someone she had no possibility of resenting. Emily doesn't want to hate Death, and he probably thinks that she's a good person, but he's wrong. She knows why he's eaten up inside. She knows why he can barely sleep at night. She knows and she hasn't told him. Agnes told her why.

It's all about his father. The other half of those gray, ever-shifting eyes of his. That's what Agnes said, at least. Death doesn't know who he is so there's no basis for being. It's the thing he's always wanted to know about himself but never been able to learn because no one, including Agnes, will tell him.

But why did she tell me?

Emily is still stumped by this, but regardless Death deserves to know. The fact that no one has told him makes Emily's blood boil, and yet she can't bring herself to do it because she's a coward. Emily knows the worst will happen if she manages to tell Death and she's unsure if she has the strength the bear the consequences.

I'm so sorry.

Death is watching her. Looking through her eyes and into the grooves of her mind where the tendrils take hold. It feels like an eternity, but in reality it is only an instant. A brief glance.

Death turns to Jeff.

"Heaven."

Jeff nods as he finishes up Anita's paperwork and turns to Emily, jots some things down and fudges some dates before handing her a piece of paper to sign.

"Sign here, here and-"

"I know. Thank you."

Emily signs. It all feels too unreal. Like, it's actually happening. Up until this point she's just been floating around as a ghost or whatever but now it's official. It's on paper in writing and signed to boot.

Dead. Destination: Heaven.

Do I deserve that? I don't think so.

It feels wrong. But Emily is too scared of the alternative. She had been too nervous to ask Death about it because she thought if she knew anything it would only make the fear worse. Now she's not so sure. The little black spot pumps icy ink into her veins.

Anita smiles and shows Emily her paperwork.

"Looks like we're stuck together for a bit longer."

Emily lets out a hollow laugh.

"Fun time's over. There should be a bus close by in just a minute. You can catch it if you hurry. Go."

Anita nods and grabs Emily's hand and starts walking out of the house.

"Let's go."

"Wait I just, Death."

"Yes?"

"Um, I uh. You're um..."

"What is it?"

Oh god, I can't do it. I can't I just can't.

"...uh it was good getting to know you. Hopefully I'll see you around."

"You probably won't."

"Oh, um-"

The front door slams shut leaving the two eternal beings alone in the house with the wailing Eric and Anita's corpse.

"You made a decision. That's new."

"You're polite as ever, Jeff."

Death turns to the demon.

"Is it just me or was that whole thing really weird?"

"What do you mean?"

"Anita. Did you notice anything with her? As soon as she died her entire attitude changed. The whole conversation with Eric was bizarre. It felt unnatural, almost scripted."

"Real life is a weird thing, Death. If you got out more, you'd know that."

"Did her record say anything? Do you have it with you?"

"It's on the access point, but it doesn't matter now. The decision's been made. She was put down as Heaven, reading the file won't change anything now."

"I suppose you're right. I just can't shake the feeling that something was off about all of this."

"Well I'm going to head out. You can finish up the souls for the rest of the day. I'm sick of this bullshit."

Jeff shoves his hands in his pocket and strolls out, but not before stopping in the doorway.

"Again, Death. It won't change anything."

Eric has calmed down a bit since the initial realization, and has done a pretty good job of cleaning up, actually. Death gets the feeling that he would make a good janitor at like an Elementary School or something if he weren't a psychotic felon. Sometimes people never become what they're supposed to be and Death finds that quite sad.

Well. I suppose it's back to the usual.

But something still doesn't feel right even after Death has turned the keys in the ignition and started driving. Something about what he saw in Anita. Those brief instances. Death is not sure what he saw and it's just on the tip of his tongue. Something is blocking it though and it's just-

Death slams on the brakes in the middle of the street. If there was a car behind him, he would have caused a major accident. Death looks into the shopping center on the right side of the road, his breathing halted as he realized what he's seeing. That look in Anita's eyes.

Recognition. She could see Emily and I. It was scripted, she was putting on a show. But how could she see us? The only way she would have been able to see me is if...

Death slams down on the accelerator and swerves into oncoming traffic as he makes a very illegal U-turn. Death zooms forward with his destination decided. He has to get there fast or else none of this will have been worth it. As Death powers along, he pulls out his phone and opens the access point and pulls up Anita's file as he glances back and forth between the phone and traffic, weaving between lanes with neglect for turn signals.

Death scrolls through the file and finds what he's looking for.

That bitch.

Death cuts a hard left through a red light and presses down on the accelerator once more. If he can make it to the freeway he just might be able to make it in time.

One of the cars that Death cut in front of pulls into the shopping center and into a parking space, the driver sighing as he exits the vehicle.

"That guy was crazy. I mean, seriously. What kind of asshole pulls a stunt like that, Christ Almighty."

The muttering about how stupid and dumb and irresponsible people are continues as he opens the door of the take-out Chinese restaurant to pick up the order for him and his wife.

Oddly enough, the place is very popular with couples.

CHAPTER SIXTY

Peter lets out another sigh of relief as he and Michael wait by the Heavenly Gates.

I was certain he knew.

But it seems like Michael doesn't know about Peter's initial attempt to sell him out. He's truly relieved, and he should be, but there's a small part of him that kind of wishes Michael had in fact found out. If he did then maybe Peter wouldn't feel the deep and inescapable guilt he's formed over the past few hours.

It's official now.

Against all odds, Michael had found something to incriminate Death and reveal his conspiring behavior. Sure, Satan was involved too but he's literally the Devil. What can you really expect him to do? It's your own fault for allowing him to get away with anything so you can't really blame him for it. Satan will likely get a small punishment, but more likely just a yelling at than anything else. Death is a different story.

This is the worst possible thing he could ever do. There isn't even an official punishment for what happens if someone takes a soul.

It wasn't until just about now that Peter realized this. Peter has no idea what God is going to concoct for Death and it's beginning to worry him. He had not thought this far ahead.

Peter scratches his knuckle.

And Michael. Peter had never really intended to do anything bad to him, but he certainly made the threat to Death.

Did I mean it? Did I really plan to let Michael take the fall for something he wasn't even remotely involved in?

Peter gulps.

He really has fallen quite a bit. It feels weird to say considering his eternal standing, but Peter is living in his own personal Hell. Judas had always reprimanded him for his brashness. Peter had always shrugged it off because it was never in the pursuit of anything bad. Peter had a love for the good things in this world and he chased them with everything he had in him, but this was different. Peter had used the people around him as stepping-stones towards some kind of atonement. Jesus supposedly forgives all, but Peter has never been the type to take things like that at face value. Not that he thinks Jesus is lying, it's just that Peter betrayed the one who is supposed to forgive. Denied him three times and then came crawling back.

It makes Peter nauseous just thinking about it. He really is loathsome. There's no turning back now, especially as he can hear the screeching of a bus in the distance. She should be on this one, at least, that's what Michael found alongside his other evidence. Death will be arriving soon as well, but Peter finds that hard to believe. Death wouldn't go out of his way for another person, especially when it incriminates him more than anything else they may have on him at the moment.

The bus rolls down the road and pulls up to the stop, letting the wheels roll back into the parked position before opening the doors in dire need of oil. The souls begin to file out.

Peter's knuckle starts to hurt from his scratching.

CHAPTER SIXTY-ONE

The crossroads have always given Death the chills. After all this time, you would think he'd get used to it or even bored. But something about them, the way they look and especially that signpost with its creepy knotted wood just freaks Death out. Today is a bit different, not that he doesn't feel a chill run down his spine as he blows past the signpost and down the road to Heaven, the suspension on his car wailing in agony, but Death has bigger things on his mind.

The trees break as Death slams the breaks and cuts the wheel, swerving the car into a stop near the entrance and rushing out towards the bus expelling a steady stream of souls. Death frantically searches through the crowd of new arrivals and those who are already waiting in line.

She has to be here, that's her bus.

Death may not have found Emily, but Anita has found him. The crowd is large and she's using it to their advantage, not giving in to her urge to push and shove through the crowd, but rather letting it sweep her and Emily up like leaves in a creek. If she plays it cool they can probably make it, and once they're inside she'll have finally done it. All of her life has been building up to this, and it made restraining herself on the bus ride almost impossible.

It had been a packed bus. Full to the brim with disgusting, hideous, boring human filth. All of them self-righteous in their own standing, laughing and conversing about the most inane things to such an extent that it made Anita physically nauseous.

"Nance, it's good to see you. Hopefully they'll have casserole in Heaven haha."

"We'll get to meet God, won't we? I wonder if He's as tall in real life."

"Do you think they have movies up here? I never got to finish 'The Sixth Sense' and I really want to know how it ends."

It was a blessing in and of itself just to get off the bus and keep those banal, prying eyes off of Emily. Her life's work is almost complete, and no one would be coming between Anita and her destiny. She had nearly been separated from Emily once, and it was then that Anita knew she had to come up with a more permanent solution. She needed to find a way in which she and Emily could stay together through all eternity. Somewhere deserving of Emily, where her pure, golden, angelic soul could remain as such and Anita could rest. And what better place for an angel than Heaven?

"What is it, Anita?"

Anita wonders if Emily could forgive her if she knew what she did. If anyone could, it would be her.

"Nope. It's just really good to see you again. I was starting to miss you."

Emily smiles.

"I was starting to miss you too."

Anita's heart sinks.

No, it can't be.

Emily's eyes, once resigned to a waking sleep now reek with a fiery suspicion. Anita wants to reach out and touch her but she restrains herself for fear of being burned up.

What is happening?

Emily is smiling with such an authenticity, but the now lucid form of the *real* her stares straight into Anita. It looks at her not with anger, not with grief, not even pity, but the disgust of one who looks down upon an insect.

Anita's god has betrayed her.

It is in this moment of realization that a hand places itself on Emily's shoulder. A tall man with close cut blonde hair and a sort of sad scowl on his face. The man turns to the short, pudgy one just behind him, and then back to Emily.

"Ma'am, I'm going to have to ask you to come with us, please."

"Oh, um. Wh-why? Did I do something wrong or-"

"You don't need to worry about anything, there are just some questions we need to ask you. Come on."

Anita feels her voice disappear. Her eyes locked on the lucid form with eyes boring into her as Emily looks back and forth between Anita and the two strange men before she notices something over her friend's shoulder. Anita turns to follow her eyeline and comes face to face with Death. She has seen him before, but for the first time she sees him for what he is.

The Grim Reaper.

His eyes, once shifting and shaping, are locked on a gray. The gray of a midnight tombstone, the gray of a scythe's cold steel, the gray of Death, and Anita feels something that she has not felt since she was a child and saw that hideous drunken man on the sidewalk tottering towards her and her family.

Fear.

The short man begins to speak.

"Death, what are you doing here?"

"Emily, I-"

"Death."

"Yes, Peter, I know. I'll come with you, can you not interrupt me, please? I don't have the braincells to deal with your lack of them right now."

The tall man snorts and receives a sharp glare from the short man.

"Death, it wasn't really her was it?...it's..."

Emily looks at Anita and back at Death.

Anita follows the eyelines as they make eye contact and Death glances at her with the same eyes as the lucid form before looking at Emily and nodding.

Emily takes a deep breath.

"Alright. Ok."

"Please, Ma'am, we need to go. Death, come on."

Death steps past Anita and the group of four begin to break through the crowd and towards the gates. Anita's eyes fall upon Emily and the lucid form, both with their back turned to her and Anita can do nothing but scream. A hoarse, animal scream. Two and a half decades worth of emotion released at once. The souls around her back away, creating an almost two-person null space in every direction. The scream rings out, making its way towards the ears of Emily and they would have made it through and into her brain and fit right into the grooves, freezing the slowly receding inky tendrils in place were it not for a now lucid spectral set of hands that cover her ears, protecting Emily from those waves of unnecessary sonic guilt.

CHAPTER SIXTY-TWO

"The Holy Church of the Damned" is empty but for two people. The front door is open to allow some of the smoke to air out from the previous night as Jeff mills about, sweeping, wiping down tables and setting up chairs while Judas leans in one of the bar stools lazily puffing on a cigarette.

The scene is peaceful, and the two give off an air of winding down after a job well done. Judas stares at the ceiling as the thin trail of unfiltered smoke twirls and dances up, up, up until it's dissipates. Jeff comes around the counter and pours a touch of scotch into two glasses and places one down in front of Judas. The green eyes make their way down from the ceiling and to the glass in front of him.

"Sorry, Jeff. I don't drink. Thank you though."

"Suit yourself. I would've thought you would want to destroy your liver."

"Oh, believe me, I do, but it's a control thing."

Jeff shrugs and taps a sip from his glass.

"So, it's tonight?"

Judas nods.

"Are you ready?"

Judas shakes his head and takes a light drag.

Jeff takes a deep breath and lets it out as a soft sigh, causing the smoke to disperse past Judas' head.

"It'll be fine, you know that, right?"

Judas nods.

"There's no hard feelings, and even if there were, you've more than made up for it."

Judas nods.

"You know he knows, right? You don't need to try and hide it."

Judas cover his face with his left hand and nods, a thin trail of smoke trickling upward from the space between his middle and forefinger.

If Jeff were a different person, he would reach over the counter to rest a hand on Judas' shoulder. Instead, Jeff continues his cleaning, the only noises left in the bar being the intermittent squirt and subsequent squeak from Jeff's spray bottle and dish rag, the occasional quiet breeze passing through the front door, and the barely audible sound of a tear striking the floor.

CHAPTER SIXTY-THREE

God sighs.

"Why am I having to talk to you in my office, Death?"

Emily glances between the three others in the room. Death, seated in the chair to her left with perfect posture and eyes locked forward on God. The Creator Himself, seated across from them with an air of exhaustion, and the young man to His right. Emily knew who he was almost immediately. Something inside of her just innately knew. He looks like his Father, but with a different look in his eyes, those multi-colored eyes that shift and shape contain a variant soul to his Father's. God's eyes lack the same hue, the same spark and burst of color. Like a peacock that should have died some time ago.

Somehow, sitting in the office of the God she's heard so much about her whole life is not incredibly surprising to Emily. Since her passing, very little has felt "surprising". Death is a person, Death has a mother with a terrible secret, human souls ride the bus to the afterlife, Anita...

You know, I feel lighter.

Emily has felt the same ever since she died, and that was the most surprising part of the whole process. You would think when you die, now being semi-ethereal, you'd feel different and probably lighter. Emily had felt as if the forces of gravity still applied to her and that she would be bound to them for the rest of time, but it feels like something is leaving her. Emily can feel the chill blackness leaving her body drop by drop. It feels like her body is being purged of lead. It was never gravity that kept her under the dark waters, always gazing up from the depths. It was this lead-like inky blackness. The feeling of lightness slowly making its way up her body from the tips of her toes creeping its way up to the grooves of her brain.

"You're having to talk to me because I did not fill out the paperwork for this soul when I first encountered her. In other words, I did not do my job."

"You're not making any sort of excuse?"

Death shakes his head.

"Do you also admit to altering the database of souls in order to cover up for your lapse in judgement."

"Yes, sir. I do."

He didn't do that. I was with him like, the entire time. What is he doing?

Emily gives Death a look and he glances at her. The ever present shifting in his eyes has calmed into a slow splash of grays, almost like a lava lamp. Two words hidden within that glance like a code.

Trust me.

God holds His head in His hands and lets out a sigh.

"And you understand that without a record to compare her to, we have no way of knowing where she is destined to go?"

"My Lord, if you don't mind, her destination is Heaven. I made sure of that."

"Can you understand that I might be a little distrusting of you right now?"

Death nods.

The entire time they have been here He has not so much looked at Emily and she is not sure whether or not to be offended, but either way, she decides to speak up. She cannot just sit idly by and watch Death take the fall for something that is not all his fault.

"Um, God, I'd just like to say that-"

"And I would first like to apologize for this one's disruption of your eternal rest. You have lived and worked some time for this. If you speak to one of the angels outside we can make sure to connect you with coupons redeemable at any Yam of God location as a form of compensation."

"Oh, no, that's not necessary at all I just-"

"And of course we will get you sorted into the right place as soon as possible. Again, thank you for your patience and understanding. Now, Death."

"Sir?"

"What do you think we should do about this?"

He didn't even let me finish a sentence. Isn't it my fate they're discussing?

"I think you should send her to Heaven. It's what was on her record, and quite frankly, it's what she deserves."

"Why is that?"

"I should think her behavior right now is enough. Not belligerent in the slightest, thoroughly understanding of the situation, perfectly content to trust the system even though her fate is on the line. Have you ever met someone destined for Hell that behaves like that?"

"You make a good point. However, I was mainly referring to what we should do about you. We discussed something very similar not long ago, and I am sure you understand how suspicious your behavior seems when we consider that?"

"Absolutely, sir."

What did they discuss? What's going on?

"So. What do you suggest as punishment?"

"I think you already know what you're going to do, but I would assume total erasure. In other words, the Void."

God nods absentmindedly.

"It's interesting you should say that. So, what to do about her?"

Jesus coughs.

"Hello. I actually have a suggestion. Emily?"

Jesus turns to Emily and looks her in the eyes, a thin non-smile on his face.

"Yes?"

"The way things work here is that all things must be just and pure. Heaven is built upon this foundation of justice and purity, and we cannot have a soul that we are not certain about living here with those who worked very hard for this eternity. Am I making sense?"

"I believe so."

"Good. So, that all goes to say that we cannot help but try to be perfectly and completely certain of your character. Now, I'm going to ask you a question. Please answer truthfully and also understand that I am speaking the truth as well. Can you do that?"

"Alright."

"Excellent. If you reside in Heaven, then we must banish Death to the Void. There must be an equal exchange. However, if you choose to descend to Hell and suffer the truest of punishment for all eternity, we can begin to discuss a more forgiving fate for Death. Which do you choose?"

God's lip twitches. Death stares straight ahead, not so much as glancing at Emily.

It's all on me now, isn't it?

Emily doesn't want to go to Hell. She doesn't feel like this is the right thing to want, but it's also far from wrong, considering the circumstances. After all, it was Death who put her in this situation in the first place. Why should she have to suffer for something he did. Emily's entire life has been suffering at the hands of others, control always just out of her reach. What's so wrong about Emily making a call that actually benefits herself? Would that really be so bad? Death wouldn't hold it against her, right? He understands, right? That's why he's staring ahead, he doesn't want to influence her decision which means that he doesn't mind if she says Heaven. After all, it's her life. It's her fate, and it's not her fault that she's sitting here in this office.

But Anita.

The idea of being near her gives Emily goosebumps and she can feel the slow expulsion of the chill blackness perhaps begin to reverse. Never again. She will never have to speak to Anita ever again. This was what she wanted wasn't it? To get Emily forever. To keep her to herself. Emily doesn't want to be the trophy of the woman who has destroyed everything Emily ever loved. Emily's life has been Hell since the day she met Anita, what difference does eternity make?

"I choose Hell in exchange for Death being given a lighter punishment."

Death lets out a deep breath.

Jesus smiles.

"Well, that's settled then."

Jesus pulls out a piece of paper and fills it out before handing it to Emily.

"If you bring this to Michael, the gatekeeper who brought you in just before, he and Peter can get you all sorted. Congratulations, and I wish you the best of luck and happiness in your eternity. You've earned it, Emily."

Emily looks down at the paper. Which appears to be some kind of executive request form and at the bottom written in simple print letters under the "Request" line:

Upon the official decree of Jesus Christ, the Lamb of God and the One True King, the person(s) in possession of this form obtains the permissions required for an eternal residence in Heaven.

"Wait, I don't-"

Death lets out a sigh of relief.

"You answered correctly."

"Wait, you said you were telling the truth. I was truthful but you lied."

"Emily, it's fine. They ask that kind of question to get a read on your character. Just take it, please. I'll be fine you just-"

Emily is done. Emily has had it. Emily is finished.

No more.

"No, fuck that, Death. He doesn't get to lie to me like that. I'm sick of people lying to me, you know? Fuck that. Fuck this. With all due respect, you sit here in this office and make calls on people's lives but when's the last time either of you actually sat down and had a conversation with anyone No, fuck that. People aren't playthings for you to lie to and toy with. I have feelings. I have experiences. You know no one really believes in you right? And why would they, you make it so hard for them. The planet has gone to shit because you don't do anything about it. I'm so fucking sick of this shit. And don't think I don't know about your secret. If Agnes was here right now, I'd yell at her too because she's not innocent either. All of you sit around and keep this from him like it's nothing. Can't you tell that Death is dying? He's being devoured from the inside out because none of you will help him. None of you will tell him the truth and that's fucked up, pardon my language. So you may be God, and again, with all due respect, but you're acting like a real coward right now. Your Son too. Agnes too. All of you are acting like complete and utter children, and I work with kids, that's not a compliment."

Emily takes a deep breath.

Silence.

Death is looking down, eyes wide.

God, mouth agape staring at Emily.

Jesus leaned back in his chair, that thin non-smile still on his face.

Oh no. Did I go too far? I went too far, right?

Upon further thought, Emily doesn't actually regret it at all. In fact she feels good. She feels light. The chill blackness is gone from the grooves in her brain. Her being feels clear and the little spot behind her lungs is empty. It's gone. It's finally gone.

"And no, before you ask, I'm not taking any of that back."

Jesus looks at Death.

"Could you hand me back that paper please."

Death takes the paper from Emily and hands it to Jesus who draws a line and jots something down before handing it back to Emily.

Upon the official decree of, Jesus Christ the Lamb of God and the One True King, the person(s) in possession of this form ~~obtains the permissions required for an eternal residence in Heaven.~~ Is sentenced to an eternal residence in Hell for blasphemy.

God speaks.

"Well. We're done with that. Death, you are sentenced to the Void. I will personally-"

"Father, forgive the interruption, but I would like to be the one to do this, please. If you will."

God pauses, as if hesitating to give his answer.

"Yes, of course."

Jesus smiles.

"Thank you."

Jesus tilts his head and calls out.

"Michael, come in here please!"

The door opens and the serious man who brought Emily here enters.

"If you could escort her to Hell, I would appreciate that. Shall we go, Death."

Death nods.

Michael grabs Emily's arm with a kind, but firm grasp.

All rise.

"No, you guys don't get to do this to him. Please, you can't. He doesn't deserve it. Don't do this."

All but God exit the office, a somber expression on His face.

"God. You can't do this to him. Don't try and be all stoic about this. You can save him so just do it you fucking coward."

The door shuts behind them.

Emily feels herself pulled to the right, Death and Jesus are walking to the left.

Emily fights back but Michael is too strong.

"Death!"

Death and Jesus turn.

"Death! Your mother told me, she told me who it is. Death, your dad is-"

Michael's hand covers Emily's mouth as she continues to fight and shout.

She has to tell him. He needs to know. It's only right that he know. It's not fair, none of this is fair.

Death and Emily make eye contact and she can see it in his eyes. An understanding, but also something she has not seen in the short time they've known one another.

Joy.

That joy manifests itself as a flash of prismic color in his irises as Death does something he has never done before. Death shouts.

"Thank you!"

Emily can feel the tears welling in the corners of her eyes as Death smiles. It looks awkward and forced, like his face is a mask that was never meant to contort like this, but it's the most reassuring thing Emily has ever seen in her entire life, and now her after-life. Death turns with Jesus and the two walk across the room before rounding a corner and disappearing from sight.

Death does not turn back once.

Emily feels the hand fall away from her mouth, bringing about a moment of calm before the choked sobs flow forth.

CHAPTER SIXTY-FOUR

The room is cold. That's the only thing Death really notices about it. It's just a room after all. The room that will soon become his grave. No windows, just a door, a dim lightbulb, a chair resembling the kind they have at the dentist, and Jesus. The door is closed and the two stand in silence, eyes on the chair which will be Death's final resting place.

The irony of the situation is not lost on either of them.

Jesus is the first to speak up.

"Are you ready?"

"I'm not entirely sure."

"That's fine. We can wait. I know you aren't trying to get out of it."

Death nods and the silence returns before Jesus breaks it once more.

"I hope you know this is not personal."

Death nods.

"And that if it could be any other way, I would not be doing this."

Death nods.

"Alright. As long as you know that."

The chair is made of that kind of vinyl that makes your thighs sweat when you wear shorts. The kind that squeaks at the faintest of muscle movements projecting outward to inform the entire room that yes, indeed the person in this chair is fidgeting.

"Do you hate me, Death?"

"I don't think so. I probably did, but I don't know any more."

"Okay. I would understand if you did. After all..."

"Yeah."

"We've never really gotten along, have we?"

"No, not really."

"You know, I never told you this, but when I died and we spent those few days together, I was really looking forward to it. Spending time with you, that is. I wanted to get to know you."

Death glances away briefly before replying.

"What does it feel like? Dying."

Jesus looks at Death.

"You don't know?"

"I never wanted to."

Jesus nods his head, gathering his thoughts.

"Well, mine was a bit unique. The lead up was bad. The process itself is often very painful and the anticipation is almost too much to bear. But once you get to the point, that moment of passing, it almost feels peaceful. The built-up stress is released in an instant and you gaze out upon eternity. It's a bit like the slow rise of a roller coaster. Climbing to top and then that moment where you can see everything around you and time seems to freeze in place to give you that little bit of extra time to feel it all before you shoot down."

Death nods.

"That was my experience. I don't know exactly what it's like for everyone else."

"Thank you."

"Are you ready?"

Death shakes his head.

"Alright. We have time."

Death takes a deep breath before attempting to speak.

"I'm sorry I never tried I just..."

"I understand."

"Do you?"

"I do."

Death sighs.

"Okay. I think I'm ready."

"Are you sure?"

Death shakes his head as he climbs into the squeaky fake-leather chair.

Jesus stands in front of him and the two make eye contact.

"It's going to be quick, but for you it's going to feel much longer. It won't exactly be painful, but it will not be comfortable. The Void is something wholly other. I am undergoing total erasure. You will cease to exist. You are not trapped somewhere, you cannot be freed. I am going to remove you from Creation itself and release you into the emptiness from which God made all. Where you are going there is no such thing as space, time, or even reality. There are no words in the creative imagination to describe where you are going and what you will feel, or what will happen to you. There are forces beyond God and beyond what we can even imagine. What it wills is beyond anything. Do you understand?"

Death nods.

"Are you ready?"

"Just a second."

Jesus nods and Death takes another deep breath and lets it out slowly and with great effort.

"It's not that I hated you. I just couldn't bear your existence. Does that make sense?"

Jesus nods and replies.

"You knew, didn't you?"

Death nods.

"You've always known?"

Death nods.

"And you never said anything."

Death nods.

"Why?"

Death face contorts into something resembling a smile, but not a smile. A tired but content twist of the lips which is only ever present when saying something that you've thought and thought and thought but never said because you just never could. You could just never get your lips to actually form the words because if you make yourself say it then it becomes real. If you keep it inside then it's just a thought. A corrosive thought that holds you down day in and day out and eats your very soul bit by bit, piece by piece until you're nothing but a hard, round ball with the best parts of you, a suffocated fetus, long dead and rotting inside.

"Because nothing will change the fact that He doesn't want me."

Jesus nods his head.

"I'm sorry we only ever had a heart to heart at a time like this."

Death nods.

"If I ever see you again, do you think we could be friends?"

"I don't know. Besides, how would we ever meet again if I'm about to vanish from existence?"

Jesus shrugs.

"The world is mysterious, Death."

"I suppose it is."

"Well, we should probably get started, shouldn't we?"

Death nods.

Jesus looks into Death's eyes and he can feel pressure on his very being. Pushing and pulling him out of his body and out of this world. Jesus's eyes begin to shift and shape in a spiral, an eternal spiral much like that of Death's ceiling fan at home. The one he would stare at each night as he fell asleep. Death experiences a feeling of nostalgia as the eternal spiral of the Christ's eyes draw him out and into the beyond. Into something new and powerful and uncharted. Out of this existence and into another.

People always talk about your life flashing before your eyes.

Everything you've ever experienced playing before you as your time ends. For Death it's different. There is no expansive slideshow because there isn't much worth remembering. Rather, Death sees a small array of images many of which are out of order.

Death and Satan watching television.

Jeff being rude to Death.

Emily crunching loudly on potato chips.

Agnes rebuking Death for not finishing his kale.

The smell of citrus.

A lone daisy on the side of the road.

God giving him his notebook and the joy and pride he felt but kept deep down where no one, especially not God, would ever see.

Emily's eyes as she listens intently to what he is saying.

The look of fear from Anita as she saw him approach.

The black waves of the ocean.

The orange juice sky.

The face of Jesus as they spoke normally for the first time.

The face Death saw in the mirror, well rested, without bags under his eyes, and something behind his irises that told him that everything would be just fine.

I wish I could have gone to that place, wherever it is.

The eternal prismic spiral intensifies and Death feels the last bits of himself being drawn out and offered up to the Void. As the last ounce of Death escapes his soul, time seems as if to slow.

Thus Spoke the Word of God: I wish we could have been real brothers, if only for a day.

The smell of citrus.

Death can feel the ocean breeze as he gazes into those gray eyes so filled with life and love and joy. Death hears a knock at the door and he turns his head.

Black.

CHAPTER SIXTY-FIVE

Emily is seated at the counter of a really gross bar in Hell. She found the place after getting all checked in and it feels like something from Vegas. Tacky, baroque, and just plain over the top. But she needed alcohol, and quick. It was after the second one that a tall demon approached her.

"Hello. Do you remember me?"

Emily nods.

"Jeff, right?"

Jeff nods.

"He wants to speak to you."

"Who?"

"Who do you think?"

Emily shrugs, nods and follows Jeff to a room behind the bar where sits the Devil.

"Hey, there. Take a seat."

"What did you want to talk about?"

"Wow, straight the point, are we?"

"It's been a long day."

"I'm sure it has, I'm sure it has. I heard about what you did. That took a lot of balls."

"Oh, that. I just got to talking and it flowed right out. If I'm being perfectly honest, it was a bit over the top and wasn't exactly intentional. Nothing too courageous."

"That's not what I'm referring to. Anyone could do that. But you tried to tell him."

"What?"

"You actually tried to tell Death who his father is."

"Oh...well. He deserved to know."

Satan nods.

"I never could've told him."

Silence.

"How would you like to work for me?"

"What?"

"You heard me. Do you want a job?"

"But don't I need to be punished for eternity?"

Satan brushes his hand to the side.

"You mean the whole blasphemy thing? You're fine. After all, you were supposed to go to Heaven. They just sent you down here to save face. You're not gonna be punished or anything like that. So how about it? Wanna work for Satan?"

A big, toothy grin.

Emily looks at the drink in her hand before gulping down the rest.

"Buy me a drink first?"

"I'll put it on my tab."

CHAPTER SIXTY-SIX

God is alone in his office. Everyone in the building is long gone, and here He is staring at the phone.

He has to make the call at some point.

God picks up the receiver and dials.

Ringgggg

Ringgggg

Ringgggg

Ringgggg

Ringg-

"Hello."

"Agnes."

"Took you long enough. I wasn't sure if you would be man enough to give me a call."

"Agnes, I...I can't do this. He's gone. He's really gone."

"He is. And whose fault is that?"

"It's my fault. I destroyed him."

"Good. At least you can still take responsibility."

Silence.

God can hear the choked voice of Agnes as she begins to sob.

"Agnes, I miss you."

"Please don't start with that right now I-"

"Sin, please. He's gone and it's our fault."

"*Our* fault? You're counting me in this? And don't you dare call by that name."

"*That name*? It's the only name you have, Sin. You can't get mad about this because you started it. Who tempted those two idiots? You really expected me to believe that was *Lucifer*? Really? That kid would've stuck his head inside an oven if I had asked him to. No, you've always hated them and you tried to use something I loved to destroy them. All because you thought he wasn't getting enough attention. But I let Lucifer take the fall, the poor son of a bitch, because I wanted my son to at least have a mother if he couldn't have a father. I gave him a job and look at what he did. You had every opportunity to stop him. Don't pretend like you didn't know."

Agnes remains silent.

"Did you really think that he would manage to get away with that? I can't just let people take souls. It's not right. I didn't want to send him away like that, but people have to know that humans can't be tossed around like poker chips. I would be a terrible God if I let–"

"For a good God, you're a terrible father."

The line goes dead.

CHAPTER SIXTY-SEVEN

Judas leans against the tree, letting the ash from his cigarette fall into the grass as he looks up at the stars. His left hand containing an envelope is shaking.

"It's been a long time."

Judas turns his head to see the approaching figure of Jesus.

"It's a bit ironic that you wanted to meet here, isn't it?"

Judas shrugs as Jesus takes a seat next to him.

"Do you mind if I have one?"

Judas holds out the box.

"Help yourself."

Jesus takes one out.

"Light, please."

Judas flicks his lighter on and Jesus ignites the tip of the unfiltered cigarette.

Jesus takes a puff and lets the smoke drift upwards in its ghastly dance.

"Is it worth asking how you've been?"

Judas shakes his head.

"Not really."

"Alright."

The stars are especially bright tonight.

"Can I have the envelope, please?"

Judas hands it over.

"Satan was on to me towards the end, so I had to ditch the digital copy, but I printed it off beforehand and stowed it separately. He has no idea you had any involvement."

"Perfect as always, Judas."

Jesus opens the envelope and gazes at the record, illuminated by the light of the moon and stars.

Judas in a hushed voice.

"Do you think he's out there?"

Jesus shakes his head.

"We have no way of knowing where he is, or even *if* he is."

"But you do, don't you."

Jesus does not answer.

"If you already knew, why did you want the file?"

"I just needed to read it. To see it for myself. If I accessed it then my Father would know that I know. And if that happens then everything has been for naught."

Judas nods.

Jesus turns to him.

"You know there's still a place for you in Heaven, right? All you have to do is say the word."

Judas nods.

"I know you've heard it before, but I forgive you."

Judas nods.

"I miss having my friend to talk to."

The stars twinkle in the sky.

"Alright, I understand. It was nice to see you, Judas."

Jesus leans in and gives Judas a soft kiss on the cheek before putting his cigarette out on the tree bark and departing.

Judas sits and stares at the stars, smoking and thinking until the sun rises.

Peter is hunched back in an uncomfortable wooden chair, entranced by the spin of his ceiling fan.

Jeff yawns, closes the book he was reading, placing it on his nightstand, turning off the lamp and rolling over on his side to await the sleep that would likely never come.

Michael pens the final line of his novel: "And even though the case remained unsolved, the detective found he only thought about it once in a while, and only ever when he mowed his lawn."

Anita is scribbling on a piece of paper, attempting and failing to record Emily's image with pinpoint accuracy. She clutches the sheet and throws it to the side, grabbing another as a small mountain of failed attempts forms around her.

God considers the towering stacks of papers on his desk, closes his eyes, massages his temples, and releases a slow, heavy sigh.

Emily opens the microwave in her dingy apartment off the main strip in Hell and retrieves the hot pocket from within, breaking it open to release the heat and giving it a quick puff before taking a bite.

Jesus flips through a photo album, pausing on a blurry group shot from a non-descript dinner party. Two boys stand at the forefront amidst the host of deities, angels, and Heaven-adjacent beings. The picture has aged poorly, causing the color of the boys' lava lamp eyes to appear as the same gray hue.

Agnes's fingers brush against the oft used doorknob, turning it with the utmost care as she pushes it open and a soft creak echoes through Death's empty home. She hesitates before pressing forward, a faint breath escaping her lips which manifests itself as a laugh. The kind of laughter which precedes tears. As she takes the painting in her hands, Agnes smiles, content with the knowledge that somewhere out there her son has found his own kind of bliss.

The eternal setting sun, the cloudless, orange juice sky. The sound of crashing waves. Death gazes down from the balcony as they curl into themselves, the resulting sea foam a deep, inky black. Death can feel a light sea breeze on his face. His breath is light and he feels rested. His eyelids aren't heavy. Death takes a deep, full breath of the salty air, allowing it to fill his lungs, free of the strange thing that once lived just behind it. There is a faint smell of citrus. Death turns around and catches a glimpse of the veil fluttering against the breeze and just beyond it, a room, and just beyond that, a door with a faint knock resonating from it. Death's hand brushes against the handle, turning it ever so slowly and drawing his arm back as the door opens with a slight creak. Upon discovering the source of the sound, Death cannot help but smile.

Made in the USA
Columbia, SC
16 November 2020

24681499R00217